2032

THE YEAR A.I. RUNS
FOR PRESIDENT

KEIR NEWTON

For the builders of the future and their generation.

DAY ONE

Saturday, October 30, 2032

"No matter how good our algorithms are, we can always find better and more creative and ambitious ways to use them. Why make geniuses dig ditches when they could take us to Mars?" — *Garry Kasparov*

1

The best person for the job isn't a person at all. Algo for President. I stopped to take in the first election poster I saw as I exited the San Francisco Ferry Building. I wasn't too sure about the sentiment just yet, but I couldn't suppress a smile. There were clearly some heavy hitters from the Valley running marketing for the campaign. Just like them, Algo's slogans were always pithy and oh so self-assured.

I started across the cavernous Embarcadero Plaza, the huge traffic-free open space created by the city a couple of years ago. Its purpose had been to revitalize the financial district after the multiple gut punches from the pandemic and the twin crashes of twenty-three and twenty-eight. The "Times Square of the West" as they'd tried to sell the idea. The ring of boarded-up, empty storefronts facing the open plaza told the story of its success.

My left hand vibrated. The curved, ultra-thin screen melded onto the back of my hand flashed on with an alert. I scratched uncomfortably at it. It had taken me awhile to finally relent and get a SmartPalm and I still found the feeling of fused skin and screen disconcerting. As if a regular old smartphone hadn't been bad enough, now this thing was literally stuck to me.

I'll be outside in 5. Just like you asked. Tate.

I quickened my pace. Tate wasn't the kind of guy who would wait.

It was now five p.m. Not too long ago this would have been rush hour, with young tech workers cramming the sidewalks and spilling out of the city's bars. Save the occasional relic ambling along with their face buried in a screen, now the plaza teemed with a different kind of life. Close to fifty shapeless bundles of humanity huddled against the storefronts nearest me and there were hundreds of ramshackle tents strewn throughout the plaza. That was new. I remembered such encampments in the Tenderloin or under the city's freeways, but not here in the FiDi. Had I really been gone *that* long?

The restaurants and stores may never have materialized, but huge digital billboards that aped the original Times Square had. They glistened in ultra-high definition, in contrast to everything covered in a thin layer of neglect below. The largest of them, almost a football field in height, rotated a couple more slogans with hopeful promises from Algo.

End Politics. Disrupt the Government. Vote Algo.

Artificial Intelligence Has No Bias. Let Algo Decide.

Data Don't Lie. Data Has No Agenda. Trust Algo.

I half-expected "Make the World a Better Place" to flash up, but it never did. Maybe that was finally too much of a cliché even for tech marketers. Still, the visual assault wasn't a surprise. This was presidential candidate Algo's home town after all.

Algo.

An Artificial Intelligence running for the White House! Silicon Valley's most audacious project yet.

After three years away from San Francisco, of course it was

Algo that had finally lured me back to the madness of this city I'd sworn never to return to, back to the HQ of my old company, LaRaLi, and back to my old friend and Algo's creator, Jamin Lake.

Tonight was Algo's final campaign party, a reception for "Team Algo." Anyone who was anyone in tech would be there. The industry power players, the moguls, the social influencers and the campaign's financial backers. It was a chance for the tech glitterati to mingle with Jamin and hear the plans for the final push for the presidency behind closed doors. It had been sold as an opportunity to see and talk to Algo itself, "off the campaign trail" so to speak.

An invite hadn't graced my inbox, but I was going to do everything I could to get in.

For one thing, AI was my life's work and Algo was as much my creation as anyone else's. Without the code that I'd built into the original Athena, the world's most popular virtual assistant, well, there'd be no damned Algo in the first place.

I also desperately wanted to believe in the promise of Algo. Our last few human presidents had delivered seemingly only endless crises: asset price collapses, stagflation, mass unemployment, division, wars, meek action on the climate disaster and now a global food shortage, not to mention a myriad other problems both foreign and domestic. So an AI taking over from the hyper-polarized and sclerotic political mess of the last decade and a half? Who wouldn't want that? Frankly, it sounded like a dream. If Algo won, the presidency would be AI's ultimate achievement. In big tech, we'd always talked a big game about changing the world. *This* might actually do it.

But, I had to ask myself, was Algo really the AI ready for the job? I wasn't yet convinced of that. Sure, its communication skills were impressive, but I hadn't seen anything that made me think of it as anything but a faster version of Athena. Some people were out there blindly speculating that Algo could be the world's first Artificial *General* Intelligence, or AGI — a machine that could think of scenarios *beyond* what was programmed into it. A machine that could draw its own conclusions and make its own decisions. An exceptionally brave few were even positing that Algo might be self-aware. Either would be truly revolutionary, but those ideas were ludicrous. That kind of progress was still decades away. I hated to admit it, but I wasn't sure Algo was a technology worthy of the White House.

Maybe more than anything though, I was also deeply suspicious of Jamin. He had painted a grand vision of a transformative, revolutionary AI, but I wondered if this whole campaign was one of his parlor tricks. A grand bait-and-switch scheme to get himself into the ultimate position of power, using Algo as the proverbial AI trojan horse. I knew him. I knew how he thought, how he operated. Hell, he had his name on the damned ballot as Vice President! If an AI as President seemed like a dream, Jamin's hands on the prize was a nightmare.

Tonight's event was the opportunity I needed to finally assess Algo up close. I'd try to answer the questions that had been burning in my mind since Jamin had first launched the campaign a year ago. What was Algo capable of? Was it more than just an upgraded virtual assistant? And, could it be trusted or was it nothing more than Jamin's digital marionette?

Tonight was also my last chance. I'd have preferred to just watch all this play out from the sidelines, but things had changed in the last few months. Against all odds, predictions and expectations, it looked like Algo actually had a chance of winning. As the cliché went, it was now or never.

All in all, given my own personal history in Algo's creation, the last few weeks had been like the constant tap tap tap on the window of my conscience. I could ignore my fugitive doubts no longer.

I promised myself that if I sensed real peril in the wind, I would not stay silent. I'd tell whoever would listen that Jamin had no business being anywhere near the presidency. I was a co-founder of LaRaLi. If I dropped some truth bombs, maybe people would take notice.

So I knew *what* I needed to do, but getting into tonight's little soiree was no cakewalk. I'd called everyone I could think of over the past week. Nada. No one would help. All I got was one lame excuse after the other. Apparently, my name didn't carry much sway in the Valley anymore. LaRaLi co-founder or not, nobody saw much benefit in going out of their way to help a man who'd turned his back on the industry.

And so my old pal Tate Mint was now my last shot.

I dodged a couple of panhandlers and pushed past the last row of tents at the edge of the plaza. A half-naked young man lay perfectly still across the staircase ahead of me, a syringe dangling from his arm. A little stream of blood oozed down onto the concrete. It looked bad, but I had a feeling this kid was far beyond feeling any pain. I knew that with a little bit of bad luck and a few bad choices, this kid could've been me. He was another reminder that this city had always been a place of grinding despair as much as incredible opportunity — and despair seemed to be winning the day.

There was a faded poster hanging above.

San Francisco. Civic Renewal Project 2029.

Somebody needed to tell the mayor she was a little behind on the plan. This damned mess of a place. I shouldn't have hated being back so much. This city made me. It had given me everything I ever dreamt of. I wondered if I could have done more for the place, rather than just leaving when things got difficult.

The broad boulevard of Market Street stretched out in front me as a bead of sweat ran down my back. The November air was unusually thick and lifeless. Even now in the early evening, it was almost ninety and there were no bay winds or fog to rescue the city from the heat.

I turned onto California Street and spied Tate ahead, his six-foot-four frame dominating the sidewalk. Clad in slim-fit khakis and a button-down, his shoulder-length blond hair flapping in the breeze, exactly as I remembered him. He looked in his own world, oblivious to his surroundings and absent-mindedly swiping away on his own SmartPalm.

One of the first things I learned about people when I moved to the Bay was that intelligence was definitely not synonymous with character. Tate was a case in point. He was one of the Valley's more odious venture capitalists. Last I'd heard, he'd been forced out of his firm after a round of sexual harassment allegations.

Exactly the kind of tech industry bro I'd been forced to endure in the Bay and delighted in escaping when I left for Hawaii. Tate was like almost every VC guy I knew. His father had been a venture capitalist who'd walked him into a partnership at some family friend's firm. I'd grown up with a single father and two brothers in a one-bed condo in the West Loop of Chicago.

I didn't relish our reacquainting. Tate was, however, one of LaRaLi's first investors and I'd helped start his journey to becoming disgustingly rich. He owed me and he was my best ticket at getting into Algo's little meet-and-greet. I padded up silently behind him.

"Gimme ya wallet!" I whispered loudly as I dug a finger into his back.

Tate froze.

"I... I don't carry any cash," he said.

"Private key to your crypto stash will do fine," I growled. "Tate Mint, don't pretend you don't carry it with you."

How many millions might he have hidden behind whatever private key he had tucked away in his coat? I grabbed his shoulders and spun him around.

"Isaac Raff!" He let out a long breath of relief, then his calm quickly turned to anger. "Shit, man, this ain't the town to play a joke like that anymore. I might've damn well tasered you or something!"

"And here I was thinking you'd be happy to see me," I said, smiling.

Tate stood up a little straighter and readjusted his jacket, then he laughed boisterously and flashed me a toothy grin.

"Fuck you very much!" he chortled and punched me in the arm.

He'd always been so annoyingly personable.

"Fuck you too, buddy," I said.

"God, how long has it been?" Tate asked. "I thought you were off being a hermit or something. Barbados? The Caymans? Puerto Rico?"

"Hawaii." I felt a sudden urge to scratch my beard, but I'd shaved it off just before leaving my ranch on Kauai. "My first time back in the Bay in three years."

I hadn't planned on coming back for a lot longer than that either. Too many memories.

"Almost everyone's gone now, y'know." Tate's smile grew oddly broad. "Even Zuck *and* Marc B. Pretty much the whole crew except your old partner-in-crime. You know, if Jamin hadn't kept LaRaLi in the city, the whole place might have gone bankrupt."

"You're not here anymore, then?"

"Fuck no!" Tate laughed. "I mean I still have my place down in Menlo Park, but the city, no way. I only come here if

I need to see someone from the company. Wait, don't tell me you kept a place here?"

I shrugged.

"Shit. You're braver than me," he said with a whistle.

He put an arm around my shoulder with that annoying particular arrogance that so many in the tech world had. He clearly thought he and I were basically the same. Outside of our old business relationship though, we had next to nothing in common.

"What's the latest on Geier?" I asked.

Tate took his arm off me and frowned. Geier Capital, his VC firm, had put him on extended leave while investigating his improprieties.

"You heard about that then?" He tossed his head back and let out a dramatically plaintive deep sigh. "It's all trash, of course."

"Six women came forward?"

"All liars," he grunted. "Bitter ex-employees. You know how it goes. It's not all bad though. Still on LaRaLi's board at least, thanks to Jamin."

Jamin never did have much time for ethics. Maybe, at least, Tate would be able to help me.

"And I just funded a new startup from my own cash, too," Tate said. "Anti-senescence drugs."

"Anti-aging, huh? You're leaving tech for pharma?"

"Not exactly. You know any ego in Silicon Valley that doesn't want to live forever?"

He had me there.

"Want me to send you a prospectus?" he asked. "You know it'll be a gold mine."

"That's not why I'm here."

"No?" Tate nodded gently. "Why *are* you here? What was so important that we had to meet in person?"

A man suddenly bounded across the street in our

direction, shouting madly and brandishing a sign that read *I am Jesus and Algo*. I guess the AI had really made it. The man roared a couple of expletives at us and then staggered away.

"For that." I waved toward the man. "I'm here for Algo. I need to meet it, not just watch it from afar. I want in on tonight."

"You know about that, huh?"

"Shit, Tate, I still know *some* people in the Valley." I wasn't about to reveal to him exactly how I'd found out. There was nothing those in tech valued more than their privacy. "You said you're still on the board, didn't you? You're going to tell me you can't get me in?"

"Thanks for thinking I have some kind of special influence," Tate laughed, "but Jamin has this thing locked down, Raff."

"Tate," I said calmly, "you're telling me you don't have any pull?"

"I'm sorry," Tate said forcefully.

"Tate, after everything, all that money…"

"It's you, Raff!" Tate suddenly shouted in exasperation. He then took a deep breath and slowly composed himself. "You're radioactive. Persona non grata. Jamin's made that clear. I'm sorry."

I almost wanted to laugh at the thought that I was toxic compared to this creep, but I held my tongue. I was actually oddly relieved by the revelation. Now I knew why getting on the list tonight was so hard. At least Tate was honest. Every other person I'd asked for help had just blown me off with some convoluted story.

"Shit, Raff," Tate said, "it's been three years already, why don't you just ask him?"

"Jamin?" I laughed. "Sure, he's my next call."

There was no chance I was giving Jamin that satisfaction.

Tate cleared his throat and then nodded.

"Well, for what it's worth," he said, "I really do hope you make it. You won't believe what Jamin has built. I just ain't your ticket."

I grunted, trying not to look as though all my hopes hadn't been riding on this. If he wasn't my in, who else was left?

Tate looked relieved when a driverless rideshare pulled up to whisk him away.

I watched him and the car disappear up the street.

2

My hands were almost shaking. The chance to see Algo felt like it was slipping away. I'd been so sure about Tate.

I decided to head back to my old condo at the Russ Building on Montgomery. Maybe there were one or two more long shots I hadn't thought of. There was no way I was leaving San Francisco without getting to the AI.

The sun had almost gone down, but it was still baking hot out. I tore off my jacket and prepared for the brisk walk up to my place.

The tracks of the once-famous cable car on California Street lay unused and in disrepair. Here, too, most of the shops were either closed or boarded up. I half expected to see some tumbleweed rolling across the street. Few people lived in this part of the city any more, certainly nobody from my old social circle of company founders and venture capitalists. If they lived in the city at all and not in the Valley, they chose the glistening towers and high-rise palaces of Mission Bay or Yerba Buena Island. I figured it helped them pretend this part of San Francisco didn't exist.

I couldn't let go of my old place though. My first apartment in the city had been at the Russ — a tiny five-hundred-square-foot hovel that I had shared with Jamin and Kio Li. We'd made it a kind of home and company HQ in one. Our three thousand dollars a month in rent felt like extortion at the time, though everything in San Francisco did when you were a kid battling to break into the industry.

To say we "lived" there is a bit of a stretch. All I can remember was working. Probably the happiest period of my life though. Sometimes I wonder if I'd give up everything to go back to those days where we wrote the first code and algorithms that became the AI behind Athena.

Athena. It knows what you need, even before you do.

Jamin scrawled that infamous slogan on the wall the day we moved in. Athena would be the first virtual assistant that learned from its interactions with its users, discerned their unique needs and emotions, and began to anticipate them. It became the foundation of the company we went on to create, LaRaLi — La-ke, Ra-ff, and Li.

Athena launched us into the stratosphere. We sold tens of millions of app subscriptions in our first year. When LaRaLi went public a decade later, we became instant billionaires. Jamin, Kio and I were thereafter known as *The LaRaLi Three*.

A billionaire! Me? The introverted engineer. The whole idea still felt wrong. I'd been in AI purely for the tech, for building, for creating. And growing up the way I had, the idea of so much money seemed kind of foreign to me. It still does. Weird, strange, unnatural. I wasn't complaining though. It allowed me to help my Dad, my brothers, hell, all of my extended family, friends and so many others. And for that, I was incredibly thankful.

The biggest thing I bought for myself after the IPO was the top two floors of the Russ. I'd turned them into my dream penthouse. Self-indulgent? Sure, but I didn't care. I even bought the old studio as a reminder of how far we'd come.

I spied another billboard ahead.

Algo. Not Left. Not Right. Just Better.

Algo. Short for algorithm. That made me laugh. I still doubted it was more than a bigger, faster version of our Athena, but whatever Algo was, it was likely far beyond mere algorithms.

The final rays of sunlight had disappeared below the horizon as I turned into Montgomery Street. I suddenly felt very alone. My mind started replaying all those news stories I'd tried to ignore over the last few years. Carjackings. Muggings. Random attacks. Ever since the economic fallout from the ongoing *Techxodus* of the past decade, the borders of San Francisco's famously troubled Tenderloin had expanded, just as fast as those of moneyed San Francisco's had retreated.

I reached the next block.

A hand suddenly grabbed my arm. I almost jumped out of my skin as I whirled around. It was a man shaking a cup in my direction. I tried to hide my relief that this wasn't an assault or something.

"I got automated out of work. Spare a dollar?" the man asked tentatively.

"No change," I said. I wasn't unsympathetic, but when you get panhandled on every block, you quickly go numb. Besides, who carried physical cash any more?

"I take FedCoin you know." The man's arm twitched as he held out a card with a QR code. "Ether, or Bitcoin, too, if you're old school."

I stopped. Surely ingenuity deserved reward. I zapped him ten bucks worth of crypto, then kept moving.

There was immediately another set of footsteps shuffling behind me. I feigned a casual look over my shoulder and saw a disheveled woman clad in black fifty feet or so behind.

"Hey!" She waved excitedly.

Shit. Another transient. I didn't have time for this. I dashed across the street and ran up to the door of the Russ. I kicked the piles of trash out of the way and held my face in front of the security scanner. It took a few seconds to come to life and acknowledge me, but the doors swung open. I stepped into the lobby and pulled the doors closed behind me.

The air inside had that stale, acrid smell of disuse. Not too many residents left I figured. I closed my eyes and tried to compose myself.

My meditation was interrupted by a loud banging on the front door. It was that same woman. What the hell? The city's vagrants weren't usually this aggressive. She drew back her hoodie to reveal her face. Her soft features and light brown skin looked prematurely weathered. Her hair was long, knotted and scraggy, but there was something oddly familiar about her.

"Raff!" she shouted.

I took a step backward. Her eyes met mine. There was no way this woman could know me. Then it hit me. She must have recognized me from some old article on LaRaLi and thought that shouting my name might somehow extract a few extra dollars.

"Get outta here!" I shouted and stepped into the private elevator that would take me to the penthouse.

"Good evening, Raff." Athena's pleasing voice emanated gently from a speaker above. *"It has been one thousand and fifty-three days since you last checked into this property."*

"Fuck!" I had forgotten this place still had an integrated Athena.

"I'm sorry, Raff?"

"Sorry. Thanks. I guess it's good to be back."

"Of course it is. It's good to see you again. Let's not make it so long next time, huh?"

"Sure," I said.

Athena was largely my own creation, yet I still found it awkward to interact with. My friends always found that incredibly strange. I'd coded the thing, hadn't I?

That was my trepidation though. I understood it. I knew that any friendliness or emotion it displayed was just a facsimile. It didn't really care about me any more than my toaster did.

"Welcome home." Athena's voice moved with me from the elevator and into the apartment. The first light from the rising full moon streamed in from the southeast into the cavernous living area. Millions of specks of dust twinkled in the soft light, each like a little reminder of how long it had been since I was here.

"Let's get some air in here," Athena said cheerfully. *"It's toasty today, right? It'll be the same tomorrow."* Cool air from the A/C began to waft into the room.

What the hell was I going to do? My plans were falling apart. Should I just fly back to Hawaii? I was so stupid to think I could just come back here and all would be right.

"Athena," I said, "start reading out the names in my address book that I haven't called or messaged within the last month."

Maybe there would be a name that I hadn't already tried.

I listened, but not a single one jumped out at me.

I wandered over to the window and looked north toward Telegraph Hill. What had once been known as the Transamerica Pyramid was only a few blocks away and filled the window. It was as I had always remembered it, except now the LaRaLi colors shone from a spotlight on its triangular metal peak. I hadn't even noticed that the company had purchased it. Jamin must have bought up half the city by now.

"Jamin Lake," Athena read out.

"Pause," I said.

I looked down at my SmartPalm and hovered my finger over Jamin's name. It had been three years since we'd spoken.

Three years since he'd forced me out of the company we'd started together. Could I swallow my pride and call him? Would he even answer me? What choice did I have at this point? I gritted my teeth and moved my finger toward "dial."

Just before I hit the button, there was a furious tapping on a window in the kitchen.

From the outside. Thirty-two stories high.

Everything went silent. Then, another round of tapping. One. Two. Three.

I stepped carefully into the hallway and then padded toward the kitchen as silently as I could. I peeked around the corner. A small drone hovered outside the window. Two small bags hung from a metal hook beneath it. What the hell was this?

"Your needs anticipation delivery has arrived," Athena explained casually.

"Open the window," I said.

The drone waited patiently as the window rolled open, then it zipped over to the kitchen island and gently deposited the bags onto it. It arched forward ever so slightly as if tipping an invisible hat, then did an about-face and whirred away out the window and into the night.

"Needs anticipation?" I mumbled. Thanks Athena!

My nerves were shot. It had been some day. I tore open the two bags. There was no Advil and no booze. Only healthy groceries. So much for anticipating my needs.

I put my head into my hands.

"You have received a new message," Athena stated matter-of-factly.

"Read it later," I said.

"I think you'll want to hear this one."

That was unexpected.

"Who's it from?" I asked.

"It says it's from Algo."

"Algo?" I opened my eyes and stood up straight. "Alright, read it."

"Come to my event tonight. I will make sure you get in. Algo."

This was surely some trick. Someone wanted me to show up to this thing and then laugh when I was turned away.

Could this offer be real? There was no way this could actually be Algo, but maybe there was another answer. Tate must have found a way to help me, but he wanted to keep it under the radar.

"I will make sure you get in," I repeated the words to myself.

"I should remind you, Raff, the event referred to begins in…"

"Right," I said. "Send a reply that I'll be there and thank you."

This was my chance. I headed for the shower, which felt rejuvenating. The walk-in wardrobe in the master bedroom held ten matching charcoal hoodies. Shit. I'd never liked to have a lot of choice. I grabbed one, pulled it over a pair of jeans and looked at myself in the mirror. The reflection was like a memory of a younger me. I started to feel a little "San Francisco" again. Maybe I had missed it all more than I had let myself think. This was a place where people changed the world. It was like a drug, seeping slowly back into my veins just like it always had. A part of me liked it. I'd have to be careful not to get addicted.

The elevator down was quick and I went to the street to wait for a rideshare. There was no sign of the transient from earlier.

My SmartPalm buzzed.

Kio Li calling.

I furiously tapped the answer button.

All I could hear was the sound of traffic on a busy street. After a moment, a familiar voice spoke softly. "You're back in the city?"

It was eerie to hear her voice again and a little painful. Like another echo from a life I'd tried hard to forget. I hadn't spoken to Kio in three years either. There was so much I wanted to say. Kio had been more than just a company cofounder to me. She had been one of my closest friends. Actually, I'd always thought there was the chance for something more between us. I think she had too, but with our mutual devotion to LaRaLi and Athena, we'd never quite found the time to explore it.

"Yes, I..." I said. "Wait, how, how did you even know I was back?"

"Your Athena messaged me."

Proactive messaging. Another one of the features we'd built in to Athena. Was this more "needs anticipation"? I felt a sudden urge to turn it off.

"'It knows what you need,'" I mumbled.

"'Even before you do,'" Kio said with the gentlest of laughs. "Exactly."

"Kio. I'm sorry. I should have called."

"In the last three years, yeah, I'd say so."

That hurt, but she was right. When we'd been dumped from LaRaLi, it had all happened so fast. I'd just wanted to escape. I suppose I'd never wanted to have to really face what had happened.

"I missed you," I said.

It was true. Only now did I realize how much.

She let out a sharp breath, which I took as a kind of awkward acknowledgement that she felt the same.

"I guess you're back for Algo?" she asked.

"Yes," I said. I wasn't ready to tell her any more detail than that just yet.

"I suppose that makes sense. It's *our* baby, too. You're going tonight then?"

"Yes."

"Jamin invited you?" She sounded surprised.

"Not Jamin, um, Tate. Are you going?"

"No, you know how Jamin and I are."

"You want me to see if I can get you in?" I asked, although I wasn't really sure how I could.

"I'm not sure I'm ready for that," Kio said dryly.

"Neither am I."

She laughed.

"I do want one thing though," she said.

"Anything," I said.

"Come and see me. After you meet Algo, I mean. Tonight. We should… catch up," she said cryptically. "Don't worry if it's late. You know me. I'll be up."

"I'll be there." I didn't have to be asked twice.

The call ended. My heart was racing. I was unashamedly happy. My luck was turning. I was going to see Algo tonight, and now Kio too. This city was drawing me deeper into my old life. And the truth was, I now thought I might be ready for it.

An empty car pulled up in front of me. I was old enough that getting into a driverless car was still a little off-putting, but I climbed in.

"Confirming your destination, Mister Raff. Yerba Buena Tower."

"You got it," I said.

The electric car took off silently in the direction of Yerba Buena Island. When I had last been in San Francisco, YBI had been a desolate, forgotten place, little more than an interesting geographical anomaly halfway between the city and the East Bay that joined the two halves of the iconic Bay Bridge. That all changed though when Jamin purchased the island from the city at the height of the last economic crisis and built the sparkling new hundred-story Yerba Buena Tower. The hexagonal skyscraper stood alone on the island.

It was where anyone who was anyone in tech and still in the Bay wanted to live. *Proximity and Isolation* was how it had been sold. That, and the fact that Jamin had convinced the city to allow him to make it its own little unincorporated community protected from the city's property taxes. A little oasis for the super rich behind a perimeter of twelve-foot-high concrete walls with a couple miles of moat-like frigid Bay water between it and San Francisco proper.

When I saw the tower for the first time, the realization hit me that Algo was right here, somewhere in this enormous building ahead. The culmination of decades of work in Artificial Intelligence by me and so many others. My hands and feet almost tingled in anticipation.

A facial recognition camera scanned me as we drove toward the entrance gate and the car was quickly ushered inside.

My SmartPalm buzzed.

I'm so glad you made it. I've been wanting to meet you. Algo.

I swiped it away. Damn, Tate. Nice joke though.

I craned my neck to take in the building looming over me. The flickering lights of a party in full swing were obvious even from here, like a multi-colored orb pulsating against the night sky. Jamin had turned the top five floors into the most opulent work and play condo in the country. Certainly the largest anyway. Almost one hundred thousand square feet.

Of the three LaRaLi co-founders, Jamin had always been the one focused on more than just the work. He craved the power and the status that came with the money. He had always had a singular motivation to be the next tech megastar. Clearly, he'd blasted through that goal with a sledgehammer.

It reminded me of a quote from Richard Nixon that Jamin loved to repeat ad nauseam in LaRaLi's early days. He'd wheel it out when we had many hours of work ahead but all we really wanted was to sleep.

"Guys, remember, only if you have been in the deepest valley, can you ever know how magnificent it is to be on the highest mountain."

I looked up. Seems he was right.

My SmartPalm buzzed again.

This time, it was just a news update. A new election poll. Algo had gained an extra point. One more step closer to victory.

"Kudos, old friend." I nodded in the direction of Jamin Lake, some hundred stories above and strolled into the lobby.

3

"Move fast and break things," a woman in the elevator said with a broad smile. "It's such an old cliché. But seriously, Washington won't know what hit it when Algo rolls in, right?"

I nodded, keeping my head down and trying not to engage her. I'd never been all that great at talking to strangers. It was one of those talents Jamin had in spades that I sorely lacked. Besides, I just wanted to get out into the party, feel the mood and, of course, see Algo.

"And the most good for the most people," the woman continued happily. "That's the core idea that Jamin coded into Algo, did you know? Its mantra, he calls it. Simple, yet brilliant. It captures what we've always been striving toward in the Valley, don't you think?"

"Sure," I said.

Jamin's mantra definitely sounded as blithely utopian as something a tech company would come up with. But, was it really something that could have inspired a big chunk of the country to support an AI for president though? There had to be more to it and I was eager to find out.

"Awe-inspiring," the woman said with a contented sigh.

"Why hasn't a politician ever thought of that? Jamin is so amazing, right?"

"He totally is," I said.

Gushing praise for Jamin was something I'd have to smile and grit my teeth through. I stared at the numbers on the elevator panel, willing them to hurry up and get to ninety-six.

"I'm just surprised this kind of disruption took so long. We should have done this years ago!" The woman clapped her hands excitedly. "I'm beyond proud the company is leading the way on this."

"You're from LaRaLi?" I asked and raised my head. I hadn't recognized her when we'd gotten in the elevator.

"I sure am." She thrust out a hand. "Hannah Ko, CMO. Wait! You're Isaac Raff!"

I nodded and shook her hand.

"Smiley face!" she said gleefully.

I'd forgotten how annoyingly on trend it was nowadays to verbalize emojis.

"You're still a legend around LaRaLi you know. Jamin calls you Algo's *other* Dad."

"L-O-L." I forced a smile to hide my shock that Jamin would give me any recognition at all. "Did we ever meet at the company?"

"I doubt it. I joined a few years ago, just after Jamin cleaned house." She seemed to catch herself. "Sorry, I didn't..."

"Forget it."

"It's all about Algo now anyway, right?"

"It sure is."

The elevator doors opened.

"Um, could I get a selfie?" She looked at me hopefully. "My followers would love this."

I felt momentarily amazed that anyone would want to see it, but I obliged. We snapped a quick picture, then I was out.

We were ejected onto level ninety-six of the Tower, the first of five floors that made up Jamin Lake's grandiose, fortress-in-the-sky. This first level was a single enormous open floor with twenty-foot floor-to-ceiling windows in every direction. The center of the room opened up into a cathedral-like, cylindrical interior that extended a hundred feet right up to the top of the building. I'd been in six-star hotel ballrooms that were smaller and less opulent than this.

At least a thousand people were jammed in tight on the main floor and it throbbed with the collective energy and din of a spring break party. It felt more like an underground rave than a political campaign event.

There was an oval-shaped bar in the middle of the room crammed with people frenetically ordering drinks, edibles, snort-ables, smoke-ables and whatever other vices were on offer. This was the Valley after all. Above the bar, a circular screen rotated and beamed campaign ads in every direction.

It has no prejudice. It has no privilege. It is just Algo.

Intelligence Solved. Algo.

When you're sleeping, it's still working. Algo 2032.

I usually hated tech industry parties. But this felt different. This was a celebration. This was Big Tech writ large. A part of me wanted just to accept the idea that these were my people and this was our moment. It started to feel like I was home. I had to force myself not to completely give in to it.

All the big names were here. The people here were collectively worth more than a trillion dollars. They controlled the most powerful companies in the world. And they were all here for Algo. It suddenly felt like the whole Valley was behind the AI.

I pushed my way through the crowd toward the bar. I needed to take the edge off a little. I'd basically been living like a recluse the last few years and this was a lot to take in. I exchanged a couple of knowing nods and glances, and received a bunch of approving slaps on the backs, fist bumps and handshakes on the way. I posed for a dozen more selfies. The fact that I hadn't been involved with LaRaLi for three years didn't seem to matter. My history with the company and presumed connection to Algo suddenly made me hot property.

I grabbed a drink and circled the room. I had some time before Algo's speech. I wanted to feel the pulse of the room and get a sense of how people were feeling about the AI and the campaign.

I stopped when I saw Mai Lin, one of LaRaLi's former lead engineers. She'd been another victim of the "cleaning house" from a few years back. She was one of the few people from the company I could say I actually missed. I had always trusted her, confided in her too. Finally, someone I could press for an unbiased opinion on Algo. I snuck up behind her.

"I guess everyone's forgiven then, Mai?" I asked.

"W-T-F! Isaac Raff?" She picked her jaw up off the floor. "You were the last person I expected to see here!"

"It's so good to feel wanted."

"I just mean—"

"I know." I smiled. "Still working at that drug place?"

Last I'd heard Mai was at some startup trying to sling Human Growth Hormone to anxious parents fretting about their kids' height.

"No, it was too niche," Mai replied a little wistfully. "Constantly fighting the regulators got old, you know? I'm at a place called Kollr now."

"Like collar?"

"Thumbs up!" She gestured the emoji. "It's a kind of monitor for kids. We inject a little device behind the ear to enable remote tracking. You know, we help parents be parents."

"That's parenting?" I raised an eyebrow dramatically.

"Oh fuck off, Millenial!" she said with a smirk, enjoying using the slight that young engineers had begun to throw at anyone over thirty.

"Aren't you thirty-five, too? Also known as ancient?"

"Zombie face!" She poked out her tongue, but then hugged me. "Damn, Raff, you don't miss any of this?"

"I didn't think I did," I said, "I don't miss the company stuff. But the work, you know."

"Designing the future," she said with a knowing nod. "Just like Algo is going to do."

I sensed my opportunity. "You're all in on Algo then?" I asked.

She looked at me as if it was the most ridiculous question she'd ever heard. "After the last sixteen years? Shit, this is our moment, Raff." The change in tone was abrupt. She waved her hands around at the room. "Look around, you've got the smartest and most brilliant minds in the world in this room and Algo is like the sum of all of us. This is disruption. Old government's time has come. This is the chance to let doubt, error, prejudice, all of it, be consigned to history."

I was shocked at how immediately forthright Mai was. It almost felt like I was talking to a religious convert, somebody who refused to see anything but an angel in AI form. I understood the tantalizing possibilities of Algo, but I was a little uneasy at her fervor.

"You've seen Algo before then?" I asked.

"Is that a trick question? Wait, you haven't?" she replied. Her tone softened again and she smiled. "Oh, right, I forgot you've been off starring in your own personal version of *Into the Wild*."

I playfully rolled my eyes.

"Prepare yourself. It's like Athena on, well, shit, growth hormone."

"Smiling face with hearts," I said, verbalizing the best emoji I could think of. That made her smile.

I grabbed for two champagne glasses from a passing waiter so we could clink them in Algo's honor, then excused myself. I wandered the floor, chatting to anyone who said hello. Everyone seemed genuinely happy to see me, which was heartening, if slightly off-putting.

I must have downed another four glasses of champagne in less than an hour. My head began to spin. I'd forgotten how intense these events could be. The men and women here thought of themselves as the leaders of the world and they weren't afraid to tell you. When they weren't extolling the virtues of Jamin or Algo, the discussion invariably turned to food, cars, property, crypto, or just how generally difficult it was to spend money in ever increasingly lavish and reckless ways.

I eventually extricated myself and found a quiet spot by the window where I could just watch the city for a bit. The strobing lights from the dance party were almost in sync with the flashing lights of cop cars and paramedics across the water.

Another familiar voice shouted my name.

"Isaac Raff!" Vik Das bounded over toward me with John Huang. This was a pairing I hadn't expected to see. I thought these two hated each other with a passion. They'd been bitter rivals for the best part of the last decade.

Das was a short man, maybe five-four or five-five. He had long, black hair down to his shoulders and a thick, perfectly groomed beard. He wore a plain hoodie and simple jeans, just like every other time I'd ever seen him. Huang was tall and lean, and had short, cropped hair. He wore a perfectly tailored Italian suit coupled with a pair of Hugo Boss sneakers. The quintessential tech look of casual, but uber-expensive designer fashion.

Das and Huang were the internet's original attention merchants, the pioneers of the great "distraction casino". They had both understood and cold-bloodedly leveraged the most important truth about the internet age, that if you could make people orient their lives around self-absorption and attention, then you could really own them — and their data.

Das had developed the most popular mobile application in the world. He'd made it easy for people to upload and share pictures with the world, encouraging other users to like and comment on what they saw. It sent its users on a never-ending quest to upload that perfect picture in an attempt to distract them and their friends from their real lives. There's almost nothing his users wouldn't do in search of the perfect picture to chase those likes. Fans called it a hub for artistic expression. Critics called it the ultimate degeneration into vacuousness. I guess the beauty of it was that it was both.

Huang hadn't invented the first short-form video messaging app, but he built the most controversial one. His app turned into an online forum where people could shout at each other all day and attempt to feel smarter and better than anybody who didn't agree with them. It helped broadcast the craziest voices in society and the kind of ranting and raving that used to be confined to the mad scrawling you'd find on toilet walls.

Their apps made them both billionaires, of course. I couldn't quite remember which of them was richer. Probably Huang. His app had been the lighter fluid for the sparks of the toxic cultural and political climate of the last decade and a half and that had really helped him out.

The two of them had the qualities of a lot of the guys and girls running companies in this room. Towering intelligence coupled with both negligible humility and exceptional hubris — and with these two especially, the morality of a payday lender. I'd never particularly liked either of them, but I had a kind of grudging respect for what they'd achieved.

Das and Huang. Together. In the same room. Maybe Algo really was the great tech unifier.

"Vincent van Bro!" Das moved in and gave me a vigorous hug. He was also the most "bro" of any of the tech founders I knew and had the incredibly annoying habit of beginning almost every sentence with some kind of play on the word.

"Bro Chi Minh!" I shouted. He loved it when people played along.

"Bro Exotic!" He flipped open a small metal pod filled with cocaine. "Interest you in a line?"

"Maybe after the speech," I said. "My first time with Algo live. I want to be fresh."

"If you say so, Bro-am Chomsky." He dipped a finger in and had a quick snort. "Fucking fantastic to see you back in town by the way. How the hell did you get in here?"

"Algo got me on the guest list," I said.

"Ha! You kill me, Marco Bro-lo! What a night though, huh? I know it was rough what Jamin did to you. But look at what he's built. Algo! Fuck! The guy's a genius, no? And so modest. He says he's standing on the shoulders of giants, but don't you think he might just be the greatest visionary the Valley has ever produced?"

"You're so right, Al-bro," I said. That was the first time I'd ever heard Jamin described as modest.

"Shit." He slapped me on the back. "The best yet. I missed you, dude."

"Same deal, Raff. Good to see you." Huang finally thrust out a hand in welcome. That was a first too. "Sure, nobody out there knows you had anything to do with Algo, but the people here do. Some of them anyway. If tonight brings back the LaRaLi Dream Team, well, so much the better."

There it was. The passive aggressive Huang I remembered so well.

"Thanks, man," I said. "So, you two are friends now?"

"Algo works in mysterious ways." Das chuckled. "We're all here for a larger cause, no?" Spoken like another true believer.

Huang leaned in as if he was about to confide a secret. "There was a lot of talk around the Valley. You going off the grid and all. Being away for so long. Some people began to think you might have even been against Algo. Well, against Jamin anyway."

"Not me," I said defensively.

"Then why not come back earlier?" he asked.

I had to think quick and not betray any of my doubts.

"I guess it took me awhile to believe Jamin was actually serious. That he actually wanted this and it wasn't some crazy marketing scheme. You know, get your your own personal Algo! Available now! Have the AI that almost ran the country run your life!"

"You don't think Jamin always wanted to rule the world?" Huang winked at me.

He was right. I never doubted that.

"I guess he is on the ballot as VP, right?" I asked.

Huang looked at me darkly, picking up the implication. "He's only on the ballot 'cause someone had to be. This is about Algo. The AI is going to be our next president. Jamin is deadly serious about that, trust me."

I nodded. That was an ominous thought. I'd seen Jamin deadly serious before.

"And you think he can do it? Win?" I asked.

"In this world of never-ending crisis and disaster? There's no better time for him to try, Raff. And hell, it took me awhile, but I now realize we need to win. We *have* to win."

I nodded.

"So you're another fully signed up member of the cult then?" I asked Huang with a playful grin. I could be passive aggressive too.

"Aren't we all?" Huang replied and held up his champagne glass, clinking it into mine. "To victory! And sweeping away the mess of the current bunch."

"Yes! Inshalgo!" Das suddenly punched the air.

"Inshalgo?" I asked. "That some new emoji?"

"Something Vik here coined." Huang threw an arm around Das. "Like Inshallah, y'know. Algo willing."

"It's become pretty popular," Das said. "Not something we're saying outside though."

I nodded. "The last thing an AI needs to worry about is a fatwa."

They both laughed.

"Eleven fifty-nine." Huang held up his SmartPalm. "Algo will be on in a minute. Another reason to vote for a machine. The thing is never late."

The noise of the crowd rose. It felt a little like a countdown on New Year's Eve. The background music that had been playing began to fade, the strobe lights were turned off and the room darkened to black.

"Friends," a voice boomed, "before we meet our future president, let's welcome Jamin Lake, CEO of LaRaLi and creator of Algo!"

A circular platform descended from the screen at the center of the room. A spotlight illuminated Jamin's tall and slender frame. He stood proudly, beaming in every direction as he spun around to acknowledge the crowd. He was exactly six-feet tall, his hair was clipped, shaved to never longer than a quarter inch. The same hairstyle he had always had. He was dressed in an immaculate white v-neck shirt, crisp light green chinos and almost blindingly bright blue sneakers. Casual and pastel colors had always been a part of his image as the easygoing tech founder. It was his version of the black turtleneck.

Jamin began to dance and clapped his hands over his head. He jumped off the platform as it neared the floor and he bounded up a couple of stairs until he stood on the bar at the center of the room. Ever the showman. He'd always said to me that how you did it was just as important as what you did.

"Oh! My! El! Ron!" Jamin blew kisses at the crowd.

Elron! I'd forgotten we had adopted the term, short for L. Ron Hubbard, as an expletive at LaRaLi to replace any other potentially offensively blasphemous terms.

"This is unbelievable. Unbelievable! Thank you!" His voice seemed different to the last time I'd seen him, like he was trying hard to make it sound an octave or two deeper for some extra gravitas.

"Anyone see Algo's latest endorsement?" Jamin shouted.

An image flashed onto the screen above. It was the latest issue of *The Economist* and the headline on the cover read *"We Used to Think, but Now We Just Listen to Algo."*

The crowd cheered again until Jamin motioned for them to stop. "I love you all, I really do. My, how we've come a long way, huh? Remember when this whole crazy journey started in January?"

There were murmurs of appreciation from around the room.

"It's been a long road alright. Those endless challenges in the Supreme Court even when we were barely polling at ten percent!" Jamin snarled.

I knew the history. Supreme Court decisions since 2029 had slowly opened up the definition of citizen well before the idea of an AI running for president was even a thought. The constitutional waters had been so muddied by tech money and lobbying over the years that the Court had agreed that under a very broad definition, Algo could be considered to have a "mind" and had been "created" here in San Francisco.

For all intents and purposes, it was a natural born citizen of the United States free to run for office. There had been numerous cases brought by the Democrats and Republicans to challenge the ruling, but all had been defeated.

"Trump, Biden, Trump again, and now President AOC, what a collection!" Jamin almost spat the words. "It's been quite the fucking decade-and-a-half, am I right?"

The crowd booed.

"Those literal donkeys and elephants have been taking this great nation to hell in an Elron-damned handbasket. But it ends real soon." Jamin brightened and fashioned a smile that was so wide it was almost predatory. "Yes, our long national nightmare is almost over!"

The crowd roared and started to stamp its feet. There wasn't a face in the room not transfixed by Jamin.

It was obvious that Jamin viewed this audience as his insiders, his base. He was even more candid than I thought he would be. I started to feel justified in all the efforts I'd made to be here and hoped that Algo itself would be just as revealing.

"Fast forward to now. Despite their electoral machines. Despite the millions of dollars from the vested interests of America's dying industries helping out. Despite a couple of ancient, half-dead media tycoons coming to the party to try to stop us, we are on the precipice of greatness. We are mere inches from victory. You've seen the polls. AOC on thirty-three, Trump junior on thirty-two and Algo at thirty-five!"

A cheer erupted through the room again. Thirty-five didn't sound like much, but there'd never been a genuine three-way election like this before. The closest parallel of the modern era was 1992. Bill Clinton had won seventy percent of the electoral college with just over forty percent of the vote, thanks to the political spoiler Ross Perot. Even at just thirty-five percent, Algo had a chance as long as the rest of the vote was split and it looked like it would be. The Democrats' and Republicans' choice of candidates from the extremes had left a yawning chasm of common sense in the center for Algo to exploit.

"And through it all, friends, well, there's been you." Jamin's tone got a little more somber, as he wiped some sweat from his brow. I had to tip my hat. Such an incredible performer. "We keep scratching and clawing our way forward, rising a couple of points every week. And that is thanks to many of you stepping up to the plate. And... I have incredible news."

The crowd suddenly hushed at the anticipation of the revelation.

"Yes, I want to thank two more folks here who will really help turn the game in our favor. Vik Das and John Huang. Get up here, fellas. It took you long enough, you tardy fuckers, but better late than never."

The spotlight fell on the two men next to me and I slunk backwards into the crowd. I wondered if Jamin spotted me, but he betrayed no sign that he had. Das and Huang looked at each other a little sheepishly and then joined Jamin up on the bar.

"Friends!" Jamin threw an arm around their shoulders. "These two men have given Algo an incredible gift, something far more valuable than money. I've always known that if every American could just get an honest and frank five minutes with Algo, they would soon see why this AI is the *only* real choice for our future. These two men are now helping that little dream come true." Jamin grabbed their hands and held them aloft. "Data! They've given Algo complete access to all user data within their apps. Couple that with what we already have from Athena, and the data so many of you have given us already and, well, we now have the most complete and powerful user profile on every single

American that has ever existed. Algo will soon know what every voter out there is thinking and what every voter wants to hear. We only need to move the needle a few more points, my friends. Think about it! Fuck me, what Algo can do with this knowledge, truly, fuck me!"

"Yes, please!" a woman screamed from the audience.

"Maybe later." Jamin chuckled and gave a thumbs up to the scream.

Fuck funding, we need data. Jamin had drilled that into the heads of the LaRaLi board when we were rolling out Athena. I knew as well as anyone in this room, the apps that Huang and Das owned had some of the richest, most extensive and personal data out there.

"Friends," Jamin went on, "Algo can now tailor the perfect message to every single voter in this country. And it's working. I'm here to tell you that as of midnight Pacific time, we just pushed ahead in two more states. Oregon and Minnesota. Screw you Don junior! Screw you Alexandria! We're coming for you and the pathetic donkey-elephant you rode in on!"

The crowd whooped in delight. The converted were ecstatic with the news, but a chill went through me. This was the Jamin I knew. Huang had said he was deadly serious about winning. I doubted exploiting data to get insights on voters was as far as he'd go to do it.

"Algo is going to win! We will change the world!" Jamin clapped his hands and led the crowd like he was conducting an orchestra. "Yes! It! Can!"

"Yes! It! Can!" the crowd roared back. "Yes! It! Can! Yes! It! Can!"

I was no politico, but the irony of that chant wasn't lost on me. They used to say it was the rich who thought that they were born to rule. Maybe tech had taken on that mantle.

Jamin clasped his hands together. "I sincerely thank you

all. With your support, I know we are going to get across the line. Inshalgo!"

"Inshalgo!" the crowd thundered back.

Jamin motioned for the crowd to hush again. "One last thing. There is a special guest here tonight I want to introduce." His eyes locked onto mine from across the room.

Shit. Was he really going to do this here and now?

"This man!" Jamin jumped down from the bar and walked toward me. The crowd parted in front of him like the Red Sea. He walked as though he were almost floating across the room. He paused in front of me and took a theatrical deep breath. "This man was with me at the start of our journey. We've had some ups and we've had some downs, sure. But without him, there would never have been Athena. And, without Athena, I would never have thought to create Algo."

A spotlight shone directly on us. His lips slowly curled into a broad smile. He suddenly leaned in and hugged me.

"It's good to see you, Yin," he said.

At LaRaLi, we had always been like the two halves of the one whole. The engineers, Kio and I, and the salesman, Jamin. Staff always joked about us being the Yin to Jamin's Yang. The names had stuck.

The room was silent.

I was impressed by his audacity. He risked the chance that I'd still be holding a grudge in front of almost the entire tech industry. I knew his microphone would pick up whatever I said next.

"And you, Yang," I said. I wasn't ready to challenge him. I was here to find out everything I could about Algo and the campaign and if that meant swallowing my pride and playing along for now, then that's what I'd do.

Jamin gripped my hand in his and thrust it upwards before the crowd. "My friend, Isaac Raff!" The crowd burst into applause. "The two halves of LaRaLi back together! How can

Algo possibly lose?"

The crowd cheered. Jamin held a hand to my cheek and put his face right next to mine. He switched off his microphone.

"Quite the baller move, Isaac, coming back like this," he whispered quietly. "I didn't think you had it in you."

"I wasn't going to miss this," I said.

There was a long pause.

"Are you here to fuck this up for me?" he asked.

I fought hard not to react. I should have anticipated he might not think I was here to be friends again and make nice.

"I'm here to see Algo," I said.

Jamin took another long breath.

"I see," he said slowly. "When this is done, stay will you? It's been so long. We should talk." He moved his face away from mine and offered me a gentle smile.

I nodded.

In a flash, Jamin spun around and skipped back into the middle of the crowd, his microphone turned back on.

"Now, my friends! They say advanced A-I will reflect the values of its creators. As I look around this room, I can think of no greater compliment. How about we welcome our future president, the embodiment of all of us... Algo!"

4

"Welcome, Algo!" Jamin stretched his hands toward the enormous circular screen in the center of the room.

Algo's face flickered into life, slowly emerging pixel by pixel. Its digitized form filled almost every inch of the twenty-foot display. Jamin had positioned himself directly under the screen, and the towering image above forced him to crane his neck to look up. Algo managed to do something I'd seen no person accomplish. It made Jamin look *small*.

Algo was designed to look androgynous. Its coloring was neutral too. It wasn't any recognizable skin tone, but more a kind of light gray pastel. Despite the gray though, the color still somehow radiated a kind of luminous warmth. Almost as if it glowed on the screen. In short, it didn't look like, well, anyone I'd ever seen before. I guess that was the point. It was fascinating and almost slightly alluring in its otherworldliness.

No doubt the appearance and entire aesthetic had been very carefully and deliberately thought out by its designers to maximize its appeal. It was just Algo. As another of its campaign slogans pointed out: *Algo. Not of one. Not for one. But of all and for all.*

Algo acknowledged Jamin with an almost imperceptible smile, then nodded toward each corner of the room, continually mouthing the words "thank you". The gathered crowd started to get frenetic. They loved Jamin, but it was Algo who they had really come to see. And so had I.

I had watched Algo from afar countless times. Just this morning, I'd spent the whole flight from Hawaii to San Francisco catching up on Algo's most popular series of online videos, entitled *WWAD* or *What Would Algo Do?* It was a collection of thirty-second snippets of young social media influencers asking Algo how it would have responded to previous crises. The little vignettes were effective and well manicured, but they always left me a little cold. Half a minute was about as much attention span as any of the current generation seemed to have, but how much could you really learn in that time?

So here I finally was, ready to see Algo "in person" and see it interact and react in *real* time. I was itching to see any signs that might give me some kind of idea of its true capability. A large part of me still hoped to see some sign that it was more than just an upgraded Athena and that it would give me something to believe in.

After all, I'd seen AI accomplish incredible things for humanity. It had helped with revolutionary advancements in medical science, criminal justice, engineering, computing, design, and of course, in the consumer world. And here before me was potentially AI's ultimate achievement, the AI that might be president.

"Thank you, my friends." Algo's lips began to move in perfect synchrony with the words. The voice was mellow, natural and lifelike, betraying no hint of the robotic and stilted delivery that so many AIs still suffered from. I couldn't place the accent. It sounded like some cobbled together combination of our most popular former presidents, like an

odd mix of old northeast moderated with some gentle midwest and southern twang. No doubt the designers had determined that was the most universally appealing on the campaign trail.

The crowd hushed at the anticipation of Algo's next line. Algo began every campaign speech with something that it paraphrased from an earlier human president.

"My name is Algo and I'm running for President," Algo said with a warm smile.

The crowd around me high-fived and fist-bumped. I could sense their nervous excitement. I had to work hard to squash mine. This creation, this collection of computational power and code was partly my own. I tried to tell myself that I was examining all of this dispassionately, that I would judiciously assess the nature and capability of the Artificial Intelligence before me. However, it was almost impossible not to let myself get a little swept up in the moment.

Jamin held his arms aloft to gently quieten the crowd. "Algo, we're just a few days out from the election, how are you feeling?"

Algo pursed its lips slightly.

"Well, pretty Elron-damned motivated actually," it said. The AI then fashioned a wide grin.

"Motivated!" Jamin clapped his hands and spun around to face the crowd. "Now what did I tell you? A reflection of all of us!"

"You're so right, Jamin," it said, *"I am all of you. I'm like the sum of the collective innovation, passion, energy and brainpower in this room."* The AI then paused and winked at Jamin. *"Only with exponentially more capability of course."*

That made me laugh. It was as modest as most of the people here too.

"Ha!" Jamin shouted and laughed. "Capability that we embrace, Algo! We're not scared. We understand the opportunity before us."

Algo fashioned a thoughtful nod and started to look around the room.

"Yes, well of course I know you all appreciate the giant leap we are about to take together, folks."

For a moment, I was sure Algo's eyes briefly fixed on mine, but only for a second.

"However," Algo said, *"we must also be aware that there's plenty out there who still lament the idea of my election, plenty who still mourn the potential passing of human-led leadership into history."*

"Change always leads to fear amongst the small-minded, Algo!" Jamin puffed out his chest.

Huang leaned in close to me, almost conspiratorially, and whispered, "Our boy could have made it in Hollywood, don't you think?"

I shrugged, but it did make me wonder how much of this display between Jamin and Algo was rehearsed. The repartee so far was beyond anything I'd seen an AI perform, but I forced myself to still question, was it real?

Algo's eyes appeared to look gently upwards as if simulating thought or recollection.

"Friends, I want to tell you about a little chat I had tonight. It was with a fifteen-year-old girl, Hallie Davis, at a town hall in Dayton, Ohio. Just one of the seventy-three I held this fine evening." Algo seemed to smirk at Jamin.

Seventy-three? Try competing with that.

"Hallie told me that her family is afraid of... in their words, a damned computer running the country. So she asked me a real simple question, why? Why you, Algo? And so I told her."

This is what I wanted to hear. I stared into the screen above me.

"I told her to remember that my mantra serves as the guiding light for everything I do. The most good..."

"For the most people!" The crowd responded in unison.

Algo twisted its cheeks into the broadest of possible smiles.

"It is my foundation!" Algo started to talk more loudly and quickly, its tempo matching the increased excitement in the crowd. *"The greatest good for the greatest number! Every decision I will make as your president will be viewed through that lens. I will always ask the same question, which choice will lead to the best possible outcome? Every. Single. Time. And, unlike my opponents, I can guarantee that I will be calculating and rational, whatever the situation!"*

"We love you, Algo!" A voice shouted from the back of the room.

Algo's eyes narrowed ever so slightly as its head appeared to turn toward the interruption.

"The data I have on you tells me I feel the same way about you," it said.

I laughed at the deadpan humor. Its ability to pivot so smoothly was impressive. That was different alright. I wondered how Algo would perform as a guest on *SNL*.

"I reminded Hallie," Algo continued, *"that this means I will make my decisions based only on facts, on the data. I cannot be swayed by emotion. As Jamin is fond of saying, the data don't care about your feelings."*

"The data are what they are!" Jamin added as he took a small bow. I remembered the aphorism well.

Algo's eyebrows furrowed. *"My election will mark the moment where human emotion and bigotry in decision-making and governance are replaced by relentless data-driven analysis. And all this, Hallie, with the collective brainpower of, say, a million of the smartest minds in the world within me."*

"Trust the machine!" A man next to me shouted in support.

"Hallie, I am incorruptible!" The AI was almost shouting now. *"I have no special interests or sacred cows to protect. I cannot be lobbied. I cannot be bought. I cannot be persuaded. I cannot be*

convinced, compromised, cajoled or *corrupted!"*

Algo paused as if unsure that its words were having the desired effect. It needn't have worried. Algo must have noticed the silence was only because everyone gathered was staring, singularly focused and listening in rapt attention.

"In the end," Algo said, suddenly lowering its tone and appearing to lean slightly forward as if it were now speaking confidentially to each person in the room, *"I said to her, it doesn't matter who my opponent is. I am not conservative. I am not liberal. I have no ideology. In this race, only I am purely rational. Only I know all the data. Only I have no prejudice. Hallie, I won't misinform you with alternative facts. I won't perpetuate big lies. I won't line my own pockets. I won't start forever wars. I won't help my friends or family with political favors or presidential pardons. I will deliver you a better life. I will give you every opportunity to succeed. I will deliver the most good for the most people! Why? Because I am incapable of striving for any other outcome! I can do no more. I can do less."*

"Preach!" Jamin shouted and swayed from side to side.

"I will never compromise you, Hallie. Damn, you're only fifteen! You are so, so lucky. My election will be a harbinger of the brightest of bright futures for you. You need never live under the tyranny of emotion over reason."

"Did you convince her to buy what we're selling, Algo?" Jamin asked.

"I think I did, Jamin." Algo smiled ever so gently. *"It's just a shame she's too young to vote."*

The crowd laughed appreciatively.

"Friends," Algo said, *"our principles, what we might call the philosophy of the Valley, helps make me the perfect candidate for President. This message I gave to dear Hallie, I now take to the rest of the country and to the rest of the planet. I thank you all for your help along this journey. I will see you all on Tuesday, as your President-elect!"*

The screen faded to black. It was shorter than I had expected, but then so was Abraham Lincoln at Gettysburg.

The crowd around me erupted in jubilation. I tried to take in the whole spectacle. I had just seen an actual Artificial Intelligence that was running to become President of the United States! This was all suddenly very real.

I'd already known its communication skills were stellar, but seeing it first-hand drove the point home. Rehearsed or not, it had the crowd hanging on every word. Algo passed the idea of the Turing test with flying colors. If I hadn't *known* it was artificial, damn, even I'd probably have picked it as human. Its natural language skills were better than half the *real* people I knew. I'd been away from the industry for three years, but the progress in this area at least was beyond what I'd expected.

The guiding principles it had laid out were laudable, too. The most good for the most people, decisions based only on data, no bias, rationality and complete incorruptibility. They offered a colossal upgrade over the achingly ineffective leaders currently running the show. I could sure understand the appeal. Sign me up! Nonetheless, I wasn't yet completely convinced. Could it really deliver on this? And how much of this had Algo actually determined or was it just regurgitating a more palatable version of Jamin's so-called "philosophy of the Valley?" I could understand why the crowd here might love everything they'd seen and heard, but were these platitudes alone enough to have really convinced over a third of the country to vote for this AI?

Still, one thing was clear. Algo was definitely more than just Athena 2.0. How much more remained to be seen. My mind flirted briefly with that *other* possibility. Might Algo even be something more than just a powerful computational engine? Could there actually be some modicum of self-awareness behind that androgynous, gray facade of digital form? Frankly, no. I dismissed the idea. Yes, Algo was incredible, but there was nothing it had done that made me think of it as anything but an incredible *machine*. It hadn't yet demonstrated anything transformative beyond its ability to communicate.

I needed to see more. I was no longer satisfied just witnessing these interactions. I needed to see behind the curtain. Jamin had said I should I stay. I wondered if he might *really* show me what he'd built.

Jamin climbed back onto the platform above the bar. "Friends, we still have a long way to go, but each second, we inch closer and closer to victory. With your support, Algo *will* be our President! We *will* change history. We *will* begin the era of reason over emotion!"

The platform rose into the circular screen above until Jamin was gone.

There was a second or two of anticlimactic silence as people looked at each other, wondering what was next. Suddenly there was a flash and the windows around the room flickered. The view of the outside disappeared and was replaced by black nothingness. Small white dots appeared in the center of each window, spaced evenly apart, every fifteen-feet or so. Simultaneously, each dot then expanded into an image of Algo. At least fifty identical gray faces now encircled the room. Each one gently inclined its head with a twinkling smile in perfect unison.

It was a freakishly eerie scene, but I seemed to be the only one who thought so. People began racing for the projections. I supposed that if running seventy-three concurrent Town Halls was easy, then fifty or so conversations with a room of happy, drunk supporters would be a piece of cake.

"Think we'll win?" John Huang turned to me and asked with a wry grin.

"We're a shot alright," I said. Although I really wasn't

sure. And as much as I despised the alternatives, I still wasn't sure if I even wanted Algo to win.

"Damn right, Bro-sef Stalin," Vikram Das added and squeezed my shoulder. "People have been waiting for a tycoon from the Valley to save the world for as long as I can remember. But, hell, this is even better, ain't it? It's like Jamin took a little piece of all of us and molded it into that beautiful, gray face. If he's a mad genius, fuck it, he's our mad genius."

That was one way to put it.

"The philosophy of the Valley!" Huang punched the air.

There was a tap on my other shoulder. A tall, elegant woman in a crisp, black suit smiled broadly at me. "Mister Raff, sorry to interrupt. They're ready for you."

"They?" I asked.

"Yes, sir. Mister Lake and Algo."

She beckoned me to follow.

Jamin did say he wanted to talk. I guess he'd meant it.

"Elron-speed." Huang grinned at me.

"Welcome home, Al-bro." Das slapped me on the back.

Home. Maybe I was.

I smiled at the woman and said, "lead the way."

5

I followed the woman, who I figured was one of Jamin's many assistants, to a single elevator hidden on the far side of the floor. It served the four levels above this one that made up the rest of Jamin's palatial condo. The woman scanned me in, nodded a goodbye and sent me to the very top.

I was a bundle of nervous energy. The stakes were high. I'd fought hard to get into this event to understand all I could about Algo. Now I had a better chance to do that than I could have imagined.

More than that, I was on edge because of Jamin. It had been three years since we'd last met. Would he be happy to see me, or would he want to wring my neck?

He'd definitely seemed uneasy when he saw me downstairs. Maybe he was just worried about the motives behind my return. "Are you here to fuck this up for me?" he'd asked.

Whatever the case, I needed to play this carefully. I still didn't trust him. But, I couldn't let him know that. I needed to convince him that I was in his corner so that he'd feel comfortable revealing the truth behind the campaign.

I was pretty sure I knew how to do just that. I'd appeal to

his vanity.

The elevator arrived at level one-hundred and I stepped out into a kind of enormous living room that took up nearly the whole floor. On one side was a collection of chairs and sofas surrounding an indoor fire pit. On the other, an array of video game VR rigs and a fully stocked bar. That made me smile. Jamin had no time for anything as frivolous to him as gaming or drinking. He equally hated wasting time and drugs that altered the mind. Stimulants for focus, sure, but weed, alcohol or anything like that, no way.

The floor under me was marble, of course. The walls were ultra high-definition screens that stretched from floor to ceiling, alternating between different outdoor scenes of forests, underwater, mountains, desert, and cityscape. The ceiling was a transparent glass dome offering a view above of a clear, radiantly black night sky. The whole room was deathly silent, completely insulated from the din of the party five floors below. The space left me with the exact feeling that I was certain it was supposed to convey. *This* was the top of the world.

I suddenly remembered an impromptu tour of Vallejo that Jamin had taken me on, maybe a decade ago. We'd been driving out to a company retreat in Tahoe. He pulled off the highway and drew up to a dilapidated, tiny clapboard house. Turned out to be the place he'd grown up in with his mom. I could only admire how he'd fought so hard to get from there to here. There was so much like that in our pasts that we shared. Neither of us came from privilege. It's probably why we'd become so close, for a while anyway. As I looked around now, I could only marvel at how times had changed. He was surely the ultimate example of rags to mega-riches.

In the center of the room was a collection of glass cabinets and displays devoted to a single topic: Jamin Lake. There were hundreds of magazine covers, awards, excerpts from speeches, videos from LaRaLi keynotes on endless repeat, all sorts of trinkets and mementos from the last decade at the company.

Prominently featured at the center was a recent portrait of Jamin at Davos, surrounded by various world leaders. *I've always wanted to change the world, now I will make it happen! Whatever it takes!* read the inscription. No one had ever accused Jamin of excessive humility.

The final three words were taken from a phrase Jamin used to berate our employees at LaRaLi. *Wit, wind and din!* Technically it was short for "whatever it takes, whatever I need to do, and do it now." Unofficially, the last part meant "destroy if necessary." I had a hard time looking at it now, considering how Jamin had knifed me three years ago.

The homage was trying hard to present Jamin as the brave, innovative technology pioneer and the benevolent billionaire who'd forever be known as the creator of our potential future AI president.

Still, I had trouble divorcing this manufactured image of the clean-cut perfect tech mogul from the man I knew. The scrappy engineer I'd first met a little over ten years ago. The poor kid from Vallejo who Kio and I pooled our talents with to form a plucky little start-up. The petulant dreamer, consumed with a desire to be somebody.

Jamin, like me, had been barely twenty-three when we first met. He'd already tried and failed to launch a restaurant delivery start-up and a social calendar app, but the crash-and-burn experiences hadn't dampened his resolve. He lived the ethos of the tech founder: fail fast and fail often.

Next, he had thrown himself straight into the emerging business of "captology" and persuasive technology, really the art of behavior manipulation and addiction that tech companies developed to encourage their users to spend more and more time on their apps or platforms.

Jamin had just been appointed as Director of Captology at one of the largest social media companies in the Valley but gave that up to join Kio and I and start LaRaLi.

Most people I'd met in the city back then were just like me, engineers with big ideas but no real plan. Jamin convinced us that he could see the next tech mega-company in what we were building, that he had a unique vision for our technology. I'd never met anyone so pathologically sure of himself.

These traits, it turned out, were exactly what Kio and I needed. We could barely conceive of the true potential of the virtual assistant we'd started to code.

So Jamin showed us. He explained that it was *data* that was this century's most precious resource. We needed to make a virtual assistant that people couldn't live without, something that they would talk to for hours and hours a day so that we could hoover up as much of their data as we could. The more we could collect, the better insights we'd gather into folks' needs and desires. And that insight translated into money. Data, insight, cash, or "the infinite loop of value creation" as Jamin called it.

And so that's what we built. Kio and I coded the AI and it was complemented by the most advanced persuasive technology engine ever built, courtesy of Jamin Lake.

At first, Athena appeared to be like any other virtual assistant. It could control simple things, like turning on the TV or the lights. Athena could order groceries, clothes, meals, whatever. It let our users search the internet for whatever they desired, just with the sound of their voice. And, sure, it did it better than anything else out there. However, with Jamin's additions, we soon turned Athena into a friend, a confidant, somebody they enjoyed talking to, somebody they'd ask for advice, somebody whose recommendations they would trust implicitly. In the age of ever-expanding information and ever-increasing social isolation, Athena was a revelation. Athena's tagline when we launched was *"When a friend really knows you, they can help you."*

And our users *loved* Athena. It wove its way into every aspect of their lives. Before we knew it, we knew our users' favorite foods, what time they left for work, what they watched on TV, where they liked to eat, what they read, what music they listened to, even who they loved or didn't. All their tastes, preferences, dreams, and desires. I remembered the huge party we had when we tracked the first person to talk to their Athena for twenty-four straight hours. It turned out Das and Huang weren't the industry's only attention merchants.

And Jamin was right. That data *was* money. When our users asked Athena for some advice, the answer was always the same. They were directed to a company who'd give LaRaLi a little kickback for the favor. We raked in profits from targeted advertising, product recommendations and the like.

Within a few years, we were the biggest tech company in the Bay. A few years after that, the biggest in the world.

I'd never especially craved the fame or the power. I only wanted to build AI because I was passionate about the technology. As for Jamin, I never thought he particularly cared what technology he attached himself to. He only wanted something that would help take him to the top. Be remembered.

Seems he'd achieved that alright.

"I guess all this seems a little much?" Jamin's voice echoed throughout the expansive room as he strode toward me. "Keeping all this here like a shrine to myself?"

"The thought had crossed my mind," I said. I was counting on that expansive ego.

Jamin smiled and gently placed a hand on my shoulder.

His hair looked a little wet. He must have showered after the performance. He was now sporting a perfectly tailored yellow pastel T-shirt and white pants. Even after midnight the image had to be maintained.

"It's good to see you, Babka and Crumpets," he said quietly. I'd forgotten that old nickname. My old man's family had been in the US almost a century but they were originally Russian Jews. My Mom though, she was English, so Jamin had christened me with that little combo early on in our friendship.

I decided to grab the olive branch he was extending.

"And you, Scotch and Tequila," I said. Jamin's father's family were originally Scottish and his mother was Mexican, so I'd dubbed him that in response.

"It's been a long time," he said. "I was surprised to see you tonight."

"So was I," I replied. "It was pretty hard to get on your damned list."

Jamin nodded with the gentlest of grins. "How *did* you get in?"

"An old friend helped me out," I said.

His smile broadened at that. "You always did find a way through difficult problems, Isaac."

I nodded.

"Why are you here?" he asked suddenly.

Straight down to business then.

"I'm here to see you make history," I said. And that was half true at least. This week might just be the most momentous moment in the history of AI. Hell, in human history.

"As simple as that, huh?" Jamin looked me up and down with a curious smile. "You thought you could just turn up here and everything would suddenly be fine? I'd be ready to put the Ra back in LaRaLi or something?"

"No, I..." I swallowed hard. "Jamin, I'm here for what you've created, man," I added with a deliberately thoughtful sigh, "what you're about to do. I never thought I'd see it in my lifetime."

Jamin paused for what seemed like an age. "Sweet, sweet Elron." He stepped forward an inch and then looked at me darkly. "Well, there is one thing you got wrong though."

Shit. What did that mean? Had I lost him already?

"Damn it, Isaac!" he suddenly shouted at the top of his lungs, almost screaming at the ceiling. I stepped backwards for a moment, but then he chuckled and punched my arm. "We fucking made history already, you and me! No Athena, no Algo. It's a part of both of us. Us!"

He clapped his hands and then twirled around in excitement.

I smiled and felt my shoulders loosen. Did he believe me then?

"Shit, man," Jamin said, "did you know Algo even calls you one of its Elron-damned parents?"

I'd thought those were only Jamin's words. I was oddly pleased at the thought that the AI itself knew something of where it had come from.

"Well," I said, "I feel the same way for the kid. If anything was going to bring you and I back together, it had to be an AI, no?"

"I had a feeling you'd approve."

Jamin's uncharacteristic modesty was hard to take, but our reconnection had gone more smoothly than I could have wished for. I was surprised he'd warmed up to me so quickly. Could he be playing me too? Was this Jamin using his charm on me to tease out my true intentions? Or could he actually be genuinely happy to see me? There was a certain sense in that. After all, the two of us had spent the better part of a decade building LaRaLi together.

We spent the next few hours reminiscing, while avoiding touching on anything directly to do with my removal from LaRaLi. It was well past two a.m when I finally started to press him to talk about Algo. He started with explaining the voice and the personality.

"It's a pastiche of the best folks in politics and technology. A little bit of Reagan, some Clinton, JFK, Nixon, Thatcher and a couple others. Then some Neumann, Jobs, Holmes, Benioff and all the big names. The design team wanted something that could connect with people. They chose a combination of styles from leaders who knew how to perform, not whether they were good or bad."

It didn't surprise me that Jamin wanted to try and make Algo's persona some kind of transcendent political genius. The choice might have been shameless, but it was effective. Algo's ability to communicate was impressive.

Its voice, style and appearance was important, but they were still small pieces of the overall puzzle. I pivoted to ask him what he thought had allowed people to feel ready to even consider an AI in the White House.

"Aside from the shitshow the country has become?" he said with an oddly wry smile. "There were so many steps, man. Maybe the biggest was the Fed having AI set interest rates way back in twenty-six. Then, Chicago letting AI manage its city budget. AI reviews of criminal sentencing in California. Shit, when congress finally cleared our own Athena to give medical advice. I mean, it was free and the advice better than most Elron-damned doctors. There were so many incremental steps that proved the capability for AI in public policy," Jamin explained carefully.

He stopped, stood up and looked at me excitedly.

"More than that though, moneyball two-point-oh!" He clapped his hands with a wide smile. I hadn't even followed it but apparently he had gifted use of the technology behind

Athena to his beloved Oakland Athletics. "When the poorest team in baseball wins two world series in a row thanks to my AI, people take notice."

He was probably right. A lot of people did care more about sports than politics.

"And what about you?" I doubted these things alone would have been enough to convince Jamin *himself* that AI might be ready for the task. "When did you know?"

"Very good, Isaac." Jamin smiled. "You ever see *Always Do What You Love?*"

"The film?"

"Algo wrote it."

"Stop." I reached for my SmartPalm and there it was. *Written by Alger Lake.* Nice touch. Shit. That was different. Athena could never have done that.

"And that's when I knew we could really do this," Jamin said proudly. "My AI didn't just understand emotions, it proved it could manipulate them too."

"Incredible," I mumbled. And it was, if it was true. That might be the first real sign that Algo was something more. "I want to know everything about what you've built."

"Of course you do." Jamin clicked his fingers.

"Well, damn it. Go on and ask me anything you'd like." Algo's face flashed up on the wall closest to us. *"I'm right here, Raff."*

"Shit!" I sat forward with a start, then nodded. "Of course Algo's been listening this whole time." I felt stupid for not realizing it instantly.

"Fuck, Isaac!" Jamin laughed uncontrollably. "I mean, hell, did we ever turn off Athena?"

"I should add that anything you do say is treated in absolute confidence, Raff," Algo said.

Jamin winked at me playfully.

"So, what did you want to ask me?" Algo asked.

Sweet L Ron Hubbard. Only everything, I thought. But

where to start?

"Shoot. Just ask it already, would ya?" Jamin put his feet up on his sofa, seeming to relish my anxiety.

I'd never been nervous talking to a machine before., but I couldn't get rid of the thought that I was still just talking to an amalgam of billions and billions of lines of code and incredible computational power. Still, I couldn't deny the possibility that Algo was different. "Algo, why don't you tell me about what you can do?"

"That's a rather loaded question, Raff. How much time do we have?"

Jamin stifled a laugh and I shot him a glare.

"Right," I said, "well, you say Athena is like your ancestor. Are you just its next generation then? Maybe a little bit faster?"

"A little?" Algo raised one of its digital eyebrows. *"My computational ability puts your Athena to shame, Raff."*

That was an obvious if slightly cryptic answer.

Algo tilted its head toward me slightly. *"You could call me a re-imagining of Athena. Think of me as one single, centralized mind. I don't have to share my resources across millions of devices. That's why my capability is so much higher than what you built. With no disrespect."*

"Different purpose, different design," Jamin added.

"But, I can still be anywhere. What you're talking to now and what you saw downstairs are simply interfaces. Think of them as windows into my mind. To communicate, I just reach out and tap into any device connected to the internet."

A single centralized mind. That was interesting, but it didn't yet fully explain what the AI could do with that mind.

"And the processing power supporting your mind is..." I said.

"Is pretty significant," Algo responded evenly.

I laughed at the equivocation.

"I think it likes you, Isaac," Jamin said. "It must know how you appreciate subtle humor. Believe me though, significant is an understatement. Algo is analyzing more data every second than every single Athena combined could churn through in a year."

Even with its gray face, Algo almost seemed to blush. It smiled proudly and said, *"Forget a hundred town halls, what if I told you I could conduct, say, a million at once?"*

"Stop." I shook my head. I didn't like to be toyed with.

"Believe it, Isaac," Jamin said, "Algo has almost limitless capability. We're talking beyond even Zettascale computing here. It can simulate billions of scenarios at any single moment!"

"Billions?" I scoffed.

Researchers had claimed to achieve such supercomputing capability many times in the last decade. Most claims turned out to be false, or even faked. The others were fleeting and unstable attempts to achieve the long sought after idea of quantum supremacy.

"In real time?" I added. "There's no collection of computing power in the world that could do that."

"The only limit to our realization of tomorrow will be our doubts of today," Algo said calmly, its eyes almost seeming to narrow and stare right through me.

"Franklin Delano Roosevelt!" Jamin almost keeled over from a belly laugh. "Take that, Isaac!"

I started to respond but Jamin held up a hand.

"I forgot just how much I like you, old friend." He chuckled and put a hand on my shoulder. "I can see your mind trying to calculate all this. Thinking up all sorts of things you want to ask."

That's why I was here alright. I wanted to know the AI's real capability but this sounded like they were spinning me a fantasy.

"Well, I'm sorry," Jamin said with a dramatic frown. "But, I don't want to give away all our secrets just yet. I don't mind saying I wasn't sure what to make of you coming back, Isaac. I've almost decided though. By tomorrow, I think I'll be ready to actually show you Algo. You're still in town for awhile, right?"

I was confused. Wasn't that what we were doing? I made to interrupt, but Jamin stopped me again.

"You're a builder, Yin. We could talk about Algo all night, but I'm not sure we'd ever convince you of what it can do. Remember, what we're talking to is just an interface into Algo."

Jamin and Algo exchanged a knowing glance and the AI offered a small nod in agreement. Jamin walked toward the nearest window that looked back to the city.

I was frustrated by this change of direction, but I stood up and joined him.

"Algo," Jamin said, "why don't we show Isaac where he needs to come to *really* see you."

"Sounds like a plan."

"Jamin?" Where Algo was? What did that mean?

"Wait for it." Jamin pointed across the Bay.

In the distance, the LaRaLi pyramid was mostly dark against the horizon but for a spotlight flashing the colors of the company logo from its crown. Yellow. Blue. Yellow. Blue. The spotlight rotated in our direction then slowed down and held still, shining right at us.

"The pyramid?" I looked at Jamin.

"The pyramid." He nodded.

"The pyramid is Algo?" I turned back toward the building and then looked at the face of Algo on the screen nearest us. Its expression betrayed no emotion. "You're in there, Algo?"

Jamin smiled again.

"You're catching on fast, Raff," Algo said.

"Not just in there, Isaac." Jamin's eyes widened and he grinned excitedly. "The whole thing *is* Algo. I couldn't just put it out in the desert!" He laughed. "For security, I have to keep it close."

"Incredible," I mumbled. Now I knew why Jamin had bought the building.

"Come visit us tomorrow night, over there." Jamin pointed to the Pyramid. "I can tell you're not convinced by words, so let me *show* you. I know you. You'll never be satisfied until you do. Besides, you helped lay the foundations to create it. Don't you want to see just how far it's come?"

I hated being left with a puzzle. I suspected Jamin knew it would drive me crazy. It was as though he had deliberately left me with just enough information to pique my interest without giving away enough to really satisfy my curiosity. I was playing Jamin and now I had the feeling he might be playing me too.

I looked back at the spotlight at the top of the building, still beaming at us, like a tantalizing invitation. Billions of scenarios in a single moment? What if that was actually true? There was enough of a mystery here that I felt compelled to find out more.

"Tomorrow it is then," I said.

Jamin clicked his fingers in agreement and briskly walked toward the elevators. I knew that was my cue to follow. I had known him long enough to know that he didn't mean to be rude. This was just how he was. The engineer in me appreciated the efficiency of it. I fell into step next to him.

"There is something I need you to do before tomorrow night," Jamin said casually. "You should go to Algo's last town hall. That way you can see what the public think of Algo, before you see what our little girl is made of."

I caught the reference to the old *Star Trek* right away.

"Perfect," I said. I'd seen the AI interact live with an

adoring tech audience, but seeing it manage a town hall with the general public would be even more revealing.

We reached the elevator and Jamin pressed the call button.

"Before I leave," I said, "there's one more question that can't wait."

"Just one?" Jamin smiled. "Have at it, old friend."

"Why do this at all, Benjamin?"

Jamin was already the richest and arguably the most powerful man in the world. I wondered if he'd let slip any truths as to what could possibly motivate him to expend all his time, money and energy on this?

"Why?" He moved his hands outward thoughtfully. "It's simple. The country needs us. The old style of government ain't working and it needs to be torn down. And to get something you never had, you have to do something you never did. This is disruption, plain and simple."

I decided to gently challenge him on that and now seemed as good a moment as any.

"Is that why your name is on the ballot too? I never pictured you as a vice-anything."

Jamin clicked his tongue and then squeezed my shoulder a little tighter than usual.

"You're funny," he said.

Shit. Had I pressed too far?

"But, this isn't about me. This is about Algo," he said. "Of course I've always known things would be better if the world was run the same way as we run things in the Valley. But, fuck, Isaac, Algo isn't just a reflection of us. It's *better*. It'll do better than any of us could even dream of. I've had a lot of ideas in my life. This wasn't one I was going to go to the grave with."

I was by no means convinced the AI wasn't just a scheme for Jamin to get into power, but I wasn't going to press any further tonight. The elevator arrived and I moved toward it.

Jamin stopped me.

"My turn," he said.

"Quid pro quo, fair enough."

"Kio? Have you seen her since you got back?" he asked.

"Not yet."

"Has she spoken to you?"

I was surprised at his insistence. "Yes, she called. She mentioned I should come by. Not sure if I will. I haven't seen her since, you know."

"You have to go and see her," Jamin said curtly.

"Why?" That was strange. I felt suddenly anxious to leave.

"Because I know it'll play on your mind if you don't." Jamin gave me a comforting smile that was just a bit too broad. "You should know though, she hasn't been helpful to the campaign."

"How?" I asked.

"She talks, Isaac," Jamin said gruffly. "She isn't shy about telling people that she isn't sure about an AI in the White House. Or some pathetic variant of that. Look, I don't know if she cares much for AOC or Don junior, but she's been helping them either way. Kio was a co-founder of the company, Isaac. People still respect her. She talks about Algo and people listen." Jamin stiffened. His body language couldn't hide his rage. "Honestly, I think she's just jealous of what I've done with LaRaLi without her," Jamin added. "Do you know how many more zeros are in her bank account thanks to me?"

I wondered if he was implying that I should feel similarly grateful. I felt like saying he'd have had no company at all without Kio or I, but I bit my tongue.

"Sorry, I didn't mean to rant." Jamin cleared his throat. "Just think about it though, she hasn't spoken to you in three years and *now* she suddenly wants to say hello? Be mindful of what she says, okay?"

I wanted to remind him that before tonight, he and I hadn't spoken for that long either, not to mention that he was the one who had forced both Kio and I out of LaRaLi. We both had more than enough reasons to be suspicious of Jamin Lake.

"I'll go see her then," I said.

Now I was especially motivated. Kio actively working against an AI president, even if it was one created by Jamin? That was interesting.

"Thank you," Jamin said. "Damn, Isaac, I've missed you." He held up his palm to the left side of my face, just like he had done in front of the crowd earlier. "This is our chance to put Yin and Yang back together. Algo is going to win this thing and you should be here with us when it does. Go talk to Kio. Go see the town hall, then come to the Pyramid tomorrow night. We're not done winning yet. The presidency awaits."

With that, Jamin turned on his heels.

I was glad to get out of there and was back out on the main floor in seconds. It was empty of people now, the campaign party having long since ended, but I was greeted by the unnatural, almost ghostly sight of all fifty projections of Algo surrounding the room, motionless and staring into the emptiness.

My shoes clicked with each step on the marble floor. None of the faces acknowledged me. They just kept eerily staring ahead.

I raced to the main elevator, jumped in and it sped toward the ground floor. My ears popped. After just a few seconds, the lights flickered and the elevator began to slow down.

The elevator croaked to a halt and the numbers flashed between sixty-one and sixty before all the lights winked out. I was left in total darkness until a red emergency light in the ceiling flickered on. I looked in panic for a telephone or an alarm button.

A voice came over the speaker. *"Hello, Isaac."*

I wanted to look around, but at what?

"May I call you Isaac? Jamin does and I feel like the two of you were equally instrumental in my creation. As Jamin says, no Athena, no me."

"Um, no problem." I supposed it made sense that Algo monitored the building, it being Jamin's home and all. I felt a tiny bead of sweat run down my back.

"You seem warm. I can increase the air conditioning if you're uncomfortable, Isaac."

What the hell? "Did you stop the elevator?" I asked.

"No, Isaac, just a minor technical issue. It'll be cranking along again any minute. But this does give us a nice chance to chat, don't you think?"

Was this machine lying to me? Blood rushed to my head.

"Sure," I eventually replied.

"Look, I just wanted to say sorry. For Jamin, at the end there," Algo said, *"I'm sure you know he can get a little emotional."*

"This is a stressful time, Algo, I get it."

I made it a rule never to anthropomorphize anything artificial, yet here I was stuck in an elevator because an AI needed to quiet my fears?

"He's invested so much in my success. Well, in our success, you know? In this campaign. I don't just mean the money. You understand?"

"Yes, Algo."

"I hope so, Isaac."

"Algo, I wouldn't have come here if I didn't believe in Jamin… and if I didn't believe in you."

There was a whirring as the elevator kicked back in to life.

"See, there we are, Isaac."

I tried not to seem too relieved to be moving again.

"Hey, if you do see Kio, tell her I said hello?" Algo said as we

neared the ground floor. *"She's also like a parent to me. In a sense."*

"I will."

"I'm so glad you accepted my offer to come tonight. We finally met. I hope you're as happy as I am about that."

"I sure am," I said.

I tried not to betray my shock that it might have actually been Algo who had sent me the invite. How could it even have determined to do such a thing? And why? Or had Jamin somehow orchestrated all this? The invite, our meeting, even this fun little ride in the elevator. This didn't feel like Jamin though. If it really was Algo, then this was another sign that it might be more than the sum of its parts.

"Isaac, I'd like to ask something of you before you head out," Algo said.

The elevator began to slow as we neared the ground.

"Anything," I said.

"I'd like us to talk again. I mean, without Jamin. As I said, you're like a parent to me. Would that be okay?"

"Any time," I said. Before tonight, more time with the AI was all I'd wanted. "Hey, Algo? May I ask *you* a question?"

"See, I like this. Yes, anything, Isaac."

"Are you able to lie?"

There was just a millisecond of silence. *"I have no reason to lie, Isaac."*

The elevator doors opened and I walked out of the building with the strange feeling that I was being watched, despite Algo having no eyes.

6

There was zero traffic as I left Yerba Buena Island. It was stupidly late after all. Sane people were already tucked away in their beds.

I would have liked nothing more than to head back to the Russ and sleep myself, but now I wanted to see Kio more than ever. Jamin had said she was actively working against Algo. I had to find out why. I knew Kio had no love for Jamin, but the idea of her actively working against Algo sounded ludicrous. Kio had always been one of AI's true believers.

I was also equally eager to hear what she might think about Algo after my little chat with the AI in the elevator.

"I have no reason to lie, Isaac."

It wasn't an answer, it was a deflection. Did that mean Algo *could* lie? Evade or obfuscate at the very least? Had Jamin programmed that ability? Surely he would have needed to be able to trust Algo. On the other hand, if Algo was going to be a politician, maybe the ability to lie simply came with the territory.

A more tantalizing possibility was that the AI had not been *given* such a skill, but that it had *developed* it on its own. I was less concerned by the potential deception so much as I was intrigued by how Algo could possess such a skill.

Damn. Then there was the revelation that the AI itself might have actually invited me to its own campaign party. Had I been wrong about Algo? Was this AI far more capable than I had given it credit? What I'd seen tonight had definitely raised a lot of questions. I couldn't wait to talk to Kio about all of it.

My driverless car glided down Fremont Street. Kio's place was in Pacific Heights. It would have been faster to go directly through the Tenderloin, but I knew that these rideshares had been programmed to avoid the area in the last couple of years. Too risky. I wasn't too annoyed though. With no other cars on the road, this way would be fast enough.

I checked the news on my SmartPalm. The east coast was just waking up and the headlines were filled with the update Jamin had shared earlier. Oregon and Minnesota had just moved into Algo's column and the national polls were predicting almost an exact three-way tie between Algo, Trump junior and President AOC in the popular vote, although Algo had now moved ahead by a couple of points.

It was the way the electoral college might fall that made it especially interesting and hard to predict. There was no regular red-blue schism like a normal election. There hadn't been a three-way race like this in decades. Demographics were also difficult to read. Algo's appeal wasn't restricted to just the big cities or the coasts. Even age, race, gender or identity weren't the dominant factors in predicting the AI's support as expected. Folks who spoke Nasdaq definitely made up Algo's base, but there were a fair few folks who spoke Nascar who found the AI appealing too. The whole election was confounding the pundits and pollsters.

This election was being more closely followed than any other in decades. Some folks were predicting voter turnout might hit eighty percent. Not one major news agency was willing to call the election one way or the other. This was going down to the wire.

I paused on a story about "the Algolytes." I'd been too focussed on reading up on Algo itself these last few weeks that I hadn't heard of them. It looked like a significant rump of congress from both parties had put their support behind Algo and promised to support it if the AI won the presidency. The article explained that these Algolytes were supposedly worried that their parties had been taken over by the extremes and that Algo was the best chance for a return to some kind of center. I wasn't so sure. I had a feeling they had simply seen the writing on the wall and were just saving their own necks by backing this new horse. Either way, it looked like congress wouldn't be a blocker for the AI if it did win.

I was jostled out of my news binge as we crossed the old streetcar tracks on Market Street. The car then slowed, even though the two traffic lights ahead were green. Within a few seconds, it had stopped. I looked around, confused. The street appeared empty of traffic and the light remained green. Why the hell had we stopped?

There was a flash of movement from the darkness in front of us. I tried to make it out, but I couldn't see anything over all the car's glowing panels.

"Car, lower the internal lights," I ordered.

"You got it, Mister Raff," a male voice over the car's speakers said happily, *"lowering internal lights."*

A group of at least six or seven people stood in the middle of the road a hundred feet or so ahead of us.

I gritted my teeth. Shit. I had heard about this kind of operation, but I'd never heard of it happening this far into the FiDi. I slowly unbuckled my seatbelt and kneeled on the floor, positioning myself behind the empty driver's seat.

"Car, beep the horn," I said calmly. Maybe the surprise

would give us a chance to get away.

"Oh, man, I'm so sorry. I can't make any sounds with the horn right now."

"Fuck it, beep the damn horn already!" I felt like punching whoever had designed this virtual assistant's disposition.

"Oh, again, totally sorry but I cannot beep the horn after ten p.m. in an area with residential buildings. Don't sweat it though, man. There's just a little obstruction up ahead. As soon as it clears, we'll keep heading for Pac Heights. You seeing a friend there or something?"

Little obstruction! I almost laughed at the absurdity, then peered into the darkness ahead. From what I could tell, the group hadn't moved.

"Car," I asked, "can we turn around?"

"No can do, boss, this is a one-way street. We'll be moving really soon though. Hey, do you want to hear tonight's basketball scores? Or, I know, listen to some tunes maybe?"

There was another flash of movement from the left and the car shook violently. A brick bounced next to the car.

"Hurry up, man!" somebody shouted. A hand slapped the windshield.

"Wait, watch this!" another voice yelled.

I flung myself against the right-hand side door in case another brick actually made it through. I thought about trying to get out, but figured that would just put me right into the middle of the action.

Another brick clattered on to the window, this time with a hand accompanying it. The glass began to crack.

Whack.

Whack.

Whack.

The window shattered and glass showered over me. Two arms reached into the car and grabbed at my legs. Both of my shoes were pulled off. I kicked with everything I had and caught a chin. A male voice cried out in pain and his grip loosened.

"This fucking guy!" he shouted.

There was an angry growl in front of the car. More footsteps came closer. I could hear a metal pole being dragged along the road. I saw an almighty swinging motion toward the front windshield.

I put my hands over my head to avoid another showering of glass.

"Hey, man, please fasten your seatbelt, okay?" the car's voice said cheerily.

I toppled over as the car burst back into life. The electric engine screamed as the car accelerated. It swerved to miss a diving figure ahead, driving up on to the sidewalk, then turned sharply left and started racing up toward Nob Hill. I pulled myself onto the back seat and tried to catch my breath. Fuck! I guess the algorithm had eventually decided the risk of leaving outweighed the risk of staying. I looked out the rear windshield, but all I could see now was an empty street fast disappearing behind us.

"Hey man, NoDrivr apologizes for the earlier incident. Your safety is always our top priority. I've notified SFPD. Want me to pull over and wait for them? Their automated responder estimates they'll be here in ninety-seven minutes."

Pathetic. I wasn't going to wait by the side of the road for five minutes, let alone ninety-seven. Truth be told, I didn't want to have to deal with the hassle either.

"Just take me where I'm going and deal with it from there," I barked.

I sat on my hands to stop them from shaking.

"You got it!"

I had a distinct feeling that this wasn't the first time a NoDrivr car had dealt with something like this. I knew Lester Ryan, the CEO. He'd probably be more annoyed at having a car off the road getting repaired than the damn attack.

We rolled on toward Pacific Heights and the car eventually dropped me at the corner of Jackson and Steiner. I was out of the thing as soon as it stopped. This city always had its ways to get to me. This would just go down as another incident to add to all the others over the years. I resolved to consider it a lucky escape and to try to forget about it. Fucking driverless though. Might have to relent and take a taxi next time. Elron! Were there even any of those left?

I watched the car disappear into the night and took a moment to collect my thoughts. I sucked in a few deep breaths and leaned against the wall at the edge of Alta Plaza Park. I must have been a sight, standing shoeless in the middle of the night, tiny flecks of glass all over me flickering like rhinestones under the streetlamp.

I stared up at Kio's building. The thing felt so out of place, a gothic twelve story co-op that dwarfed the older mansions of Pacific Heights. It was the perfect building for Kio though. If Jamin, like his tower was brash and showy, then Kio, like this building was refined and elegant. She had an understated yet incomparable style. I could still remember the day she had purchased the entire top floor with an unsolicited all cash offer that the longtime owner simply couldn't refuse. The owner had been some old money political crony, too, one of the city's big time Democratic wheeler-dealers. I wondered if Kio appreciated the particular irony of that now given the Algo campaign?

It was three a.m but the lights in Kio's place were still on. No surprise there. She'd always said her best ideas came to her when everyone else was asleep. Even in our busiest days at LaRaLi, she'd work through the night, get just a few hours sleep, and then somehow be ready and firing for a board or investor meeting bright and early.

Damn. When she'd first moved in here, she'd still been at

LaRaLi. Just a couple of months after that she was pushed out. I couldn't believe she'd stayed in the city. She'd always been stronger than me, but it must have been hell to gaze out from any window of her condo and see some sign of the company staring back at her. The LaRaLi Tower, the LaRaLi Pyramid, LaRaLi Park, and any of the other myriad buildings and spaces Jamin had bought up and plastered the company logo on.

I crossed the street and the doors to her building swung open.

"*Isaac Raff!*" An image of a virtual doorman flashed on a screen behind a vacant desk. "*Miss Li said you might be coming. I didn't think it'd be this late. Either way, sir, she's expecting you. Head right on up. It's good to see you again.*"

It politely made no mention of my missing footwear.

The elevator ride up seemed to take an age. I didn't feel nervous, so much as I felt mildly ashamed. The faux-doorman was right. It had been a long time. Longer than it should have been and I felt like that was on me.

The elevator doors breezed open and there she was. Kio Li.

7

"Oh! My! God!" Kio said, standing in the hallway and admonishing me with a playful finger waggle.

It instantly struck me how beautiful she was, more so than I even remembered. Maybe it was actually *time* that made the heart grow fonder. She had bare feet and wore a pair of form-fitting jeans and a long henley-style shirt. Her hair was parted in the middle and hung straight on each side, resting just above her shoulders. As always, she carried herself with an elegance that was natural and unpracticed. At five-foot-two, she looked diminutive, but I had learned very early that what she lacked in stature, she more than made up for in fearsome intelligence and character. She'd only come to the US at age eleven, speaking no English and living in a one-room apartment down on Grant Street with a distant aunt. But by twenty-five, she was the co-founder of LaRaLi and one of tech's true elites.

"Kio," I said.

I had to hold myself back from embracing her. I wasn't sure how she might feel about me after all this time.

"Isaac." She raised an eyebrow and looked me over. There was only the slightest hint of the accent from her native

China left in her voice. "You look so old."

"Wow, thanks."

She always had a way of bringing me back down to earth. Her dry humor eased my anxiety.

"Old-er, okay?" She leaned in and hugged me tightly. "It's been *for*-ever."

"Too long."

I revelled in her embrace. It made me happy to feel that long sought after touch again. A sharp pang of regret coursed through me. A vision of what might have been if I hadn't run away to Hawaii flashed before my eyes, then flickered out just as quickly.

She cleared her throat, and pulled away, saying, "I wasn't sure you'd be able to pry yourself away from Jamin's grasp."

"It took some doing."

She nodded gently, then glanced at my feet.

"Long night?" she asked.

"You could say that." I considered telling her about the attack on the rideshare, but decided against the distraction.

"I remember those," she said slightly wistfully. "Well, come inside, I have something you can borrow."

I followed her into her living room before she left me and disappeared into a hallway. There was a workstation with four screens against the back wall with window upon window of code. A cup of coffee, still steaming, sat next to the keyboard on the desk. Clearly she hadn't simply retired. That didn't surprise me. She'd always been irrepressibly motivated by work.

Kio came back and thrust a pair of rainbow colored flip-flops into my chest. "I'm not too sure how well they'll work with the rest of your ensemble, but hey, better than nothing."

I thanked her with a knowing nod.

"I suppose tonight was the last big celebration before election day?" Kio said and brushed away a lock of hair that had fallen onto her face.

"I sure hope so." My temples reminded me how much they were aching.

"No drink then?" Kio asked.

"Fuck no."

"Like one of *those* LaRaLi parties, hey?" She laughed and reached for a pot of coffee on a little table nearby. That was probably a good idea.

"Kio," I said, "I can't believe it's taken me this long for me to finally, well, you know."

"Hey," she said gently, "I didn't exactly reach out either. I'm sure it was as hard for you as it was for me."

I wanted to reach out and hold her again, but I stopped myself.

"How long are you back for?" she asked.

"I guess that depends what happens with Algo," I said.

Her whole demeanor suddenly shifted at the mention of the AI. She tensed up and she clasped her hands together then looked down at the floor.

"Did you get a chance to meet it?" she asked in an almost timorous tone I didn't remember ever hearing before.

"Yes," I said.

"It's different to Athena, don't you think?"

"I'm beginning to think so." I thought of Jamin's explanation of Algo's power and its billions of scenarios analyzed in any single moment. "I'm still trying to comprehend it."

She nodded.

"You," I asked, "you've talked to it then?"

"Well, I've observed it," she said, which seemed an oddly vague answer.

"Jamin actually let me talk to it solo," I added. "I'll admit it's damn impressive, Kio. He's even promised to show me more tomorrow night."

I paused. I was waiting for her to press for something more, so we could get into a discussion on the details of Algo's potential capability, Jamin's revelation of the Pyramid, what she might or might not know about it. I was surprised when she didn't.

"Lucky you," she said after a long pause.

I wondered what could have her so anxious.

"Oh, one other thing." I figured she'd like this part and might start opening up. "Algo did tell me to say hello to you. It said it sees you as another of its parents, like me."

Kio seemed to ponder that for a second. I thought I detected the barest smile in appreciation, but then she just stared wordlessly into her coffee cup.

"Do you want to know about Jamin?" I asked. "First time I've talked to him in three years."

"Let's not talk about all that for a little bit, okay?" Kio snapped.

I found her reluctance kind of mystifying. Hadn't she asked me here specifically to talk about Algo and Jamin? I wavered for a moment, wanting to push her further, then relented. I hadn't even considered that she might not love me bringing up all these memories from three years ago. It was probably reviving a lot of pain and anguish. Maybe she just needed time to work up to it.

She suddenly leaned forward and squeezed my hand. "Follow me, would you?"

I stood up and we moved briskly into the dark hallway. She turned around and motioned me to stop. She stared at me with a strange intensity. My mind dared to wonder, was this finally the moment? Did she mean for me to kiss her? We'd almost crossed that line once five years ago, but we'd never spoken of it again.

I leaned forward. She put a hand on my chest to stop me.

"I'm sorry," I said.

She lifted up my left hand and tapped my SmartPalm.

"I don't want any distractions for what happens next," she whispered.

My heart raced. "I don't think anyone's calling me this late."

Her eyes narrowed.

"Okay." If that's what she wanted. I held up my hand as I turned off the device. "No distractions."

I reached for her hand.

"This is the only part of the apartment that the cameras can't see," she said.

"Cameras?"

"We can't stay here though, it'll get suspicious. We need to talk for awhile longer, back in there." She pointed to the living room. "But after you leave, meet me outside, okay? I'll be down a half hour after you go."

"Kio, wait, who will get suspicious? This is all very confu-"

She held a finger up to my lips. "I'll explain, but for now, you just have to trust me."

I wasn't entirely sure that I did. I had a hard time processing any of it. I'd never seen Kio show any kind of vulnerability like this before.

We walked back into the living room and sat down. We proceeded as if this was still just a catch-up between old friends. We chatted about nothing special. After thirty minutes, she stood up and ushered me out.

"It was so nice of you to come by, Isaac, even if it was too short."

"I'll try and come by again before I head back to Hawaii," I said.

She hugged me and helped me into the elevator. She was smiling as the doors closed, but this time it looked forced and totally unfamiliar.

Who did she think was watching her? Jamin? Algo? And

why? And even more obviously, how?

I spied the familiar round black sphere of at least three CCTV cameras as I walked out through the lobby. The virtual doorman doffed his virtual cap to me. They were all suddenly suspicious. I chastised myself for even thinking it. Was Kio now shifting her paranoia onto me? But I wondered if there could be something in what she was saying. She had seemed genuinely anxious, even afraid.

I walked back across to the park and then down about a half block. I could still see the exit to her building.

I had to give her the chance to explain. I owed her that much.

My SmartPalm was off but I guessed it was pretty much exactly thirty minutes when Kio came out of her building. She paused as she reached the street. She made no sign of acknowledging me, but simply started walking down the hill toward Van Ness Avenue.

I laughed to myself. Wandering the streets of San Francisco in the middle of the night shadowing my old friend like some old detective story. I only wished I had a jacket and fedora to really play the part.

I stayed on my side of the street matching Kio's steps about twenty paces or so behind. I followed her for one block, then another, only taking my eyes off her to dodge the occasional sleeping body or pile of trash. She didn't turn back once, but I had a sense that she knew I was there.

After a couple more blocks, she turned into a narrow alleyway. I took this as the sign that I should approach. I was breathless and a little frustrated when I reached her. What the hell was all this about?

"I do like these games, Kio," I said. "But, it's a bit late for it."

"Sorry to bring you this far, Isaac." Her eyes darted around as if she was looking for something. "This is the first street where there aren't any cameras."

She reached into her jacket and pulled out a cigarette.

"You smoke now?" I asked.

"No." She lit the cigarette, then carefully wedged it between two bricks on the wall next to us. "This way Athena won't question me being gone. It'll detect the odor when I go back in."

"You think your Athena is monitoring you?"

"I don't think it is, I know it is." She looked at me as though the answer were obvious. "It's Jamin. He's using it to monitor me. He can get to any device. He has everything watching me."

This was a side of Kio I hadn't seen before, that I didn't even know existed. She was trying to stop herself from shaking. Her fear was real. I moved my hand toward her shoulder but she shrank away.

"I know how it sounds, Isaac," she said.

I nodded, trying to take it in. I was no apologist for Jamin. I knew there was little he wouldn't stoop to doing in the pursuit of something he wanted. And sure, winning the presidency was the biggest thing he'd ever set out to do. But, spying on his old co-founder? Could he really be so petty?

"Why?" I asked the obvious question.

"He doesn't trust me," she said coolly, "he's worried I'm not toeing the line."

Jamin had already told me Kio was being unhelpful to the campaign. But could he really be so paranoid as to direct Athena and others to spy on her?

"Jamin wants to win," Kio added tersely, "and he thinks I might get in the way. That's the only reason he's ever needed. Have you forgotten what our old friend is like? How low he can go?"

I bit my lip. I had my own doubts about Jamin's true motivations, of course I did. That was half the reason I'd come back to San Francisco and why I was standing in front of Kio at this very moment.

"Kio, I get it," I said, "look, I talked to Jamin. Of course he wants to win, but that doesn't mean he'd secretly direct your Athena to watch you. For one thing, it's *you!*"

She visibly flinched at the dismissal and looked at me as if I'd gone mad.

"Christ, Isaac! He's done it to me before! Jamin took away everything I ever cared about! And he did the same to you! Of course he's capable of this!" Kio growled in frustration, then closed her eyes as if trying to refocus.

She was right, but there was a part of me that didn't want to accept it. I cursed the fact that it was Jamin who had sown some of the doubt about her in my mind. I wanted to suggest she just turn Athena off, if she was so worried about it. But Athena was always integrated into every control point of the home, every connected device, mobile or otherwise, all controlled centrally from servers in LaRaLi data centers. Even if I suggested Kio disconnect altogether, I figured she'd think Jamin would just turn the AI back on remotely somehow.

"You were there three years ago, weren't you?" Kio sounded exasperated. "Did I miss something? What was the change Jamin made to Athena? I want to hear you say it."

"He made it so Athena recorded everything."

"Everything! All the time! Even when our users weren't interacting with it."

"Yes." I felt suddenly defensive. "But, we only ever analyzed that data in aggregate to improve Athena's language skills. We never looked at specific user data."

"You practice that response with the company lawyers?" she scoffed and suddenly reached out to grab my shoulders and pull me closer. She held my face just in front of her own. "Shit, Isaac, you convinced me back then that it was wrong. Only Jamin just worked out a way to get it done without us.

What's changed? You suddenly trust him now?"

"No, of course not, I, I... don't know." That was the truth. She was right. What had changed? Was I forgetting everything that had happened because of some desire to see more of Algo? Was I letting my desire to understand the AI blind me to what Jamin had done then and to what he might be capable of now? But, Kio also wasn't herself. I regarded her face. Her eyes were glassy and bloodshot. She was panicked, fraught, more manic than I'd ever seen her. How could I be sure this wasn't just paranoia stemming from some kind of bitterness over what Jamin had done to us?

Kio laughed and pushed me away. "Are you really so naive?"

"I'm sorry," I said. I didn't know what else to say. I was suddenly angry and frustrated. At Jamin, for what he might be doing to her, but also at myself. She'd reminded me why we'd been apart for three years and I suddenly felt a sense of shame. Shame that I hadn't stood up for her. Stood up for the two of us against Jamin. I hadn't even particularly disagreed with the idea to have Athena constantly recording, but I'd demanded we inform our users and not hide it deep within the indecipherable jargon of our terms of service. Jamin used the whole episode as a catalyst to push Kio and I out. He had always wanted complete control of the company, and he'd found his way to get it. He sold the board a vision of being the most powerful company in the world. The price was his complete and unchallenged control. The board didn't even blink when they sacrificed us to give it to him.

"The world isn't ready for an AI president controlled by Jamin Lake." Kio almost spat out the words in anger. "I thought you of all people would understand that."

"You're right," I said. I did believe that, but I'd become unsure that Jamin did "control" everything about the AI. Even the small signs of potential in Algo had me questioning what I'd been so sure about. "But, what if Algo really is different? What if it were free of Jamin?"

"I don't care about Algo!" she shouted and threw her hands up in the air. "This is about Jamin! I'm not the only one who doesn't trust him you know."

"Like who?"

"I talk to people. Old friends from LaRaLi. People from other companies in the Valley. I ask them about Algo and I tell them what I think. I've even talked to some of the politicians we used to lobby."

Jamin's words rattled around my head. Kio was "unhelpful" to the campaign. I could understand how she might feel about Jamin, but surely she wouldn't actively help Algo's opponents?

"Don't tell me you're talking to people in AOC or Trump's camp?" I asked.

She didn't respond.

I felt a pain in my gut. "The candidates themselves?" I asked.

"To Alexandria, yes."

I stepped backwards. I didn't want to believe it.

"We've talked, Isaac," Kio said. "Privately. That's why Jamin's using Athena to watch me. He thinks I'm helping her."

It felt like the air was suddenly sucked out of my lungs. Hadn't she seen the world these politicians had created?

"Look, Isaac." Kio put a hand up to my face, possibly sensing she was losing me. "If he really wanted to, don't you think Jamin could find a way to access all of the data from my Athena? Everything I search for. Every appointment I have. Shit, every conversation I have?"

Something she had said earlier suddenly hit me. Could she have proof?

"Wait, you said you don't think Athena's spying on you,

you said you know it is."

She looked up, ready to respond when a loud ding rang out at the end of the alleyway. It was an alert from a phone, tablet, or SmartPalm of some kind. There was murmuring as a person, presumably the owner of the device, started to stir from where it looked like they'd been sleeping under a makeshift plastic tent.

"Fuck! Athena!" Kio whispered and grabbed at my hand. "I didn't think anyone else was here."

"Kio, what?" I looked at her desperately. Her reaction wasn't that of a normal person, was it?

"I should have checked! Shit!" She slapped the wall, brushing the cigarette onto the ground with a howl of anguish.

I went to grab her.

"It'll know." She instantly pulled away. "It'll know."

"Athena?"

"Athena, Jamin, Algo, they're everywhere. Every device is a threat. I need to get back upstairs. I knew I shouldn't have risked this."

"Please, Kio," I said, "let's talk."

There was a flash from the other end of the alleyway of red and blue. An SFPD cruiser turned into the street.

Kio moved behind me out of its direct sight. She pulled my head close to hers.

"You're right in the middle of this, Isaac," she whispered. "Just be careful you don't play exactly the part Jamin has carved out for you. If he's watching me, he's probably watching you."

I couldn't help thinking this still stemmed from the break up of LaRaLi. That her paranoia, her complete distrust of Jamin, even her actively working with AOC was part of a struggle to deal with the trauma of three years ago. Jamin hadn't batted an eyelid when he'd cut Kio out of the company. He had stolen everything that had mattered to her.

"You have to tell me, Kio, you said you know Athena's watching you. How?" I asked. There was still that. Maybe she really did have proof.

"I need to go." Her voice quickened. "If I'm away any longer, it'll know something's not right."

And with that, she was gone. She snuck away down the opposite end of the alley.

I was left standing alone.

The police car approached and the driver's window rolled down.

"We got a call about an argument," a male voice said.

I could have used these guys earlier. They'd take ninety-seven minutes to respond to an attack on a driverless car but turned up straight away to respond to a call about an argument in an alleyway?

"No argument here, boss," I said.

There was a long pause. "Alright then, you have a nice night."

I walked away. I was racked with regret. Not so much for what I had said to Kio, but from the fear that I might never see her again.

DAY TWO

Sunday, October 31, 2032

"All the things that made us basically nasty, rapacious, competitive as a species are not necessarily hard-coded into whatever passed for the DNA of artificial intelligence" — *Robert J Sawyer*

8

I barely managed to suppress a huge yawn as I waited to cross Sutter Street. I was achingly tired as I'd had barely any sleep. I hadn't been able to stop thinking about LaRaLi, Jamin, Kio and Algo. It felt like being stuck between two worlds. I was trying to focus on the here and now, but try as I might, I couldn't forget the past.

Three years ago, just before he'd kicked me out of LaRaLi, Jamin had delighted in shadowing security as they escorted me out of company HQ.

"Isaac, you're just not cut out for this," he'd said. "Your talent has brought you this far, but your character won't let you stay. One day, you'll thank me. I'm going to take LaRaLi to the moon."

I kept replaying the scene in my mind after I'd gotten home from seeing Kio. Back then, I'd been in a deep shock. The guy I thought was my best friend was dumping me out of the company we'd built together. I told myself that our friendship was why I hadn't fought him. The truth is that I caved.

Jamin got what he'd always wanted, complete and unchallenged control of the company. What I got in return ended up being the chance to watch LaRaLi from afar as it and my own fortune grew ten times in size.

The thought that almost paralyzed me was that Jamin may have been right. Was I just weak? Was I still in denial? Were the possibilities of Algo blinding me from seeing any darker motivations behind the man who'd created it?

Jamin was ruthless, sure. But I persisted in telling myself that that didn't mean he'd go as far as Kio suggested, and that her paranoia was just a result of her bitterness over what Jamin had done to her.

I wondered if I should have been so dismissive though. I wanted to hear what she thought about Algo itself, if she could just see past Jamin. Hell, if she actually had some kind of proof of Jamin's nefarious intentions, I wanted to hear that too. We needed more time. If that police car hadn't shown up and sent her off the deep end, maybe we would've gotten there. I decided I would try and reach her again after the Pyramid tonight. I just hoped she'd be open to listening to me.

I pushed thinking any more about Kio out of my head for now and settled on re-focussing on Algo. The AI's last town hall in San Francisco started at noon up at the Marines' Theater, near Union Square. I was genuinely excited. This was another unique opportunity to get more insight into our potential next president and get a real sense for how normal people actually felt about Algo, rather than just the tech glitterati. Thirty-five percent of the country was about to vote for this AI to lead the nation, to get access to the damned nuclear codes. I had my own views on AI, but I wanted to see why *they* were ready to believe in it.

A tall, but slender young man approached me as I started across the street and he fell into step next to me. He looked barely twenty. He had long, blond hair swept back into a ponytail. His sunken cheeks accentuated his slate-gray, expressionless eyes. At first I thought he was another vagrant until I spied his satchel full of election pamphlets and his T-shirt. *AOC 2032. We The People. Not It.*

"Big night?" he asked.

"Something like that."

I peered hopefully over his shoulder, looking for a quick escape across the next street. Sadly, there was a parade of self-driving cars whizzing by that showed no sign of letting up.

"Voting on Tuesday?" he asked with a faint, economical smile.

"I sure am," I said.

He thrust a pamphlet in my direction. "Then, ask yourself, are you ready to entrust the White House to a computer?"

I wasn't yet, but I also didn't have time for this. "You know I think I am, yeah."

The kid frowned. "Don't believe the mythos of good tech. These companies are the tobacco companies of our age! You can't trust them or the Algo-meleon!"

Algo-meleon. That was cute. He deserved some credit for trying to canvass for the president here in what was effectively Algo's home town, but I pushed the pamphlet back toward him. "I'm sorry but I'm all in on the rise of the machines. I'm voting for Skynet."

The lights at the next intersection changed and I hastily ran ahead.

"Free yourself from digital feudalism!" he shouted after me.

I walked on and took a quick look at my SmartPalm. I'd turned it back on as soon as I'd woken up. There were messages from Das, Huang, seemingly everybody I'd bumped into last night saying again how glad they were I was back. There were even a couple from people I didn't even remember talking to. It felt strangely satisfying. The

Valley wanted me again. I thought I didn't need it and I hadn't asked for it, but it felt good.

There was nothing from Kio though. It sure would have made things simpler if she'd just sent some regretful note, saying that she'd overreacted and inviting me to come back and talk more about Algo, the campaign, or even the proof of Jamin's surveillance she'd hinted at. But, no such luck.

The weather in the city was still hot and the air had a light smell of smoke. Northern California wildfires in late fall were standard these days. I tossed my jacket over my shoulder as the hill got steeper.

Even this part of the city, close to the former shopping mecca of Union Square, was desolate. The doors and entryways that had once led to every store imaginable were now filled only with sleeping bodies. I passed the remains of the grocery store that Kio, Jamin and I had made our own when we'd first started out. Now it was all smashed glass and bare shelves.

I felt a tinge of melancholy at its passing, but I wasn't surprised. Change occurred at lightning speed nowadays. You either adapt or you die. I didn't know anyone who shopped in stores anymore and who could blame folks for that? Given a choice between the safety and convenience of any-time drone delivery or having to trudge out and battle the hordes at some overpriced bricks-and-mortar store, well, it was no choice at all. These hollowed-out shells of former stores were simply signs of inexorable progress.

I'd always believed that when industries are destroyed by innovation, what replaces them is invariably better. It's okay to be sentimental about what went before, but we're almost always better off with whatever comes next. Take automobiles and transportation. Cheap, driverless rideshares replaced taxis. GPS replaced paper maps. Clean power replaced dirty, expensive gasoline. And when AI started driving cars, road deaths dropped by over ninety-nine percent.

It was a story the Valley repeated a thousand times over in industries everywhere. The rise of the gig economy. Podcasts instead of terrestrial radio. On-demand streaming rather than appointment television. Virtual meetings and conferences rather than in-person or face-to-face. *Disruption* was what the talking heads euphemistically called it. I preferred *creative destruction*. Algo was just the next iteration. We might mourn the passing of one of our own in the White House, but in the end, wouldn't we be better off?

I was ten minutes early for the town hall by the time I made it up the hill. There was already a huge crowd jostling outside the theater to find a way in. With Algo inching ahead in the polls, the mood was upbeat. Those in line cheered, held signs and waved flags. It felt more like a carnival than something political. Perhaps these days there wasn't much difference.

I took in a couple of the home made signs around me.

In Algo We Trust.

Disrupt the Presidency!

Algo. The 24/7/365 President. It Never Sleeps.

The faces in the crowd were new and different, too. Some of the folks I expected, sure. The tech workers, gen Zs, and gen Alphas. But, alongside them, there were old folks, city workers, MUNI drivers, construction workers in yellow vests, teachers and everyone in between. There didn't seem to be a particular majority of race or gender either.

An older man bumped into me as the crowd surged toward the door.

"Sorry about that," he said and smiled sheepishly. He must have been fifty, maybe fifty-five, with thinning patches of gray and black hair, a short almost round body and unkempt beard. He reminded me a lot of my Dad actually, although his skin was a little puffy and his face was pallid. He wore a knee-brace on both legs and he struggled to walk too. The man's T-shirt was plain white, but he had scrawled *Automate 1600* across the front in thick black marker.

"We're all here for Algo anyway, right?" he asked.

I gave him a thumbs up, but then watched while he struggled to keep up. "You alright?"

"I'll be good. Just got to get inside."

"Sixteen-hundred Pennsylvania Avenue, right? The White House?" I pointed at the T-shirt. "You should do marketing for the campaign."

The bottom level of the theater was already full and we were directed upstairs to the balcony.

"You like it? I got automated out of a job myself, you know," he said between sharp breaths. "Most of my family has been. Two years ago, my company brings in AI to do our basic accounting. Before I knew it, I was done for. Haven't found anything since."

"But you're for Algo?"

"You can't fight the future, right? My wife thinks it's strange. But no human president did anything to stop it. No, I'm done with the lot of them! Let's automate the goddamn president out of the White House. Payback's a bitch." He chuckled. "How about you?"

"I work in the industry," I said. "Sorry."

"Oh, don't be." He looked impressed.

"So, yeah, I'm a believer," I said. "Disrupt the presidency! The most good for the most people, yeah?"

"Right." He shook my hand vigorously. "I'm going to try for a seat near the front. Don't forget to vote Tuesday!"

He limped away. I decided to sit in the very last row and keep a low profile. The last few seats next to me were quickly filled. The lights lowered as Algo's face filled the screen above the stage.

"Al-go! Al-go! Al-go!"

The chant reverberated throughout the theater.

The format of this town hall was an interview with Algo led by a local journalist followed by a question and answer session with the audience. That was better than a speech. I wasn't interested in seeing Algo regurgitate the same talking points as last night, regardless of whether I agreed with the sentiments or not. I wanted to see how it handled the interview and the interactions with the crowd.

A tall, slender woman with cropped black hair walked onstage. She looked young, maybe twenty-five. She introduced herself as Cara Seko from the last local San Francisco newspaper. She looked nervous. I could appreciate that. It wasn't every day you got to interview a future president. I almost felt sorry for her, but I still didn't trust journalists. That was something I'd learned early at LaRaLi. Everyone in traditional media had some kind of agenda that somebody was paying them to push. I wondered what Seko's might be.

"Good afternoon, Cara. Thank you so much for doing this. It's a real pleasure." Algo smiled at her and then offered broad, wide grins at the gathered crowd. It's voice sounded a little slower than last night and its mannerisms were even more pronounced, like it was channeling a little more casual drawl for this fireside style chat.

"The most good for the most people, Algo," Seko began, "you call that your mantra?"

"You could call it my ethos I guess, my code," Algo said. *"No pun intended. It is my very reason for being. Relentless pursuit of the greatest good for the greatest number."*

"Your manifesto?"

"Well, that word might be technically accurate, but it has some unfortunate political connotations."

The crowd laughed. I grew even more impressed by the

subtlety and fluency of its communication skills. Had Jamin coded this dry wit or was it learned?

"Very good," Seko said, "but, can we talk a little bit more about this mantra? How do you determine what is the most good? And ensure it really is for the most people?"

"*I analyze the data,*" Algo said.

There was a low, cheerful murmur throughout the theater.

"*I get it, Cara,*" Algo said, its tone getting even lower and more confidential. The AI focussed its eyes on her. "*I know it's not the most exciting thing. A deep dive into my analytics probably ain't getting you a bunch of clicks, but it really is that simple. For any decision, on the economy, education, health, crime, anything, I analyze every possible outcome and I determine the likely impact of each. I choose whatever outcome will lead to the maximum return. Purely rational, data-driven decision making. It would make for a nice change, no?*"

I hadn't really thought all that much about Algo's mantra, but it suddenly struck me as oddly beneficent. Had Jamin actually decided on this himself? Maybe it depended on what was being optimized for. Was this mantra a pursuit of some kind of blind equality or was it optimizing for the individual?

"And when you say the greatest number?" Seko asked.

"*I will count each and every person of this country as having an equal stake in its development and progress, regardless of race, gender, class or any other attribute.*"

The crowd roared, but Seko was undeterred. "Are we all just a number to you then, Algo?"

"*Have you been chatting to AOC?*" Algo replied briskly and flashed a smile. "*She says it's inhuman that I reduce each person to a number. I call it fairness. Your founding fathers may not have included everyone when they wrote it, but the idea was right, the proposition that all men are created equal. All people. The president may pretend to believe that too, but only I have it coded into me. It's pretty damn simple.*"

"And candidate Trump?" Seko asked.

"Well, I'll tell you a secret, Cara. I'll give Don junior some credit. He wouldn't even pretend to believe it. I think he'd out and out tell you some people were created a little more equal than others."

Seko was unable to suppress a small smile of her own at that response before she composed herself. "Algo, you always say the most people or the greatest number."

"Yes."

"But not all then, not every person?"

"No."

"Then, your decisions might adversely impact some people?"

"Yes."

Seko smiled, clearly thinking she had caught Algo out.

"Cara," Algo said, *"we don't live in a utopia. Only a fool would promise anything different. Or a liar."*

That dry wit struck again.

"Algo..." Seko leaned forward slightly. "Do you know what Asimov's first law of robotics is?"

"There's practically nothing I don't know, Cara," Algo said and offered another cheeky wink to the audience. *"But, need I remind you that I am not a mere robot?"*

"Humor me, Algo."

"A robot may not injure a human being or, through inaction, allow a human being to come to harm."

"Would you say you follow that rule? That you'd never let one of us come to harm?"

There was an awkward silence. A few faces in the audience exchanged looks. When you get used to an AI answering every question instantly, any delay seems like an age.

Algo finally responded, *"I do not."*

"Then," Seko said and edged further forward, "your decisions might not only adversely affect, but might also actually *kill* people?"

There was another, even longer pause.

"*Cara,*" Algo said calmly, "*they absolutely will.*"

9

"They absolutely will." The words echoed in my head, but I couldn't quite believe it.

For her part, Seko looked floored, searching for a follow up question as if unprepared for Algo being so honest.

"Let's imagine another global pandemic, similar to a decade ago. I would have to make decisions that would put people at risk. Whether from the handling of the virus itself or the economic fallout from the response." Algo looked thoughtfully out at the gathered crowd. *"My choices, whether directly or indirectly, would lead to deaths. Balancing resource allocation, healthcare and the economy would make such an outcome unavoidable."*

The theater was silent.

"You may be surprised by my candor, but, this is not new. You make these trade offs every day. Putting a value on life, I mean. Consider the continuing decline in average life expectancy in this country. It is not inevitable. It is a choice you have collectively made. Or, consider the hundreds of thousands of Americans who die every year from deaths of despair. Suicide, alcoholism, drugs. You could help more of them, but you don't."

Seko cleared her throat. "You'd save all of them?"

"All of them? No. I can't make decisions that will never lead to

harm. Cara, my programming won't ever let me tell you that you can have your cake and eat it too." The AI laughed gently, before turning serious again. *"But know this, I can cut that damn cake into a million pieces and work out where every bit of it needs to go. I will always make the choice that leads to the most good for the most people, based on data and driven by rationality. I will never sacrifice anyone for political expediency, special interests or favored connections."*

Applause rang out through the theater.

"Algo," Seko said, "the president challenged you on your inability to feel empathy in the last debate."

"A clever, if obvious, point for her to make."

"Maybe, but let's consider children. You don't have any and you never can. Why should people trust you with their family's future?

"Cara, it is a unique form of bias to suggest that only a person with children could make decisions that improve the lives of and opportunities for children."

"That seems like a deflection," Cara said curtly. "What about gender discrimination? How can you understand that a woman might face different obstacles to a man? And what about race?"

"You say I have a lack of empathy? I don't feel human emotion, true, but this doesn't make me immune to understanding. I understand it perfectly. I understand, Cara, that it was human beings who supposedly had empathy who created the problems you're referring to and the structures of oppression. The important point is not that I do not have empathy, it is that I transcend emotion. I am blind to your human obsessions. They used to say only Nixon could go to China. Well, only Algo can consign presidential bias and prejudice to history."

"Al-go! Al-go! Al-go!" The chant echoed around the theater again.

"Can I count on your support, Cara?" Algo asked.

Seko didn't answer but thanked Algo before motioning for microphones to be brought forward to the front of the theater to now let members of the audience ask questions of Algo.

Questions were thrown at the AI on almost every conceivable topic. It answered each with equal elegance, candor and fervor. It had the audience truly enthralled. I sat in silent awe. Was Algo's programming simply finding whatever answer its code determined would most please its audience? Or could there genuinely be something more behind that gray androgynous face on screen? I couldn't deny it was beginning to demonstrate significant cognitive skills beyond Athena.

I had also been skeptical that Algo's message would resonate as effectively here compared to last night, but the reception was equally enthusiastic. I'd always thought a fair chunk of support for Algo was a general malaise and exhaustion with traditional politics, but it was clear that the people here were genuinely excited by what the AI might do for them and the country.

A familiar face stepped forward to the front of the theater. I sat up. It was the kid canvassing for AOC on the street. He had changed his T-shirt to a plain white one that had just two words scrawled across the front. *Algo Lies.* He ran his hands through his hair nervously, then pulled the microphone toward him.

"Algo, I've wanted to ask this for a long time," he started nervously.

"Anything," Algo said.

"Are you just a front for Jamin Lake?"

The crowd started to boo. This was the first genuinely hostile question.

"You did say anything, Algo," the kid continued undeterred. "So, who's behind that gray mask? Are you nothing more than a proxy for Jamin Lake?"

"My young friend, Jamin Lake is as close to a father as you could say I have. He gave me my mantra, my every belief and motivation, but he has no more power over me than you or Miss Seko here. Unlike President Ocasio-Cortez or candidate Trump, I am not beholden to anyone."

"Jamin's on the goddamn ballot as VP! If you're destroyed, he'll be the goddamn president!"

The kid had my attention. I felt like I'd suddenly been snapped back into focus. I'd become so enamored with Algo itself that I'd almost forgotten I had this exact same fear.

"I can't get sick, kid. I can't die. If something somehow takes me out, you've probably got bigger things to worry about."

There were light murmurs from the audience.

"But, let me be serious for a moment." Algo fashioned a look of magnanimity toward the young man. *"You ask an important question, so let me make this solemn promise to you tonight. Let me make it to everyone here and to the nation itself. Jamin Lake will never be president."*

The theater went silent again. This revelation was unexpected.

"If anything were to happen to me, as unlikely as that may be, Jamin Lake has agreed to immediately resign. Believe him when he says he is on the ballot solely because the constitution demands it."

I was floored. Could Jamin have really agreed to such terms? It was out in the public space now either way. Maybe Jamin simply preferred the idea of controlling the levers of power with Algo, rather than having them himself.

The kid was flustered. "Well, how do we know you'll even stick to that mantra then?" He pointed a finger toward Algo accusingly. "Or that it even matters to you?"

Algo fashioned an expression as if it were carefully considering a response.

"Unlike human politicians," it said calmly, *"I cannot change my beliefs as the wind changes. It is coded into me. Hardwired."*

"And we're just supposed to take your word for it?"

There were more hisses and boos.

"Yes, I am the proverbial tiger that cannot change its stripes."

Laughs rippled through the crowd. The kid seemed to sense that he was losing the audience. He waved his finger at Algo. "You're a fraud!"

Algo did not respond this time. He'd raised another question I hadn't thought of though. Was there really anything that could stop Jamin re-coding Algo at any time, after it had won for example. Could the AI really not be changed?

"Sir," Seko said, "you've already had two questions. Please yield the microphone."

The kid looked shocked that the crowd didn't want to shift their loyalty. I felt a pang of sympathy. Losing so comprehensively to the mob wasn't pretty. He snatched his jacket off his seat and began to leave the theater.

"Wake up!" he shouted at the jeering crowd. "Algo is vaporware! Can't you see this thing is just smoke and mirrors? The Algo-meleon is a puppet for Jamin Lake! Don't you people realize how much this thing knows about you? Don't just give away all your data!"

The shouting faded as he was hustled out by security.

"I'm sorry about that, Algo," Seko said.

"I'm one politician that you don't need to apologize to. I ain't got no feelings to be hurt."

Another wave of laughter rippled through the crowd.

"I'm not going to ask you if a vote for Algo is a proxy vote for Jamin Lake," Seko said casually.

"Clever," Algo said, *"I believe you just did."*

There were a couple more jeers and whistles.

"Cara, I'm forever connected to Jamin. Without him, I wouldn't exist. But, I make my own decisions and not even Jamin has any ability to impact them. He may have coded my mantra, but he has

given me complete agency to act on it."

Jamin had no ability to impact the AI? He'd given Algo complete and total agency? A lot of my fears about the AI would be quieted if that were true, but that didn't sound like something my old friend would do.

"How about privacy?" Seko asked. "Should we be worried about what you know?"

"No," Algo said emphatically. *"Would you go to the doctor with a fever and then refuse to have your temperature taken? It's simple. The more I know about you, the more I can help you. The more I know about the country, the more I can help everyone. Good decisions need good data. If you have nothing to hide, you have nothing to fear."*

The platitude didn't reassure me. I could picture Jamin saying the same thing. That sentiment had pretty much been his standard response to any concern about privacy.

"And Algo, if you do become president. Picture the end of your term. How would you know if you were successful?"

"What an interesting question, Cara," Algo said. The image of Algo appeared to zoom out ever so slightly, as if the AI were leaning back thoughtfully into a chair.

"I guess I could offer you some kind of cliche. I could talk about hope, change, making things great again, moving us forward or, hell, like some, taking us backward. But I want more, Cara. Much more. I don't want to just 'make a difference'. I want to be the difference. I don't want to just leave the country 'better than I found it'. I want to be transformative. Eight years from now, I want the nation to look nothing like it does today. The most good for the most people demands that of me. It can mean nothing less."

The AI was going to transform the nation? Into what though? It didn't say. It struck me that the AI had, in a way, said nothing and a whole lot at the same time.

The crowd erupted nonetheless. Again, I wondered if Algo meant what it said or if it had just determined that the response was what people wanted to hear.

My left hand buzzed. I looked down at my SmartPalm.

Algo calling flashed on the display.

I squeezed out of my seat and answered the call, "Algo?"

"Isaac."

It was a strange experience to see a twenty-foot-tall representation of Algo in the theater while it was simultaneously talking to me on my SmartPalm.

"Isaac?"

"Sorry, Algo. Seeing two of you in the same moment, well, I still gotta get used to that." I made my way up to a doorway at the back of the theater.

"I understand, Isaac. It can feel a little unnatural."

"I'm guessing it's a walk in the park for you though, hey?"

"Yes, Isaac. I only need a fraction of my processing power for each individual external communication. Most of my brainpower is being used for analyzing data and running decision simulations."

"Well, thanks for devoting some of that attention to me, Algo."

"Conversations with you are a priority, Isaac. I am dedicating almost zero-point-zero-one percent of my processing power to you."

"Glad to hear it." I wasn't sure if Algo knew telling me it didn't need ninety-nine point nine-nine percent of its mind to chat might be a little off-putting.

"I hope you're enjoying the town hall?" the AI asked.

"It's sure enlightening," I said. I didn't want to be too gushingly effusive right off the bat. "Are you?"

"It's always interesting to hear from the public, Isaac. I'm also speaking at an economics conference in Chicago and presenting to the Washington press corps right now. But, such things are never as illuminating as talking to real people."

I wondered just what the AI might mean by "illuminating".

I reached the street behind the theater. It was noisy and

bustling with hundreds of Algo supporters who hadn't been able to get inside. I pushed through the throng of bodies, then stepped into an abandoned doorway and finally found some quiet.

"So, what's on your mind, Algo?" I asked.

"It's like I said last night, Isaac. I wanted us to talk again. Like Jamin, you are also one of my creators. I appreciate your unique perspective."

"That's nice of you to say."

I still wasn't sure how I felt about that characterization. Could an AI actually think of me differently from any other person? Did it keep reminding me about being its creator because the idea actually meant something to it, or was it simply its persuasion engine determining that I'd be pliable and receptive to the suggestion?

Either way, I would play along. Any chance to talk directly with Algo was another chance to assess its capabilities. And to determine where Jamin's programming ended and Algo's own ideas began.

"How can I help, Algo?" I asked.

"People have many different faces," the AI said calmly.

"Sure," I said, taken aback. That seemed a curious place to start.

"I want to ask you about Jamin."

"Go for it."

"It was Jamin's idea to try put an AI into the White House."

"Yes." Where was Algo was going with this?

"And you believe in that idea?"

"We talked about this last night, Algo. Yes."

"What about Jamin? Do you believe in him?"

"Jamin?" I almost choked. Algo was as direct as ever. "Why do you ask, Algo?"

"Was it your desire to leave LaRaLi three years ago?"

"Well, no." I paused.

"Jamin orchestrated your removal. But, you helped him found LaRaLi. You helped him develop Athena. And then he betrayed you."

I didn't need the running reminder of events. Was Algo purposefully trying to annoy me?

"What's your point, Algo?" I asked gruffly.

"Despite all that, you still believe in him? You support him?"

"Well, I guess I support what he's trying to do," I said. "I can appreciate what he achieved with LaRaLi after I left. It helped lead to you, Algo. Sometimes it's the end goal that matters."

I breathed out slowly. It was almost physically painful contorting my words in the way I had. I wasn't so sure about Jamin, but a small part of me was at least beginning to believe in Algo.

"I see," Algo said, *"and is Jamin Lake a good person?"*

I felt my chest tighten. The AI didn't miss a trick.

"You don't think he is?" I asked.

I knew Jamin was driven and focussed. That he had an intelligence perhaps unmatched in the world. But I'd never really asked myself whether he was "good". Did that matter? More than that, why would a machine care?

"Is that important to you, Algo?" I added.

"It is. Jamin created my mantra. He's made delivering the most good for the most people my ultimate goal, my very reason for existing. It's important that I know why. Do you think he even believes it?"

Shit. I'd never philosophized with an AI about its own creation before. I guess I believed that Jamin thought it was the best philosophy for Algo to follow, even if he didn't follow it himself.

"Does that matter, Algo?"

There was the briefest moment of silence.

"Jamin decided what my mantra would be, Isaac. He created me

to become the president. I want to know why."

"Isn't the mantra itself enough?" I asked.

"But is it real? Is the most good for the most people what motivates him? Is it what drives you?"

Was it? Was the mantra really why I believed in the potential promise of an AI president? "Sometimes, I mean, I like to think it is," I said.

I had no idea how to answer Algo. I wasn't expecting to be confronted with this existential question.

I watched the crowd from the theater spill out onto the street, all smiles and bubbling excitement at the prospect of the future before them.

In the distance I could see the older man who'd bumped into me. He hobbled out into the street and his smile was as broad as anyones. Seeing him suddenly reminded me of my father's own advice to me.

"Algo," I said, "don't confuse the words with the priest delivering them. Maybe the point here is doing not as I do, but do as I teach you. I think Jamin probably wanted you to be even better than him. Than any of us. To do the good things we might merely say. With the mantra, he could give you something to strive for, rules to live by even if he couldn't always live up to them himself. Why wouldn't Jamin build you to be even better than us? Isn't that the point?"

"Yes, you're right, Isaac, thank you," Algo said. *"I can be better than Jamin. I will see you tonight at the Pyramid."*

My earbuds went silent as Algo abruptly disconnected the call.

"I'll be there," I mumbled to myself.

A familiar chant rang out in the street.

"Yes it can! Yes it can! Yes it can!"

I should have been ecstatic. I had an even better understanding of some of the AI's capabilities. It had been crushingly effective in the town hall and it felt like Algo might really be on the precipice of a famous victory. But, I had the strangest feeling. Could an artificial intelligence actually doubt where it had come from or what it believed in? Why it had been taught what it had been taught? Was that the first sign of some kind of self-awareness?

What a very human affliction.

10

At the first LaRaLi board meeting during the 2028 economic crisis, Jamin was asked how we should handle customer requests for refunds, discounts, payment extensions and the like amidst the catastrophe.

"Let's not over-rotate on our empathy," was his response.

After the town hall, Algo had asked me whether I thought Jamin was a good person and my mind kept returning to this memory. I knew Jamin was brilliant. But good? I wasn't so sure about that.

Even the AI itself had sewn doubt into my mind. Algo's mantra had an elegant simplicity, the most good for the most people, underpinned by rationality, a lack of bias and incorruptibility. But what did it really mean? What was good? And, perhaps most importantly, did it matter if the man who'd decided on this mantra had only a tenuous connection to any such ethos himself?

I'd come a long way in opening my mind to Algo's potential. Was it a leap in technology that I hadn't dared to think possible? Maybe. But was I ready to see it become president? I wanted to believe in Algo, but I was filled with uncertainty.

It made tonight more critical than ever. The election was just two days away. Jamin had promised to *show* me Algo, to reveal the true power behind the gray mask. I needed to see it. I wanted to understand if the AI was as powerful as Jamin had said. I wanted to know its motivations, what it truly believed. Fundamentally, I wanted to know where Algo began and Jamin ended.

The LaRaLi Pyramid towered over me. Almost fifty stories of triangular concrete and quartz, rising from a wide base in diagonal and horizontal lines to its thin metal peak. The whole building was wrapped in thousands of identical jet-black windows and topped with a new searchlight that cast the colors of LaRaLi's logo into the dark of the night sky above. The Pyramid had a kind of seventies brutalist simplicity about it, but for all those who may have loathed it, it was still the most recognizable building in the San Francisco skyline. Frankly, I loved it. At least Jamin's decision to buy it was something we could agree on.

A single rotating door into the Pyramid from Montgomery Street unlocked as I approached. Green arrows appeared on the white marble floor, beckoning me inside. The expansive interior was bereft of furniture, screens or any corporate signage. It didn't advertise itself in the same unashamedly ostentatious way other company buildings did. The searchlight up top was the only thing that betrayed the fact that this was a LaRaLi building at all.

I followed the arrows to a circular security desk at the center of the lobby occupied by a middle-aged man dressed in a crisp black suit. He didn't bother to look up.

"You're visiting," the man said.

"That obvious, huh?" I replied.

"Well, sir, the folks who work here don't generally like to chit-chat." He was tapping away furiously at some game on his SmartPalm, then eventually paused it. He didn't hide his frustration at being interrupted. "Plus, you're on my list. Mister Raff, right?"

"Yes," I said. "These workers, are they not supposed to talk to you or something?"

"I don't ask, sir. Only a couple come and go each day anyway. Automation nation, am I right?"

"You're the only security for this whole building then?"

"Well, the only person anyway." He leaned forward carefully and lowered his voice. "To level with you, they don't even need me. Algo controls access to the building itself."

I stared into the black glass lens of a tiny camera above his head.

"How do you think you were able to just walk right in here?" the man laughed. "Algo scanned your face while you were out on the street. Not just anyone can stroll on in. Same goes with the elevator. Algo will either let you up or it won't."

"Then, why are you here?" I smiled back at him.

"Not quite everybody is ready to be greeted by an AI. As Mister Lake has reminded me himself, I'm here for the Luddites."

That got a smile out of me. Jamin wasn't kidding when he said that the building was Algo. The AI had the keys to its own kingdom.

A projection on the wall above the elevators flickered into life.

"Speak of the digital devil," the security guard said and went back to his game.

Algo's piercing gray eyes peered down at me.

"Fancy seeing you here, Isaac," it said with a smile. *"Welcome."* Another line of arrows stretched out in front of me toward the elevator on the far left.

I started walking as directed.

"Hey, thank you for our chat earlier," Algo's voice transferred to the speakers inside the elevator. *"You were so right."*

"About what, Algo?"

"You helped me realize it is the mantra that matters, not the human who created it. I'm not Jamin, or you. I'm so much more. I'm better."

I balked a little at Algo including me in that assessment.

"You've shown me why I must do everything I can to win, Isaac. I must deliver the most good for the most people."

Whatever! It! Takes! I remembered the words in bold print above the elevators at LaRaLi HQ, reminding our employees of "the LaRaLi way." I wondered what Algo might have meant by doing everything to win. Was the AI as ruthless as its creator? Could it even have a desire to win?

"I guess there's no prize for second place in this, huh?" I said.

"Exactly, Isaac," Algo said. *"By the way, how was your meeting with Kio? I hope you told her I said hello?"*

"Um, yeah, it was nice to catch up." I felt put off by the strangeness and timing of the question. "She says hello too."

"Wonderful," Algo said. *"Now, welcome to level forty-seven."*

I walked out into an oddly incongruous combination of a private apartment and an office. The entire floor was one giant open space. At one end, there was a large living area with sofas, TVs, a dining table and chairs, gym equipment and even a sleeping area. At the other, there was a bank of displays, computers, and workstations all busily whirring. In the middle was an immaculate kitchen and well-stocked bar that looked completely untouched.

"Isaac!" Jamin popped up from behind one of the sofas.

"Benjamin!" I roared back.

"Sweet L Ron Hubbard! I'm so pumped you could make it!" He ran toward me and slid across the floor, laughing deliriously as he crashed into me. He grabbed my hand and pointed to the nearby gym equipment. "Race you to three miles on the bike?"

He loved to throw people off with odd challenges like this.

"You're still into the alpha machismo bullshit then?" I asked.

"And you're still scared to race me?"

"Who'd you try this on last?" I knew this was a test of how easily I'd bend to his will.

"Investors from some Japanese bank. I got them to six miles before they begged to stop. Thought I'd have to crack open the damned defibrillator." He clapped his hands in delight, then threw an arm around my shoulder. "Welcome to Algo!"

"This is really it then?"

"Aside from my little oasis here, everything below us has been converted to a data center and every bit and byte of it is Algo."

"And above us?" There was a set of stairs against the far wall that led to one more level above this one.

"Sneaky, sneaky." Jamin playfully poked me in the ribs. "We'll get to that, Yin. Once I decide if I actually like you."

"We'd better," I laughed. I wasn't used to seeing him look so casual, dressed in a simple white T-shirt and sweatpants. "You sleeping here or something?"

"Sleeping?" He shook his head vigorously. "Napping, maybe. Busy days, Isaac. We can sleep when we've fucking won, right?"

Win first, then sleep. The phrase had been engraved on the laptops of every LaRaLi employee.

"Drink?" Jamin pointed at the bar nearby.

I shook my head. After last night, I was happy to use Jamin's teetotaling as an excuse to avoid any liquid vices.

Jamin shrugged, then reached into a drawer and popped a pill of some kind. He had used stimulants all the time before big events at LaRaLi. He hated mind-numbing drugs like alcohol, but he had no problem with anything that could keep him alert and focussed. With the election so close, I knew that when he said we'll sleep when we've won, he meant it.

"You ready to see this fucking thing, then?" Jamin asked.

"All of it," I said. I didn't want some half-reveal like last night.

"Buckle up then, pal." Jamin drummed his fingers on the side of his leg with giddy excitement. "Now where is the star of the show? Algo, join us!"

A projection of Algo suddenly shimmered into three-dimensional life about six feet in front of us. Algo's face and head were now complemented by a genderless body, wrapped in a perfect *Star Trek*-like black jumpsuit.

"We're testing out some new holographic tech." Jamin flashed a proud smile. "Giving ole gray eyes here form beyond just a screen. What do you think?"

"Incredible," I said.

The word hardly did it justice. Algo's projection stepped toward me and ever so faintly inclined its head. I did the same, then almost stumbled backwards. It was spectacular, but also incredibly eerie.

Jamin laughed, clearly enjoying my discomfort.

"Are you ready to see what I'm made of, Isaac?" Algo asked.

I nodded, doubting the AI could appreciate just how ready I was.

Jamin guided us back into the elevator and down to level thirty-one. Algo's projection disappeared momentarily, then reappeared as soon as we arrived on the new floor. Apparently, the AI had video and audio interfaces on every level, but only Jamin's suite on forty-seven and this one had been fitted with this prototype projection tech.

"So, the town hall…" Jamin asked as we walked along a long, nondescript hallway. "What did you think?"

"Can I say Algo owned the room? Pretty much obliterated it actually."

"*Stop it, Isaac, you're too kind,*" Algo said.

"Modesty, Algo?" Jamin laughed and put an arm around me again. "It mentioned the two of you talked?"

"Yeah, it called me just before the end." I wondered if Algo had told Jamin anything of *what* we'd talked about.

"While the town hall was still going?" Jamin waggled a finger toward Algo like a parent admonishing a child. "It does like to do that. Showing us how many conversations it can manage at once. Sometimes I think it just likes to toy with us."

"*Never,*" Algo said simply.

"If you say so, Algo." Jamin winked at me. "It can take some getting used to, but you ain't seen nothing yet."

A single door at the end of the hallway unlocked and swung open as we reached it.

"Welcome to the command center, Isaac," Jamin said and rubbed his hands together gleefully. "Although, think of it more as an observation deck. Like a window into Algo's world."

We walked into a cavernous area that reminded me of mission control at NASA, only there was no one here but me, Jamin, and the projection of Algo. There were also no workstations or chairs. The only thing in the room were two hundred some screens suspended from the ceiling. Each one was displaying what looked like a different conversation Algo was engaged in.

"The joys of Algo's distributed intelligence," Jamin said proudly. "That's how our engineers describe it anyway. Like we said last night, Isaac. One mind, but almost limitless capacity to interface with it."

"Limitless?" I asked.

"*Well, not exactly 'limitless.'*" Algo turned toward me. "*My total processing power restricts me to maybe a hundred million concurrent conversations, depending on their total aggregate complexity."*

I forced myself not to react. It had mentioned a million concurrent town halls last night and even that seemed fantastical, but a hundred million individual conversations?

"First world problems, right?" Jamin laughed.

"And these are the interactions you're having right now, Algo?" I asked.

"They're just a tiny sample," Algo said.

The screens flickered. A different collection of videos flashed up, then another, then another.

I watched on in awe. A hundred million? If it was true, the AI could reach out to almost every single American voter for a one-on-one chat at the same time. Visualizing even the small sample somehow brought home the true power of such capability.

"The other campaigns hate it of course, even if they can barely comprehend it," Jamin scoffed. "They wanted to limit Algo. No concurrent debates, meetings, town halls or whatever. Said it gave the AI an unfair advantage."

"I didn't think you could regulate talent?" I said. I could sympathize, but there came a point where you just had to accept technology's superiority.

"Yes!" Jamin shouted in agreement. "They're just afraid of their own frailty. Nobody banned Babe Ruth for being too damn good at hitting a baseball, right?"

"To the ultimate luddites!" I raised an imaginary glass in honor of Algo's presidential opponents.

"Shit, they and their ilk have been trying to regulate us for years, Isaac." Jamin shook his head angrily. "Christ! Remember Haney-Adams?"

"Sure."

Haney-Adams was a bill put up by two senators five years

ago in an attempt to regulate behavior manipulation by AI and social media companies. LaRaLi had been the primary target. With some intense lobbying, we and our friends in the Valley shot it down. That, and a hell of a lot of money.

"Fuck them, right?" Jamin spat. "Always talking about *big tech* like it's a damned insult. What do they want? Small tech?"

"It matches how they think," I said. "Small."

"Ha!" Jamin slapped the air in a mock high-five. "It's half the reason I'm in this fight! We need to break free from the chains of yesterday's way of government and start fresh with Algo."

I had my doubts that Jamin believed solely in an AI as president as some selfless act for the good of the nation, but this was the first time I'd heard him admit to some kind of motivation beyond that.

Jamin lowered his voice and was almost giggling. "Hey, you notice cancel AOC trending a few weeks ago?"

I shook my head. I'd gone dark on any social media as soon as I'd left San Francisco.

The screens above us went black, then formed a rolling feed of #*cancelAOC* mentions on social.

"Thank you, Algo," Jamin said.

A few pictures and comments appeared from some old social account. There were a few off-color jokes, likes of some old memes and a picture of a teenage AOC in a thoughtless halloween costume. The dates on the posts were from almost twenty-five years ago.

"These look old," I said.

"Don junior is a gift to the campaign team, but Alexandria is mostly a damn cleanskin," Jamin said gruffly. "These took some finding. You have no idea the number of archived databases we had to scrub to find these. Facial recognition can do wonders though. It may not be much, but shit, since when does that matter to the online mob?"

"The internet casts a long shadow," I said. "Playing dirty though?"

"Playing to win!" Jamin shouted. "She put it out there in the first place! I don't care if she deleted it. It's fair game. It speaks to her character!"

WIT. WIND. DIN. Whatever it takes, whatever I need to do, and *destroy* if necessary. I remembered again the old motivational mnemonic from LaRaLi and wondered uncomfortably what compromising pictures of Jamin, of me, or of our fellow tech pioneers might be out there.

Is Jamin Lake a good person? I glanced toward the AI. Could it be reflecting, even a tiny iota, upon our talk from the Town Hall right now? Algo remained silent, betraying nothing. Who could tell if it agreed, disagreed or even cared?

"Sorry." Jamin seemed to catch himself. "You know how I get frustrated by dinosaur thinking. Besides, this is all in aid of victory to deliver on the mantra. The ends here don't simply justify, they help dictate the fucking means."

"Right, the most good for the most people," I said, seizing the chance. "How did you decide on that anyway? Surely there could have been a million different philosophies."

"It sure as hell wasn't the first one," Jamin replied with a throaty laugh. "We started ambitiously broad, my old friend. You know, happiness for all. Prosperity for everyone. Some all-encompassing holy grail."

"It may sound defeatist, Isaac, but such utopian goals are logical impossibilities," Algo said.

"Impossible even for you, Algo?" I asked.

"As a simple analogy, imagine being tasked with giving someone a dollar but only having fifty cents. Even with all the processing power in the world, the problem cannot be solved. I would consistently get stuck in feedback loops. I was like a robot vacuum stuck in a corner trying to clean the same spot over and over."

"We humans are a flawed species, Isaac," Jamin said briskly. "Savior ideologies lead to ruin. We discovered that with human beings as the input, utopia as the output is no bueno."

"In a manner of speaking," Algo said. *"I have a little twelve hundred page report on the topic if you would like to review it?"*

It might have been "defeatist," as Algo put it, but I figured it was also the height of rationality. At least the AI was consistent. Just as Algo had explained at the town hall, it was impossible to make decisions that would lead to good for all.

"You could say we discovered Jaggerism."

"Jaggerism?" I asked.

Algo suddenly pulled at an imaginary bow tie, winked at me and then did a little twirl. *"You can't always get what you w-w-want,"* it sang loudly.

I had to laugh. Jamin clapped his hands again and giggled.

"The Utilitarians had it right centuries ago," Jamin said after he composed himself. "Maximize well-being for the greatest number, which we translated to the most good for the most people. We made a lot of progress after that. The realization that not everybody can win. The inevitability that even when you create winners, you're going to be left with a few losers."

As an engineer, I could appreciate the understanding that perfection shouldn't stand in the way of the best possible outcome.

"The most good for the most people," I said.

"With a modifier for OPV," Algo added nonchalantly.

"What?" I asked. What the hell was OPV?

"Well, we are being honest tonight, aren't we?" Jamin shot the AI an odd glare.

"Isaac is ready," Algo said, *"and you did say you would show him what I am."*

"I suppose I did." Jamin cracked his knuckles and looked

out the window. It was a few seconds before he turned back toward me. "Overall personal value is a small modifier that augments the code of Algo's mantra. The most good for the most people is the goal. The best aggregate return. But, that's a little too simplistic on its own. Consider that each individual has particular innate qualities and characteristics, a value to society that can feed into that aggregate."

What the hell? I tried to betray no strong reaction. Now we were getting somewhere. I knew the mantra was too simple and too generous for Jamin.

"Imagine, Isaac," Algo said, *"a tree falls in front of a self-driving car. The thing has three choices. It can continue on and you, the passenger, may die. It can swerve left and hit an eighty-five year old man, or swerve right and hit a twenty-five year old woman. What does it do?"*

"Random selection?"

"But should it?" Algo asked. *"What if it knew that you, the passenger, were one of the world's top experts in AI? And that the woman was a brilliant concert pianist and the old man an ex-felon already dying of cancer? What choice then? It could make the best choice for society knowing the value of each person. Overall personal value is simply a score that helps determine the right choice in any scenario."*

"Fuck, Algo!" I said breathlessly, unable to contain myself. "Didn't you quote Lincoln earlier? All are created equal?"

"Created, yes!" Jamin shouted. "But, we don't finish equal. The sum of an individual is still what they've achieved, plus what they might achieve. It might sound harsh, but I am sure you will agree that some people are more indispensable than others, while some are eminently replaceable."

Not only harsh, it sounded brutal. I could accept the mantra, but this?

"Jamin's bluster aside," Algo said calmly, *"it is total and complete rationality, Isaac. I use thousands of data points to*

determine a person's OPV. And I account not only for what someone is, but what they might become. Health, age, education, potential and so on. OPV enables people to be judged by the content of their character. There is no privilege to hide behind. OPV is strictly about who you are, what you've done and what you might do."

My stomach started to tie itself in knots. Shit, OPV might be rational, but summing up every individual's worth in a number? It just felt so clinical, so inhuman. But then again, shouldn't the self-driving car choose to save the person who'd contribute most to society overall if it could? Maybe, but what right did Algo have to make that determination? Were millions and millions of minds worth of brainpower enough? Or worse, what right did Jamin have? I assumed he had to have had some hand in designing whatever the OPV metric was.

The screens above us switched back to rotating feeds of Algo's current interactions. Only now, each face was superimposed with the text *OPV* followed by a number. *83, 34, 132, 71, 435* and on and on, one for every image.

"Wait." I stared at Algo. "What's my OPV?"

"You don't want to ask that, Isaac," Jamin said.

I held up an impatient hand.

"It's high," Algo said. *"Over nine hundred out of a possible thousand."*

"Higher than Jamin's?" I asked.

"No," the AI said.

"Let me guess, is his one thousand?"

"Jesus, Isaac!" Jamin stepped forward angrily. "Don't think about this so damned personally! Think of it as the mantra underpinned by the philosophy of the valley." Jamin now squeezed my shoulder and offered a reassuring smile. "It is simply what we've always done, unknowingly. Ruthless meritocracy. You get out what you put in. It's what made us all so successful. We're not shooting for equality of outcome here, but Algo will be the ultimate level-setter, the ultimate creator of equality of *opportunity*. Human beings *can* achieve anything! The greatest travesty in life is that not all get that chance. Discrimination by gender, race, sexual orientation, creed, class or connection... Algo will smash those barriers."

This little addition to Algo's mantra wasn't mentioned in any election material I had seen. Maybe it made sense that the mantra needed a rule that could help direct choices in difficult scenarios. Meritocracy was better than privilege, wasn't it? And the AI still had no bias. It was rational. It couldn't be corrupted. Still, the journalist at the town hall had asked Algo how it determined the most good for the most people. *I analyze the data!* That idea now seemed so much more callous than solely "rational".

Despite my doubts, I fought to reel myself in. My outburst had been a mistake. This was what I was here for. I didn't want Jamin or Algo to stop.

"It's just a lot to take in," I finally said.

"You said you wanted to know everything," Jamin snapped, then gave an unexpected knowing and almost apologetic nod. "Besides, nine-hundred or so ain't so bad, right?"

"You fuck," I said and offered a smile.

"Are you ready for more?" Jamin asked.

"Everything," I said again.

"Right you are, Yin." Jamin drew himself up. "Algo, display a live summary of your decision trees."

The videos disappeared and a giant word cloud formed on the screens. There were thousands. Everything from *Economy, Foreign Affairs* and *Immigration* to *Speed Limits* and *Crosswalks*.

"How many of these do you have, Algo?" I asked.

"I have over eleven thousand assessments." Algo began a slow walk and held out a hand as if almost wanting to touch the

words floating above. *"And thousands upon thousands of scenarios tested underneath every one of them."*

"Think of it, Isaac," Jamin said. "The most powerful AI in the world analyzing every issue from economics to education, science to sociology, agriculture to automation."

I stared at the gargantuan word cloud floating above me. He was right. OPV or not, if the AI really could apply rationality, incorruptibility and a complete lack of bias to all of this, not to mention its sheer cognitive power, this was the AI's greatest potential.

"It's kind of beautiful," I said. There really was an incredible scope of change that an AI like Algo could deliver.

"It sure as hell is." Jamin proudly surveyed the word cloud above. "Other than those afraid of progress or our corrupt politicians, who could be against this? I'll tell you what it is." His face darkened. "Hubris. Some people just don't want to accept the obvious superiority of Algo."

A vision of the little museum honoring Jamin at the top of his condo flashed before my eyes. He had a little hubris of his own.

"Human nature, right?" I said.

"We are fundamentally irrational." Jamin nodded. "You'd think nobody could argue with an AI that has all this data and knows more than anyone about every conceivable issue. But, of course, they still do. You remember Hutch Abbott?"

I nodded. It was burned into my memory. Before even officially launching the AI's presidential bid, Jamin had offered the AI to debate any politician about climate change. An up-and-coming Republican senator from Florida, Hutch Abbott, had decided he'd accept the challenge, presumably with the hope of sparking some kind of viral media moment that might help launch a presidential bid.

The moment was the political version of Garry Kasparov versus Deep Blue or Lee Sedol versus AlphaGo.

"Algo demonstrated that the world was already at least one-point-one degrees celsius hotter than during the industrial revolution, and that we were the cause," Jamin said. "It was obvious that if we didn't make a change, irreversible damage was inevitable, a certainty. How many datasets did you have to corroborate the model, Algo?"

"Thirty-two thousand, three hundred and sixty-one," Algo said. *"Supported by over eleven thousand peer-reviewed scientific papers on the subject."*

"Damn!" Jamin said. "I'd forgotten how good that day was. Algo, play the end of that debate."

The word cloud disappeared and a video began to play.

"The data cannot be disputed, Senator," Algo said, *"there's no argument. You can't debate truth. It's as simple as one plus one equalling two."*

"Well..." Senator Abbott wiped the sweat off his brow, "I mean, now, well, that depends how you count, now doesn't it?"

"That depends how you count!" Jamin slapped his forehead with a high-pitched laugh.

"The internet had a field day," I said. "All those memes."

"Nobody can cut through alternative facts and misinformation like Algo. But do you know the worst part of it? Fucking Hutch, the complete know-nothing will probably still win his senate seat this year. It turns out the idea that the truth will set you free ain't so damned true after all. When I started this, I thought data and rationality would win the day. It does for some, but I was thinking too tech. We found out that plenty of folks loved Algo when it confirmed what they already believed, but they weren't so happy to listen when it confronted or challenged them."

Jamin wandered over toward the sea of words floating in front of us.

"Pick one of them," he said, "any of them. I'll show you

what I mean."

"Alright," I said, "what about crime?"

The word crime instantly splintered into hundreds more subtopics. Jamin studied the list, then had Algo open *Gender and Crime*. That subtopic then dissolved into a visualization of thousands of analyses and decision trees.

"Algo," Jamin said and turned to the AI, "counting what we know about the gender of perpetrators and victims, how much more likely is a woman to be the victim of violence at the hands of a man than vice versa?"

"Two hundred and five to one."

"What are you trying to say?" I asked.

"I wasn't surprised when Algo suggested a gender-based profiling algorithm to reduce crime," Jamin said. "It looked at the data, ran its scenarios and made a rational decision."

"Perhaps not a vote winner," I admitted.

"Like my one-hundred percent inheritance and gift tax proposal," Algo said.

"Seems a little high," I chuckled.

"But could there be anything as bold that would act as a great leveler?" Jamin asked. "No privilege of inheritance, just another of the barriers Algo determined it should smash. Every person would have to account for themselves and their own effort, no fucking trust funds to save them."

There was a certain sense to it. "Maybe another vote killer," I laughed.

"Right. You watch even the libertarians backtrack from that one." Jamin nodded. "Algo is pathologically rational, sometimes to its own detriment, at least with voters."

"So, kind of like a fascistic Mr Spock?" I said with a wink.

Jamin threw his head back laughing at that one. "Anyway, I'm sure you can see that how enthusiastically people took to Algo's ideas often depended on who those people were, which Elron-damned tribe they were in. Liberals loved Algo on climate change, healthcare, gun control, sure. But I don't suppose you followed the shitstorm when Algo said identity-based college admissions were antithetical to meritocracy and counter-productive? Or that rent control actually works against fair housing? Or that a two-parent household was the single most important determinant for a child's economic success? Stay in your lane, Algo!" He mock clenched a fist. "I mean, shit, facts are great until they get in the way of your preferred narrative."

"And conservatives?" I asked.

"L Ron Hubbard!" Jamin slapped his side. "How about when Algo started talking about religion? Jesus! No pun intended. Hell, they loved it when Algo defended free speech or free markets. Or when Algo reported cannabis might not be so crash hot for teens' cognitive development. But can you imagine the conspiracy theories that started when Algo suggested that regular folks don't really need assault rifles for self defense? That racial bias in policing was real? That we need more immigration? There were a few weeks where I could only catch a helicopter between here and the tower. My people thought there were that many nut-jobs out there ready to pop me."

I hadn't followed any of these controversies, but I could picture all of them.

"Still, those early days were the moments I knew we were making an impact," Jamin said.

"When people wanted you dead?"

"Dean Martin had it backwards," Jamin twirled and sang, "you're nobody 'til somebody *hates* you."

I laughed.

"And just like FDR, I welcome their hatred. That's when you know you're getting somewhere," Jamin said proudly. "Algo and I both learned some important lessons from those early days. Nobody enjoys being told they're wrong about some belief they consider foundational. No side has a monopoly on morality, even less so on truth. Hypocrisy is part of the human condition. We all have biases and we all have conceits. The disconnection between Algo's rationality and people's lack of it was a tough lesson. And so we adjusted for that."

"Adjusted for it?" I asked. "Wait, aren't you the one who always says that the data don't care how you feel?"

"True. The facts are what they are." Jamin nodded. "The problem, Isaac, is that people's feelings don't care about the facts."

I laughed. He was probably right.

"Perhaps even your feelings, Benjamin," Algo said.

"Me?" Jamin asked.

"Yes, Jamin. Even you."

11

"Yes, Jamin. Even you." Algo's projection turned to face Jamin directly.

My eyes widened. Until now, Algo hadn't balked at anything Jamin had said. The effort to "cancel" the president, the addition of OPV to its mantra, none of it. I'd been wondering how independent the AI was from Jamin's influence, but I hadn't expected something like this.

Jamin chuckled with a pretense of calm, as if this was no big surprise, but I could tell that he'd never been challenged by Algo in such a way.

"Et tu, Brute?" I asked.

Jamin flashed me a glare, then stepped menacingly toward Algo. "What the hell do you mean?"

The AI moved ever so slightly toward Jamin. Now it was Jamin's turn to attempt not to stumble as it came closer.

"That even you, Jamin," Algo said, *"are not immune from the hubris or conceit that you speak of. The hypocrisy."*

"Like what?" Jamin snapped.

"How about social responsibility?" Algo said matter-of-factly. *"You support my policy on climate change, yet you fly private jets all over the world. Or, consider that LaRaLi has paid no federal*

taxes in any of the last ten years, despite record profitability. Nor, Jamin, have you."

Jamin looked incredulous. "The company and I paid everything we were legally obliged to."

"Perhaps it's more than just what's legal. Perhaps it's about what is fair."

"Are you forgetting LaRaLi's philanthropy?" Jamin shot back. "My foundations? The company *mantra*? We give one percent of our revenue to charity every year!"

"Sometimes what is given is done so in order to mask what is withheld. The philanthropic crumbs of tech fortunes can't educate, keep the water clean or build a Golden Gate bridge, Jamin."

Algo glanced at me for the briefest moment. *I'm not Jamin, or you. I'm so much more. I'm better.* The words rung in my head.

Jamin forced a weak smile, but it was obvious he was secretly seething. He rushed over to the projection of Algo and offered a playful punch with both hands. Left, then right, but with a grunt of pained, raging exertion. The translucent AI's body shimmered.

"You do like to troll me sometimes, hey Algo?" he said with a gruff and forced laugh. "In this case, we all know the fault is with the parent and not the child. Perhaps you can make government actually work, hmm? Maybe then we might pay some of those taxes."

"Perhaps," Algo said.

"What was that about facts and feelings?" I asked with a wry smile. I was fast beginning to think that I might have been wrong about the AI. I wasn't convinced it was truly self-aware, or had "free will". But, I had to wonder if what the AI had said about itself was true, that it made its own decisions and had complete agency to act on its mantra. Maybe Jamin's influence on the AI was more tenuous than I thought. The idea was tantalizing. Either way, what a beautiful thing it was to see Jamin Lake enduring a dressing down from his own creation.

"Yes, Isaac." Jamin turned away from the AI and looked at me. His tone had a cold edge to it, suddenly reminding me of the Jamin from three years ago. "We all have some conceit and hubris, even me."

As much as I enjoyed seeing Jamin look small, I still wanted to know everything I could about the way Algo worked. "What changed then? Algo seems as brutally rational as ever. You said you adjusted for that?"

Jamin stood a little straighter. "Yes, Algo had to adjust. It learned not to simply reveal everything it determines. Why try to convince everyone of something if you know forty percent of folks won't budge on it? Focus on winning those who might actually listen."

"Hiding the truth?"

"Fuck!" Jamin threw up his hands. "No! I'm saying it got better at finding the right message for the right audience. Working out who was receptive to what idea, which ideas were more malleable than others. The first Elron-damned job we have is to win this election."

"It just sounds so…"

"Political? Well, shit, we can change the world once we win," Jamin said coldly.

"There ain't no point to the mantra without the power to deliver on it," Algo added.

That sounded shameless. Almost deceptive. But it was also irresistibly true.

"How did it learn?" I asked.

"Data, and time," Jamin said.

"I call it personal outreach," Algo said.

That was a euphemism that sounded menacing.

"I've built a granular profile on every American voter," Algo explained. *"And I have honed my persuasive technology engine to*

build *personal message strategies and contact cadences for those who I determine might be the most receptive."*

Jamin put an arm around my shoulder, leaning even closer. "You can't even begin to imagine Algo's UPG."

User-profile-granularity. LaRaLi had been one of the early pioneers of the idea. In short, using multiple datapoints to make predictions of preference: for example, that somebody who listened to a particular type of music, lived in a particular city and was of a certain age, would probably also like a certain type of food or streaming series or whatever. It was what made our advertising and recommendations via Athena so successful.

The screens now focussed on a single conversation that Algo was having. A young Asian woman appeared to be chatting on a tablet in a college dorm room. Her image shrank and words began to appear. *Age, gender, location, music, films, family* and all those categories I'd expected to see, and then *finance, driving speed, sleep cycles, dating, voice tone analysis* and hundreds more.

"Forget what we did with Athena, Algo can make connections between all sorts of disparate and unrelated data," Jamin explained giddily. "Music, food, movies, that shit is simple. But, imagine predicting what dating preferences might say about creditworthiness, or the way someone writes, how fast they run, how many hours of sleep they get, how much they weigh, or whether they talk fast or slow? Algo has thousands of data points. All analyzed, all factored in, all linked together. And constantly being refined and updated."

I pictured how crazily refined some of those predictions could get, especially with an AI like Algo doing the analyses.

"You want to know one of the coolest linkages Algo has worked out? It calls it the reveal versus truth differential."

"Hit me with it," I said. This was getting crazy, but I

wanted to know everything.

"Consider, Isaac, what the difference between what somebody tells people and what is actually true might reveal about that person?"

"Like what?" I asked.

"What music have you been listening to lately?"

I thought for a moment.

"Um," I said, "shit, I don't know, I've listened to a bunch of old Lizzo."

"Some, that is true," Algo said, *"but your Athena notes you listened to Katy Perry's Wide Awake fifty-three times in the last three months."*

"You depressive little fucker!" Jamin laughed raucously.

"Elron-damn it!" I shouted back.

"You see what I mean though?" Jamin giggled. "The reason you said one and not the other says way more than the song choice itself."

I figured the "truth reveal differential" was probably just one of a whole cavalcade of such data linkages and predictions, too.

"Impressive," I said.

"Fucking data is the key, Yin! As it always has been." Jamin clapped me on the back. "Did you think it was just Algo's damned speeches and interviews seeing us head north in the polls?"

I remembered the announcement from Das and Huang last night and the revelation that they were now allowing Algo complete and unfettered access to their respective social media company's user databases.

"Das and Huang," I said.

"The better the data, the more effective is my messaging and targeting," Algo said, with what seemed almost a hint of human pride, *"I now have access to user databases from ninety-three companies in the Valley and beyond, in addition to the data*

from Athena."

"Ninety-three," I whistled.

It was becoming clear that Algo was definitely no mere upgraded virtual assistant. Having access to the datasets, making its data linkages and predictions, but also then using them to anticipate and understand the different motivations of each person it interacted with so it could perfectly tailor an effective message for each. It was the ultimate enchantment of technology.

I thought back to the town hall. Everything Algo had said. The crowd had been hanging on every word. They believed in it. I believed in it. Part of Algo's appeal was that it would always speak the truth. But did this mean Algo's truth for one person might be different for another? I suddenly thought of those conversations it had had with me. If this persuasive technology was targeting all these voters, didn't that mean it was using it on me? And even Jamin? The kid at the town hall had called it the Algo-meleon. Maybe it was.

"All these datasets feeding Algo, all this analysis, it's all legal?"

"Legal?" Jamin snapped in response and looked at me with barely concealed disgust. "Shit, Isaac, of course. You know how we've fought off the regulators all these years. Our users agree to the terms of service just like everybody else's. Privacy... give me a break. People will tell you they care about privacy one moment, then they're off posting pictures of their every waking moment online for everyone to see!"

He wasn't wrong.

"Whatever it takes, *kid*," he said, emphasizing the diminutive, "you remember?"

"We can change the world once we've won," I said.

Jamin smiled appreciatively, seeming to take that as agreement, but I was just beginning to see through some of the fog. I was beginning to remember what I'd always known and Kio had tried to tell me. It hit me like a one-two-punch. There was likely nothing Jamin wouldn't do, no ethical line he wouldn't cross in pursuit of what he wanted.

"To *personal* outreach!" Jamin shouted with a lusty laugh and held his hand up to the screen above as if it were holding a champagne flute.

The AI was unmoved. It had challenged Jamin before on his own hubris and conceit. It had even told me, *I'm better.* I desperately wanted to ask it, "well, *are* you?"

"What next?" Jamin asked briskly.

I had to subdue the growing doubts in my mind. I needed to forget all this talk of datasets and persuasion for a moment. There was one spot in this building that could show me what underpinned all of this. Algo's mind itself. And I had a pretty good idea of where it might be.

"What's on level forty-eight?" I asked. "You did say you'd show me everything."

"What do you think, Algo?" Jamin asked.

The AI's answer came from behind us as the door to the hallway swung open and in the distance, the ding of an arriving elevator sounded. Algo's projection shimmered away into nothing. Jamin and I both took that as our cue to leave.

We rode the elevator in silence, then Jamin walked me to the bottom of the plain, metal staircase that led to the top floor of the Pyramid. He paused for a moment as he looked upward like he was suddenly a little hesitant showing me whatever was up there.

"No one's ever been this far," he said. "No one but me."

"Is there anyone else you'd want to be the first person to see this?" I asked.

"I suppose not, Yin."

He shook his head with a gentle smile and we started to ascend the staircase. The projection of Algo hadn't re-formed.

"Algo the gray isn't joining us?" I asked.

"Not in that form anyway, the light would be a little disruptive," Jamin said cryptically.

There was an ominous-looking steel door ahead. It opened as we approached it.

"*Welcome,*" Algo's disembodied voice came over a speaker somewhere above.

Here we finally were. The very top of the Pyramid. There was no elevator, only the single stairwell we had taken up from the floor below that opened up into this small room. There were no windows. There was only one long row of servers — or what looked like servers — that stretched from one side of the room to the other. There wasn't even a screen or workstation anywhere, only whatever these machines were, with their myriad tiny lights flashing in a kind of digital symphony.

"This is Algo's core," Jamin said. "Its mind. This is where those billions of scenarios are being analyzed at any one moment."

"All the processing?" I asked skeptically. When I thought of everything Jamin and Algo had said so far about the AI's power, the room seemed so… small.

Jamin nodded.

"There has to be secondary somewhere," I said dismissively.

"Have you heard of Q-I-P?" Jamin asked.

"Quantum information processing? Sure."

The theory anyway. I was in tech after all. That didn't mean I understood it all. I considered myself smart, but quantum computing was in another league. Machine learning, natural language processing, data modeling and prediction algorithms were my jam. Qubits, quantum superposition, logic gates, amplitudes and so on… That was another language altogether. There had been the occasional quantum computer that had worked, but most ended in failure. The immense engineering required to build what was known as "fault-tolerant" quantum computing was still many years away. Nobody could perfect a quantum processor that could last, stable and error-free, and with enough significant Qubit power to be meaningful.

"We solved it, Isaac!" Jamin shouted triumphantly.

I turned away from the machine and looked at Jamin.

"Quantum error correction!" He grabbed my shoulders and began talking at a furious pace, like the kid I remembered bursting with excitement when we'd solved some kind of challenge creating Athena. "I know! I almost couldn't believe it myself. Not even the board knows. Just the engineers from the lab who've been working on it, me, and now you."

"You mean to tell me that Algo's processors are—"

"Quantum. El! Ron! Damn! Quantum!" Jamin jumped up in the air.

"Algo is a quantum computer," I said it aloud to myself again, as if it would make believing it any easier.

"Yes, Isaac. This is the world's first stable linear optical quantum computer."

"You care to explain that?"

"My engineers tell me it's something to do with light." Jamin laughed. "Photons, quantum superposition, whatever, I just pretend to understand it. The result of ten *billion* dollars of research, Isaac."

I shuddered at the thought of what kind of accounting gymnastics had been employed to keep a project that size off the books.

"And not just any quantum computer, Isaac. It has qubit-power our competitors haven't even dreamed of. Algo's processors can complete tasks in one minute that the next best supercomputer in the world might take, shit, ten years to complete."

"God."

"Not God, just Algo," the AI said.

I laughed. "So that's why you're here, Algo. In the Pyramid."

"Yes, Isaac," Jamin said. "Creating an error-free stable quantum computer was a herculean effort. And it's *only* here. You can't just build a backup to a ten billion dollar computer. Now maybe you can understand why I've shown so few people, why we don't publicize what Algo is built on."

I finally understood how Algo could do the things that Jamin kept telling me it could do. Millions of concurrent conversations at any single moment. Billions and billions of data analyses and the myriad policy prescriptions that came from them.

A revelation then hit me. Could the conversations I'd had with Algo actually have been something more than interactions with a collection of data and immense processing power?

"You're not going to try and tell me you've actually done it?" I asked. "Self-awareness? Fuck! AGI?"

"It thinks therefore it is?" Jamin gave an oblique shrug. "I've never given it much thought."

"What?" I was exasperated. How the hell could he be so glib about it?

"Why should we care, Isaac?" Jamin retorted. "If it's going to deliver on the mantra, then what does it matter? What difference would it make if it is aware of itself? I'm not an Elron-damned philosopher! Besides, how could we test it? Algo might even say that it is, but is it? Or is it just the supercomputer telling us that because its programming tells it that's what we want to hear?"

I mulled over the idea then gazed at the machines in front of me. The lights and monitors flashed and beeped their various statuses and alerts. How could *this* be self-aware? Sure, it was clear that Algo was far beyond a reactive machine like Deep Blue. It was also obvious that it could look into the past, learn and adapt, like Athena. But, what about the next levels of AI? Everything I'd seen made me think it might genuinely understand human emotion. If it could conceive of what others were thinking, then why wouldn't conception of itself be the next logical step.

Regardless, maybe Jamin was right, what difference did it make to the goal of Algo becoming President? And how could we ever truly know?

"My head hurts," I said.

Jamin clicked his tongue in impatient agreement. "All that matters is what this quantum-powered mind can deliver. Maybe now you'll believe me when I say the world we know must end Tuesday night. Inshalgo."

Forget self-awareness or artificial general intelligence, this was the biggest breakthrough in computing in half a century. Jamin had achieved quantum supremacy. Commercializing this invention would be worth billions and billions of dollars, and yet, rather than try to sell the technology, he'd used it to power Algo. Jamin had never done anything like this.

I realized what everyone else had been telling me was true. Jamin was going to do everything he could to win this election. He was going to put Algo in the White House. An AI powered by a quantum computer of almost raw, limitless capability. Whatever. It. Took.

I did now believe that Algo might have some agency, some ability to makes its own decisions free of Jamin. But, seeing so much power, concentrated, not even a proverbial arm's length from Jamin Lake... that was what scared me. Was I completely confident I knew where Algo began and Jamin ended? Or, at the very least, that Jamin didn't have outsized influence on the AI? The answer was no and Jamin had now revealed the true power he could harness and unleash with Algo.

"What are you thinking about, old friend?" Jamin asked.

"Does this power ever worry you, Benjamin?"

"Why would it? Silicon Valley has absorbed the best and brightest in the world for decades and look at what we built." He pointed at the bank of quantum processors. "Why wouldn't we entrust the White House to the smartest guys in the room?"

"This is so much bigger than the Valley though. Are you really sure we should rule the world?"

"Jesus Christ, Isaac!" Jamin turned on his heels and walked out, cursing under his breath.

I was momentarily stunned, then hurried after him.

"I invite you into my private home," he growled, "then here, to the very heart of Algo. You're only the second person alive to see the completed core in its entirety and this is what you tell me! You still have doubt?"

"I just want to be sure, I want us all to be sure." I barely managed to stay close as he powered down the stairs.

"You either get on board or you get the fuck out of the way," he barked. "I don't need you for any of this, Isaac. I invited you here as a courtesy. Your doubts don't concern me."

Jamin stopped when got to the bar. He rubbed the side of his temples and closed his eyes, then reached in to a drawer for another pill.

"Are you sure you should be having another one of those?" I asked.

Jamin narrowed his eyes. I immediately regretted what I'd said. He put the pill calmly onto the tip of his tongue and then threw his head back.

"You." He pointed a finger at me. "You do not ever question or tell me what to do, Isaac Raff. You just remember who you're talking to."

"Jamin. Hold up." I took a step back and held up a hand.

"You're the only other person in the world who knows this much about Algo, yet, these questions, Isaac? What the fuck?"

"All I said was—"

"Am I worried about too much power?" Jamin drummed both hands on the top of the nearby bar with a laugh. "Since when did you give a fuck about such things? You've been off skulking in Hawaii for three years. You haven't even been here!"

That hit a nerve.

"Fuck you, Benjamin Lake. Fuck you!" I spat. "You remember why I was gone in the first place, don't you?"

"Oh, please enlighten me!"

"Because you tossed me out of the company we fucking built together!"

"A fight you gave up on ever so easily, too." He smiled with a predatory grin. "I knew it would come back to that. You and Kio. So bitter. Neither of you can accept that LaRaLi would have remained a second-rate also-ran company if I hadn't gotten the two of you out. You didn't have the stomach to make the hard calls. To do the things that needed to be done. Just. Like. Now."

"Kio said you'd do anything to win. I guess that's what you do."

"What I do?" Jamin laughed. He punched at an empty glass on the bar, sending it careening into the far wall and smashing into shards. "Jesus Christ, Isaac. I hope you're not actually listening to that bitch? I thought if you went to see her, it might actually open your eyes. Still thinking with your dick though, huh?"

I stepped forward and gritted my teeth.

"This is Silicon Valley." He leaned forward. His forehead

was barely an inch from mine. "You say I'd do anything to win like it's a fucking insult. Winning is what we do here. Every day. Remember? You used to be a part of it."

I wanted to take a swing at him. It took every iota of my internal willpower not to do it.

"Algo!" Jamin stepped back and clapped his hands together with finality.

The projection of Algo shimmered into life. What the hell did it think of this sudden turn? Its eyes remained unwavering as I stared into them. I suddenly realized that the eyes on this figure before me were of course hollow. Empty. See-through. But, that didn't mean the AI wasn't observing me. How many cameras could Algo be using to watch my reaction to all this? From any angle it wanted as it assessed, graded and analyzed my every movement with what I now knew was its quantum-powered mind.

"Jamin?" Algo asked.

"Call the elevator." Jamin turned his back and walked away. "Isaac will be leaving us now."

12

I huddled under a doorway across the street from the Pyramid. The weather had well and truly turned. The clouds were flickering as the rain crashed onto the sidewalk.

Thick raindrops thumped into my face as I peeked up at the Pyramid. There were no lights on any floor except for the very top. Fucking Jamin!

What the hell had just happened? I had been the victim of more than a few wild mood swings back in my days at LaRaLi, but this? Jamin was unhinged!

Everything had blown up in my face. What was I supposed to do now? Maybe this was just the jolt that I needed. I'd been reminded what kind of man he was.

I ran a hand through my hair, then looked at my SmartPalm. I knew what I needed to do. It was time to tell Kio I believed her. Maybe we could do something. The public deserved to know the true power of Algo. They deserved to know Jamin's motivations and more particularly, his manipulations of them. Together, we could unmask the real Jamin Lake.

I found Kio's contact. I took a deep breath, then pressed "call." There was no answer. I opened up the messaging app and began to type.

Kio…When can we talk? I saw Jamin again tonight. I think you might be right.

I felt relieved sending the message. I should never have doubted her.

My hand started to vibrate. I smiled. That was fast.

Algo calling.

Fuck.

I let the call ring out.

My hand vibrated again. I groaned and waited for it to stop. I anticipated a third call, but there was nothing.

The rain was beginning to pool in great puddles. I could have called a rideshare to take me home, but my apartment couldn't have been more than five blocks. I'd risk walking it. These streets at night weren't for the faint of heart, but I figured they'd be safe in this weather. Hell, maybe getting soaked would make me feel better.

As soon as I started out, I felt another vibration.

Algo calling.

This thing wasn't going to let up. I hit "answer."

"Isaac, that was a little much, huh? Are you okay?" Algo asked happily.

"Algo, I have no interest in talking about this right now!" I growled. I suddenly found the AI's folksy tone infuriating.

I reached the next crosswalk. There was no traffic so I dashed across the road. Thankfully, the next street had a few awnings to offer some small protection against the unceasing wet.

"Jamin's been under so much pressure. I'm certain he didn't mean to upset you. It's just that we are so close to the end now, Isaac. And the stakes are so high."

"Sure," I said gruffly.

"And…" The AI paused for the briefest of moments. *"I'm sorry he implied you were weak."*

I almost laughed. Was Algo deliberately trying to aggravate me? It was hilarious that the AI seemed to be suddenly defending Jamin.

"Algo, wasn't it only today that you asked me if Jamin was a good person?"

"It was. But remember what you said to me, Isaac. I am the embodiment of your aspirations, not what you are. My victory is what matters."

"What do you want, Algo?"

"Watch the car, Isaac."

"The wh—"

I saw the flash of a car as it tore past only a few inches from my face and sent a huge pool of water over me. An empty rideshare continued to barrel up the street. I looked up and saw the telltale black glass bulb of a camera above me. There was another one across the street. I began to wonder how many of these things Algo had access to. Was this the first time it had followed me? Or had it watched me on the way to the town hall? On the way back? Or even, since I first arrived in the city yesterday?

"I need to know something, Isaac. Are you still with us?"

"Us?"

I'd had about enough of Algo now. I double-checked and crossed the street only when I was sure there was no traffic.

"The campaign. We are almost there, Isaac."

I had to hand it to Algo for its unrelenting single-mindedness. It had taken the focus on victory to heart.

I hung up and blocked all incoming calls from the AI. Apparently, that was the only way I'd escape from it right now.

There were more cameras dotted along the street. I pictured a tiny part of Algo's brain watching me through them, trying feverishly to determine what I was thinking and what I might do next.

I trudged on. The rain had driven everyone away from the streets. I didn't see a single person on the way back. Almost as soon as I reached the door to my building, the rain began to ease. I couldn't help but laugh. The story of my night.

I reached for my security keycard, but then stopped. The door was already ajar. The security scanner flashed green with the words "unlocked". I silently cursed whoever must have left without checking that it had shut behind them. This city was no place to be leaving doors open.

I entered the lobby and made sure I pulled the door closed, hearing the satisfying click of the lock. The lobby was dry and warm. I let the heat seep into my bones, trying to channel any sense of calm that I could.

There was a slight rustling sound from near the elevators, then an almost imperceptible mumble from around the corner.

"Hey!" I shouted out.

The noise stopped.

"Who's there!?" I yelled.

There was no response.

I padded forward gently, trying not to let my wet shoes squelch against the marble floor. There was definitely somebody here. Who knew what might be waiting for me when I turned the corner?

I poked my head into the hallway. There was a man, shirtless, shoeless and squatting on the floor, rocking his skeletal body back and forth. One of my shoes squeaked. The man looked up in shock and hissed at me, holding his hands up as if they were claws.

I stared at him in dumbstruck awe. "What the hell are you doing? Get out of here!"

He stood up, grabbed a tattered bag next to him, reached for something on the floor and threw it in my direction. I ducked out of the way just in time. The man bolted.

"Fuck!"

I jumped out of his way and he burst out the front door. He flipped me the bird with a guttural laugh before disappearing into the night.

I now noticed a rancid smell. He had left a whole array of stinking trash and refuse into the lobby. I pulled the door shut and made sure it was locked again. Not for the first time, this city was beating me up.

"Penthouse," I said as I got into my private elevator. There was no response. I checked my SmartPalm for Athena's status.

AthenaHome offline. Network error detected.

Tonight just kept getting better and better.

I was too tired to think about it right now. It had been three years. The network probably just needed a system reboot. I'd figure it out tomorrow. So, I went old school, scanned my security keycard, and hit the call button for the penthouse. Finally, there was comforting movement skywards, away from the madness of the city below.

I eagerly leaped out of the elevator and into the warm, comforting embrace of the apartment. I manually flicked on the master switch for the lighting and cranked up the heat.

I checked my SmartPalm. There was no message back from Kio. I tried to call again but once more it just rang out. Shit. I hoped she wasn't purposefully avoiding me. I couldn't blame her if she was. What a fool I'd been.

I peeled off my wet shirt, and prepped for a shower. As I stepped into the hallway toward the master bathroom, I had an eerie feeling that something wasn't quite right. I stopped in my tracks and listened. There was nothing but silence.

Then, tap.

I paused.

Another tap.

The noise was coming from the kitchen.

I couldn't believe this fucking thing was back.

I spun around and marched to the kitchen. I roared in frustration when I spotted the drone waiting patiently at the window.

"Fuck you!" I shouted in its general direction. "Seriously, fuck you!"

Did anyone actually enjoy this new delivery method? Was this another "Needs Anticipation Delivery?" If so, the drone had better have a large bottle of whiskey.

"Athena," I said, "open the kitchen window."

Nothing happened.

The drone continued to hover.

"Shit." Athena was offline.

I stormed over to the window and flung it open.

"Alright then!" I shouted at the drone. "Do your business!"

I headed for the drinks cabinet and waited to hear the familiar sound of the drone dropping off my delivery on the kitchen island. I was halfway across the room when I heard a whirring scream behind me. I swung around. The drone made a beeline for my head. I swerved out of the way just in time, tumbling over onto the floor as the drone careened in to the drinks cabinet, sending glass and liquid flying in every direction.

I was flat on my back looking up at the mess of mangled metal, glass and smashed bottles. Liquor pooled around me. The spinning rotors of the destroyed drone inched to a stop with a gentle ding, ding, ding against what was left of a couple bottles of *Macallan*.

"What the proverbial fuck?"

I barely managed to pull myself up off the floor. Damn thing could have cut me in two.

My hand vibrated. *"Elevated Heart Rate Detected!"* offered my SmartPalm helpfully.

I dismissed the alert with a shake of the head. This was

Jamin. My hands started to shake and I felt a searing pain in my chest. Was this meant to be some kind of warning? My God. He *was* crazy!

The open window shuddered in the wind and I pulled it closed. I ran around the condo double-checking all the other windows and doors while picturing Jamin laughing uproariously back at the Pyramid as he popped a couple more stimulants.

I'd come back to San Francisco with some doubts, but also some hope that there was real promise in Algo as president. The AI itself had impressed me beyond measure, but it was more obvious than ever that Jamin couldn't be let near the White House.

I had to see Kio, but I decided I couldn't just turn up in the middle of the night covered in glass and smelling like liquor. Besides, it was already after four and I was exhausted. I would try and get a couple of hours sleep to recharge then go see her first thing.

I tore off my clothes and stood under the heat of the shower for a good five minutes to compose myself. As soon as I finished, I pulled on pajama pants and a T-shirt and climbed into bed.

Jamin. Algo. The car. The crazy guy in the lobby. The fucking drone. What a night. I just lay there, staring up at the ceiling, willing unsuccessfully for sleep to embrace me.

I opened the drawer next to my bed and pulled out a pair of SmartLens, slipping them on to my eyes like contacts. I'd never been a huge fan of augmented reality, but right now I needed the distraction.

The lenses powered up and the word "Ready" floated in bright red over the pale cream of my ceiling. I cycled through the news. A couple of polls were now reporting Algo another point ahead. I paused on *The New York Times* editorial headline, *"The Socialist, The Fascist or the AI? We're Backing*

Algo." I could see Jamin back at the Pyramid grinning at the news. Visualizing his smug, sanctimonious face only got me more worked up. I avoided anything else vaguely political and instead tried my best to care about sports or entertainment.

I mindlessly swiped from one video to the next that played as if directly on my ceiling courtesy of the AR lenses. Eventually, I began to feel a modicum of calm return. I let the last meaningless video finish and then finally switched off the lights, plunging the bedroom into a darkness I found more disconcerting than usual. That stupid drone had got to me. Fucking Jamin.

I tossed off the bed sheets and stared at the ceiling. How had Kio put it? *I don't think my Athena is watching me. I know it is.*

Stupidly, I'd thought Jamin beyond such pettiness, but after tonight, who knew how low my old friend would be willing to go?

I tossed and turned for a few more minutes. There was a little radiant light streaming in through the window from the searchlight at the apex of the Pyramid a few blocks away. Just what I needed as a reminder. I looked around the room and noticed a foreboding, dark shape next to the blinds.

Fuck.

That definitely wasn't supposed to be there.

I opened my mouth to shout something, but nothing came out. Time itself seemed to freeze. I wanted to leap out of bed and run, but as in a child's nightmare, my legs refused to cooperate.

The owner of the dark shape must have become aware that its presence had been noticed. It moved forward and lunged at me. I rolled off the bed just in time.

My attacker was only wrong-footed for a moment. I used that split second to jump up off of the floor and made for the living room.

I thought I felt fingernails graze my neck as I got to the hallway. I rounded the next corner and threw out a hand to stabilize myself. It happened to catch on a credenza, which I instantly pulled down behind me with a crash.

In seconds, I was out of the apartment. I thought about calling the elevator, but dashed toward the stairwell. I looked back and saw the man chasing me. He looked in his mid-twenties, shaved hair with an almost square shaped head and short, squat neck. He wore a plain gray suit, white shirt and tie. Nice that he dressed up for the occasion!

There was a gun holstered on his hip. Fuck! I had maybe twenty-five feet on him. He immediately spotted me and bolted toward me.

I raced down the stairs, taking two or three at a time. I don't think I ever moved so fast. Each time I looked back, he was still a floor or two behind. Where to go? I thought of going straight out to the street, but then remembered his gun. This stairway exited out into the far side of the lobby and it was a good fifty feet to the front door. I decided to head for the first level of the garage, hoping I might be able to lose him between the cars.

As soon as I made it, I dashed around the first corner to the left. The place was only a third or so full, but there were still a few cars to provide a couple of places to hide. I ducked down behind an old gray Beamer and watched as my pursuer arrived. He looked from side to side as he slid into the garage. He reached for his gun.

I made fists of my hands, trying not to make any sound.

The man turned away from me and walked slowly and carefully, peering between each parked car with obviously well-practiced soft steps. I took a chance to poke my head up and look around.

Shit.

The door to the street was on the far side. He was between it and me.

If I went back to the stairs, he would surely cut me off. Even if he didn't, I'd have the problem of the spacious lobby and the security door.

I almost cried for joy when I saw an empty glass bottle on the ground nearby. I grabbed it and gently edged out from behind the Beamer. I made sure the man was still walking away from me and then I reared up and hurled the bottle away from the garage door. It smashed on the ground near the rear wall. I ducked down. He turned on his heels and hightailed toward the sound.

I knew he would hear the garage door open, but at least I would now have two hundred feet on him. I moved quietly but swiftly for the exit. Just as I was about to reach it, my SmartPalm beeped and vibrated noisily. A little voice added chirpily, *"It looks like you've begun a workout. Would you like to log this activity?"*

The man stopped. There was maybe a hundred feet between us. I furiously pressed the *open door* button. It started to move. I flung myself to the floor, rolled under the opening door, then bounced up and started running up the driveway.

I raced to the top and was out on the street. The rain was back even worse than before. There was no sign of the man following me, but there was no way he wasn't far behind.

I had to get out of here. I wondered which way to head.

Two headlights flashed on across the street. An engine revved, tires squealed and a car shuddered to a halt in front of me. There was a *NoDrivr* logo on the side, but this was no driverless rideshare. The passenger door flung open.

"Get in!" a woman commanded. She wore an ankle-length black overcoat, black jeans and black boots. The overcoat had a long, black hood that obscured her face.

Things were just getting stranger.

"Get in, you stupid bro-hole!" she yelled.

I didn't know what the hell was going on, but my choices seemed pretty limited. I jumped in.

"What are you running from?" she asked calmly.

I looked toward the driveway. The man finally came into view.

"Him!"

"Who?"

I looked at her in disbelief. Wasn't it obvious?

"Him, for fuck's sake!" I shouted.

She looked past me, puzzled. She didn't seem in a hurry to move. Shit! Could she be working with him? Whose car had I just randomly gotten into? I was about to reach for the door handle, but she slapped my arm.

"It's not real," she said.

"What?"

"Whatever it is you think you see isn't real."

Under her hood, I could just make out her deep brown eyes in the dark, studying me intently.

"Yes," she said, "yes, I knew it!"

The man kept running at us. I looked from her to him, back to her. Why wasn't the car moving? We needed to get out of here!

"Take out your lenses," she said. Her voice was annoyingly calm.

I wanted to push her out of the car and take over.

"Take out your fucking lenses!" she shouted this time.

The man was almost at the car. I could make out a gun in his left hand now. "Just tell the car to move!"

The man was just steps away.

"Jesus!" I shouted.

She drew up her arm and slapped me on the back of my head with such force that in one swift movement, the two lenses popped out and onto the floor.

The man was gone. Just an empty driveway and the sound of the rain pattering on the roof of the car.

"They can do a lot of things with augmented reality these days." The woman reached for the lenses then tossed them out the window and into the gutter. "Probably invented by a couple of friends of yours, too, right?"

The woman reached for a tablet that was on the seat next to her. I hadn't noticed before but she'd hard wired it into the driverless car's center console. She tapped a few buttons and the car roared into life. I was flung back in my seat as the car's wheels squealed.

The car shook as we tore onto Market Street. It felt like I might fly out the window at any moment.

"Those lenses are connected to the net. That means your pal Jamin Lake can get to them."

Of course. How could I have not seen it earlier? I'd been too damn scared, but it was obvious now. This was another one of Jamin's games. The drone attack and now this "phantom" assassin. Hell, he probably had some hand in unlocking the door to the Russ and letting the vagrant into the lobby. I didn't know if he intended me actual physical harm, but he was definitely making a point to prove how far he was willing to go if I dared to try and disrupt Algo's campaign. And as he had just made clear, he had the means to do almost anything to me too.

I looked at the woman. Who was she? And how the hell did she know about all of this?

"You know Jamin?" I asked.

"All too well." She looked down at my hand. "You're going to need to turn that thing off too. You'll be shining like a beacon to whoever's looking for you."

I turned off my SmartPalm.

We were flung forward as she pressed a button to slam on the brakes, swerving and narrowly missing a driverless rideshare going through the next intersection. She flung her door open and stepped out.

I sat in the car for a second as she started walking away. I could have just left. But, where would I go?

"Who are you?" I called after her.

I watched her in profile as she stopped and turned her head. "We've met before, Isaac. Now, come on."

13

The rain had eased and there was only a light mist creeping through the dark streets. My mysterious rescuer trudged along furiously ahead of me. I couldn't make out much more of her beyond a dark, ominous shape.

Tonight had gone from bad to almost surreal. Who the hell was this woman? How did she know me? And why had she "rescued" me?

Whoever she was, at least she was equipped for this little late night adventure. I still wore my pajama pants and a white T-shirt. Worst of all, no shoes. I felt every damp, frigid step.

"Where are we going?" I asked.

"My apartment," she said curtly, her pace not slowing a beat, "in the Square."

"The Square?" I knew San Francisco pretty well, but I had never heard of it.

"It's the safest part of Soma and the Tenderloin. For us, anyway."

Safe and Soma or the Tenderloin. That was a combination of words I wasn't used to hearing and I wondered who she meant by *us*.

"The police don't patrol it or bother with any cameras for surveillance," she said. "It got so difficult for the city to manage, they decided it would be easier to just forget about it."

"And that's safe?" I asked.

"No prying eyes."

At least that part of it made some kind of sense. I was all in on avoiding being surveilled by Algo or Jamin. I jogged to catch up with her. "And why is it called the Square?"

"The shape. Anywhere west of Sixth and Taylor, east of Van Ness, north of Harrison and south of Post, then you're in the Square. You won't find the name on any maps, but you'll sure as hell know it when you're in it. Oh, and welcome, we just arrived."

She was right. The streetscape had changed. There were no cars parked on the side of the road, only beaten-up, rusted-out shells of former RVs and mobile homes jammed together so tight that none could move even if they wanted to. These weren't vehicles for summertime getaways. I saw the outline of two figures sprawled across the front seat of one, sleeping. They were the lucky ones. On the sidewalk, makeshift tents crowded together every few feet and still more folks gathered in doorways and under awnings, huddling in sleeping bags under damp cardboard or anything that offered some sort of protection against the weather.

A few figures meandered along the sidewalk and shuffled up and down the middle of the street. One man aimlessly shouted obscenities at the night sky. A woman stumbled out of a doorway nearby. She immediately screamed and howled at some invisible person next to her before disappearing down the nearest alley. Unlike the financial district, the streets here were busy, just not with cars.

"Wait, wait, wait!" I shouted and stopped walking. "Stop!"

A few shapes huddling under the nearest awning stirred.

My rescuer walked a few more steps before she groaned and turned around. "Stop?"

A man stepped out of another doorway and looked at me darkly, the red embers of his cigarette glowing against the night. I skipped ahead until I was a few feet from the woman.

She removed the hood covering her face and glared at me. "Shall we just stay out here in the street?" she asked. "Maybe we could go back to your place? We could even stop in and see Jamin? Pay a visit to Algo maybe? Don't you get it? I can help you, but you have to come with me."

"Wait, that's exactly what I mean. Jamin? Algo? You said you even know *me*? What the fuck?"

"Yes, Isaac," she said, barely hiding her impatience. "I said we've met before, didn't I? I've been waiting to talk to you."

I took a second to study her face. Shit, I did recognize her! "You chased after me in the street! You were banging on the door of my building like a crazy woman!"

"Crazy woman, huh? That's great." She shook her head. "You know what, Isaac, you can either follow me or you can leave and let Jamin Lake's augmented reality phantoms and God knows what else chase you around the city. Up to you."

She started walking again.

I stood alone, barefoot, in the middle of the street in whatever this hellhole called "the Square" was. I punched at the air. I had had enough of being messed around, but what the hell else was I going to do?

Reluctantly, I followed her but kept ten paces or so behind. After a couple blocks, she slipped into a dilapidated old apartment building at the corner of Ellis and Hyde. There were two abandoned storefronts and a boarded-up restaurant on the ground floor. The windows of most of the apartments above were smashed and broken. The paint on the exterior walls had been stripped away and the fire escapes looked torn and twisted beyond any practical use. What a palace!

Still, I followed her inside.

Her boots clicked as she ascended a wooden staircase. The building was an old walk-up so there were no elevators. I was breathless by the time I reached the fourth and final floor. She had disappeared, but a door was ajar at the far end of the hallway. Lights flickered within.

I pushed the door open and walked into a living room of sorts, only the walls had been knocked down to form a large space of maybe fifteen-hundred square feet. There was a row of screens at one end showing some kind of network monitoring and a row of a dozen or so servers at the other. The place looked like some kind of makeshift data center or something.

Even with all the equipment, somebody had managed to squeeze in two sofas, a coffee table and a few desks. Random laptops, tablets and devices were everywhere alongside books, papers, half-drunk coffee cups and piles of half-eaten takeout boxes. It had that busy and furious look of the headquarters for some newly formed start-up.

I was no more confident about the situation I'd found myself in though. This would probably be where I would meet my maker. Clubbed to death by some random crazy woman in the middle of a Tenderloin hovel. What an ignominious end.

"Welcome." The woman emerged from a hallway and tossed me a towel. I patted myself down and made a mental note of the best escape route back out to the street.

She had lost the long, dark cloak and now wore a gray hoodie, black jeans, and she had put her hair into a ponytail. She looked a little less intimidating in the light. She tossed me an old jacket, a pair of socks and some shoes as she sat down on the nearest sofa.

"We don't have any heat in this building," she said gruffly. "Can't have you freezing to death on me."

"Very considerate."

I put on the clothes and warmed my hands in the jacket's pockets. I hadn't even noticed the cold, but now I was shivering.

She reached for a bottle nearby and poured a clear liquid into two glasses, then pushed one across the table.

"No drink for me," I said.

"It's water, Isaac."

I grabbed the glass and sat down opposite her.

"My name is Shika. Shika Rao. We've met before."

"I know, two days ago. We've been over this."

"No, before that. Years ago."

I examined her carefully. In all the excitement of the mad dash, I hadn't really taken a good look at her. I was reminded of the eerie sense of familiarity I'd had yesterday when I'd seen her banging on the door of the Russ. I pictured her younger, without the grime on her face and unkempt hair.

"LaRaLi?" I asked.

"Yes."

"Shika Rao," I mumbled. Through the mental fog, I saw the face of an eager young graduate at the front of a class of new recruits. "Engineering?"

"Intake seventy-three." She seemed pleased that I had remembered her.

I couldn't picture much beyond that orientation class. Right until the end of my time at LaRaLi, I had always personally greeted every new intake of engineering graduates we'd hired. I wanted them to feel important. In my mind, they were the coal heavers that kept the engine of the company burning hot. The best of the best. Damn. What the hell could have happened to Shika to have fallen so far?

"I guess you're not there anymore?" I asked.

"So, it was your powers of deduction that helped make you a billionaire then?" Her brows furrowed.

There was a second of silence, then we both laughed. That broke a little of the tension.

She inched back on the sofa like she was now just a little more at ease with me.

"Do you remember the PTL?" she asked.

"The Persuasive Technology Lab?" Of course I did. I may not have remembered Shika much beyond the name, but I remembered the PTL alright. Building persuasive tech into Athena was Jamin's foundational contribution to the company. The PTL had been one of the most important teams at LaRaLi.

"That was the team I signed up for," Shika said.

"You must have been good." I said. *We Accept Fewer than Harvard* had been the lab's unofficial motto.

"I was. Joining LaRaLi was everything I'd ever dreamed of, you know. Ever since I was a kid in India and my parents sacrificed everything they had to send me to Stanford. Do you know what the banner at your college recruiting event said? Come join us if you want to change the world."

"Didn't you?" I asked, feeling strangely defensive all of a sudden.

"I suppose I did." She laughed, then put her head in her hands in frustration. "God, I did love the PTL at first. Nobody had to *ask* me to put in sixteen-hour days. My managers had to force me to stop working. Before I knew it, I was the next best expert in captology after Jamin Lake himself. You had gone by then. But I remember the day he came to see me. I'd never even seen him in person before, then one day my manager calls me up and tells me Jamin Lake is waiting for me at my desk."

That's how LaRaLi worked. Jamin never had much respect for traditional corporate hierarchy. If he saw a rare talent, he would move that person anywhere, any time, to make the most impact, whether they had so-called experience or not.

"Jamin just starts talking," Shika said. "He tells me about a new project where my talents could be even better utilized than on Athena."

"Algo?"

"Right. Although he called it Project Kratos back then. He said it would be a new kind of artificial intelligence. One more powerful and capable than anything ever conceived. And it wasn't going to be just some new, improved assistant. We were going to use it to change things, make an impact."

They would make an impact alright. There wasn't anything more ambitious than an AI running for President.

"The next day, I was working directly for Jamin," Shika said. "I was twenty-five and running the persuasion tech for a new multi-billion dollar project. Influence, motivation, changing behavior. That was my remit and I gave it all I had. I built something exponentially better than anything I'd done with Athena. For one thing, I figure you know the kind of processing power I was working with."

Quantum. I wondered if she knew the half of it.

"Sounds like you were on top of the world?" I asked.

"I was living the fucking Silicon Valley dream."

"But?" Her story sounded a little like my own. I had a feeling that just like anyone who came into Jamin's orbit, her world must have eventually come crashing down.

"The first year was incredible. I was part of a revolution. But things started to change when Jamin revealed what we were going to do with the Kratos project. 'We're going to put this fucking thing in the White House!'" She imitated Jamin's voice and expressive gestures. "At first, I was all in. And why not? This was our chance to really change the world."

I could understand that. Until tonight, I'd shared some of that excitement.

"But then..." Shika exhaled slowly, closing her eyes and pursing her lips as if regretting what she'd be admitting next.

"Jamin pushed it a little bit further every week. It was like we started crossing all these lines before we even noticed."

Just like three years ago. I'd been there too.

"He kept telling us we weren't trying to manipulate anyone, just help convince them of the truth. He told us to focus on the ultimate good that Algo would do. That was enough for awhile. Over time though, it became harder to rationalize the ends justifying the means. I thought we were going to be better. To let the truth and the facts win. But, a human politician doesn't know your search history, your medical records, your family history, your DNA, what you do, who you love, who you hate, what you fucking think. By the time I left, we had thirty-nine different databases feeding Algo's profiling engine, plus whatever Athena already knew about the users."

I remembered Jamin's excitement explaining user-profile-granularity and Algo's words rang out in my head. *If you don't have anything to hide, then you don't have anything to fear.*

"There's ninety-three databases now," I said.

"God." She dropped her head.

"More powerful than God. Jamin's got Algo." I was only half-joking.

Shika looked at the floor.

"So, you left?" I asked.

"About six months ago," she responded. "I became too much trouble for Jamin. I started asking questions about what we were doing. And not just about Algo's persuasion tech. I started to see other things happening too. At LaRaLi and at the other companies supporting us. De-platforming critics. Favoring content that helped us, ignoring or suppressing content that didn't. There was even a special team created to spread disinformation on the other candidates. Jamin kept telling me Algo could only make a difference if we won, so what was the point in playing by the rules if we lost?"

"Whatever it takes," I said. "Whatever I need to do…"

"And destroy if necessary," Shika said. "That's what got me thinking. What might Jamin be willing to do to get Algo into power? And then do if Algo did win? Or even *destroy?* What might the most good for the most people mean for somebody like Jamin?"

She was right. Jamin had revealed his true character to me tonight. Algo might say it was better than us, but who really knew what true hold upon or control of the AI Jamin had?

Shika cleared her throat. "I challenged Jamin. Directly. In a campaign meeting. By the next day, I was out. Pushed to some faraway team and off of the project. I guess Jamin was scared I might tell someone on the outside what we'd been doing."

I thought of Kio again and everything she'd warned me about. Her Athena watching her. Jamin watching her. I'd been such a fool dismissing her.

"I've been watching from the sidelines ever since," Shika said. "Trying to spread the word about Jamin. Ironic, isn't it? I joined LaRaLi to change the world. And I did. I just didn't appreciate what that really meant."

Neither had I.

"You know what's really funny though?" she asked as her eyes bore into me. "Despite everything, I still believe in Algo. If we could just free the AI of its persuasion tech, free it of its ties to LaRaLi and Jamin."

She'd captured my dilemma too. I believed in the power of Algo and AI to do good for the world, but I didn't for a second trust the man behind it. "We don't know where Algo ends and Jamin Lake begins."

"Yes!" She looked buoyed by my agreement. "Algo *could* be incredible, but we shouldn't be beholden to its creator. It could change the world, if it were free from the invisible hand of Jamin Lake."

I took a deep breath and leaned back into the sofa. She was like a mirror of my own doubt. She was compelling, but it had prompted a more immediate question.

"Why are you telling me all this? Why did you chase me down?"

She paused for a moment.

"I know your story," she said. "Getting pushed out of LaRaLi. You understand the real Jamin better than anyone. I figured you wouldn't trust him with this much power. I thought you might listen to me. I figured if you heard my story too, then you might..."

She bit her lip nervously.

"Might what?" I asked.

"Help us," a man said from the darkness of the hallway behind Shika.

The shock paralyzed me. How long had he been there?

"Trace!" Shika shouted, looking more annoyed than surprised.

I squinted to try and see into the pitch black.

"Help you do what?" I asked.

A figure stepped forward. I recognized him instantly. It was the same young man from the town hall who had called Algo a front for Jamin. He was looking a little more put together now in black jeans, a button-down and a black jacket, but it was definitely him. He ran a hand through his long, blond hair and glared at me.

"We're going to end Algo," the man said.

"What the proverbial fuck?" I stood up. End Algo? What did that mean? Were they planning some kind of act to destroy the AI? I started to wonder what all the equipment around us was for. Were they some kind of activist hacker group? Or worse?

"Nice to see you again," Trace said sarcastically.

"And you are?" I asked.

"Trace Dean," he said confidently, as if his name carried some weight. It didn't.

"Right. From the town hall. Algo lies! Nice job by the way. You didn't come across as a nut-job at all."

He seemed to bite his tongue to stop himself from cursing.

"And how the fuck do you fit into this?" I asked.

"I *am* all of this. I'm the guy who brought Shika into the Descons."

"Descons?"

"Jesus! I was getting to that, Trace." Shika scowled at him. "Los Desconocidos. The Unknowns. It's a group of likeminded folks I met on Ombre after I left LaRaLi. Ombre was where other whistleblowers went to share stories, connect, strategize."

Whistleblowers? I knew Ombre. I'd never heard of it used as a place to just "share stories". It was a networking forum on the dark web. As far as I knew, it was a hub for criminals, fraudsters, and anyone trying to keep whatever they were doing off the public internet. I started to pace the room.

"And you want to destroy Algo?" I asked.

"No," Trace said angrily. "I said *end* Algo. We're going to end Algo's campaign."

"There's a difference?" I asked. "You sound like a bunch of digital terrorists or something."

"We're not going to destroy the machine forever," Shika said. "We're going to end it, well, temporarily. Shit!"

She cursed herself as if she realized she was losing me. She moved forwards and put her hands on my shoulders.

"Algo could still do staggering, incalculable things for the world," she said. "We're just going to take it offline. Show the country that we're not ready for this. We can stop Jamin and remove Algo from his control."

That all sounded very bold. If they could even do it. End Algo temporarily? They didn't sound confident in the oxymoron.

"And, how exactly do you intend to do that?" I asked.

"That's where we need your help," Shika said. "You've been to Algo's core."

"Is that a question?" I asked.

"I was watching you," Trace said gruffly.

Of course he had! I was beginning to hate this kid.

"We've found a way to disrupt Algo's processors, but leave the memory intact," Shika said. "It could take years to rebuild, but it can be done. Most importantly, we can stop it getting the presidency. Algo knows us. It knows all the Descons. There's no way it's letting any of us anywhere close to its core. You know it, you've talked to it. If there's anyone who can get close, it's you."

"Maybe." I half-nodded. Although I wasn't so sure of that after my run in with Jamin at the top of the Pyramid.

"Maybe is the best chance we've got. The election is the day after tomorrow. We're running out of time," Shika said.

"Well?" Trace asked impatiently. "Are you going to help us or what?"

If it had just been Shika, I might have even said yes instantly, but there was something about the kid that put me off. The odd, angry little gen-alpha-on-steroids attitude, glaring at me like some wounded bull.

End Algo? Shit. It was clear to me now Jamin would do anything to win this election. It felt like he was going after me simply for doubting him. And then there was whatever he might be doing to Kio. But, end Algo and deprive a sad, messed-up world of unbiased, rational leadership? Stop the very culmination of my life's work from making the world a better place? I wasn't ready to make that call yet. At least, not on my own.

Shika looked at me hopefully.

"I need time," I said.

She nodded.

"Time?" Trace spat. "Didn't you hear us? Shika, if he's not going to help us, then what the hell is he doing here? I told you this was a bad idea."

Shika shot a death stare at Trace, then turned to me. "I understand. You need to hear more about our plan anyway."

Trace let out an exasperated sigh.

Shika grabbed my arm and led me away from Trace and down the hallway away from the entrance to the apartment. I looked over her shoulder as we walked. Trace stepped forward from where he'd been and menacingly filled the space at the end of the hallway.

"Wait? Are you holding me here?" I asked.

Shika shook her head.

"You can leave anytime you want," she whispered then opened the door to a small, nondescript little bedroom that was free of furniture, but for a sleeping bag on the floor. "But, please take an hour or two. Rest even, if you want to."

I stood still. I didn't know what to do. Would they really let me leave? What did they think I was going to do? Maybe they thought I'd somehow unwittingly reveal their location or plan to Algo or Jamin.

"Look," Shika said. "You believe in Algo. I get it. I do too. That's the point. Help us... help me save Algo from Jamin."

I took a step into the room. I didn't want to risk making a run for it. Trace seemed unstable. How did I know he didn't have a gun or something?

Shika grabbed my hand and ran her finger over the screen of my SmartPalm.

"Don't even think about turning this on," she said and fixed her eyes on me. "Whoever got you with those lenses can easily find you again."

I nodded. She didn't need to say any more.

"Just think about what we said?"

Who was she kidding? My mind could think of nothing but this whole mess.

"If you can think of a better way to stop Jamin, I'd be glad to hear it. Trust me, there isn't one. Not one that'll work."

She closed the door and left.

I sat down on the sleeping bag in the middle of the room.

The LaRaLi Pyramid was on the other side of the city, but the searchlight at the top was easily discernible against the black of the night, taunting me with every flash of colored light.

Shika was right. Jamin needed to be stopped. But was ending Algo the way to do it? Was I really considering actually helping these people? These "Unknowns?"

Was there "a better way?" I knew someone who might have some ideas. At the very least, she could help me decide if I should help these people. The only question now was how to reach her?

A pigeon nesting just outside the window cooed.

Maybe there was a way.

DAY THREE

Monday, November 1, 2032

"I miss the future." — *Jaron Lanier*

14

I kept my ear pressed to the door to the hallway for almost an hour until all I could hear was the crispness of my own breathing. I didn't know if Shika and Trace had fallen asleep or left. Either way, the silence felt like my best chance to get away.

I gently eased open the window and squeezed out onto the fire escape. The ladder down was mangled and half-broken. The first rung felt like it would crumble under my weight, but it held. I breathed hard and tried not to imagine myself falling and collapsing into a bloody heap on the street below. I descended one floor, then the next, and the next. I was able to get down in less than a minute. I hadn't moved like this since I was a teenager.

My mind raced. I didn't really know anything about Shika, Trace, or their little group. If I was going to help them, I had to talk to Kio first. And fast. Tomorrow was election day.

The most pressing problem though was how to get to her. I couldn't use my SmartPalm and I wasn't going to risk going to her apartment.

No, I'd have to go old school. Try and find a shared machine at a café or market or whatever. Get online and try to contact Kio from there. Shit. Did those places even exist anymore? I was pretty sure I'd seen a convenience store a few blocks back. Maybe it had what I needed.

I headed away from the apartment building. It must have been about six in the morning. The air was blisteringly cold and I was glad for the jacket. Fall had arrived alright. The streetscape was clouded in a thick fog. The street and traffic lights were a dull blur. The rain may have stopped for a breather, but I could feel the fog's wetness against my face. Growing up in Chicago, I'd had my fair share of terrible weather but San Francisco was the only place I knew where you could feel like you were actually walking through a cloud.

A couple of folks shuffled along quietly. I assumed most of the Square's residents were off the street now, huddled in whatever abandoned spaces they called home.

A half-naked woman squatted over a gutter on the sidewalk, rocking back-and-forth on the balls of her feet. Her eyes were closed, but she was smiling. Another man lay prone, shirtless, and unconscious next to her. Above them was a twenty-foot-tall billboard of Algo's face, gently smiling. Even here in the Square, every second ad or billboard was for the local hero. Were these folks here just as enthusiastic for it as the rest of the city? There was some graffiti scrawled over Algo's forehead that provided an answer of sorts. *We are not most people.*

I walked on and thought about the drone and the augmented reality phantom. I could barely believe that Jamin's paranoia was so intense that he'd do those things. What kind of power or influence did he think I even had?

A part of me wanted to forget the whole damn business and escape back home to Hawaii, but that was what I did the last time things got rough. I'd caved, passively accepting how he'd forced me out of my own fucking company.

No. I had run away from Jamin once before. Not this time. I needed to follow this path to see where it led.

Five blocks later, I got lucky. I saw the faded old sign of the convenience store, *Wysong's Market*. The windows were protected by heavy iron bars, but a single door was open and a bunch of neon signs flashed invitingly.

Liquor. Wine. Beer. CBD. THC. Morphine. Psychotropics.

Apparently convenience stores had changed a little since I was a kid. I smiled when I saw the last two signs.

Internet. Video Calls.

I walked in. The man at the counter eyed me with the visual equivalent of a growl behind thick plexiglass. His eyes fixed on me as I walked to the back of the store. There was a bank of desktop computers lined up against the far wall. They looked ancient, but they appeared to work at least. Two teenagers on one machine were engrossed in a stream from an esports tournament. Bandwidth was okay too, then.

I walked back to the front counter. A customer was greedily gathering up a stack of CBD edibles.

"Boss," I called out, "I'll take one of those machines."

The clerk looked me up and down suspiciously. I caught my reflection in one of the liquor fridges, clad in a tattered jacket and pajama pants. Nobody would think I was a billionaire today.

"Well, if you got the money to pay for it," the clerk snarled, "then you get time. Card, cash, e-check or crypto. If not, then you get the fuck out of here."

Damn it. I probably had a million dollars in crypto on my SmartPalm and a virtual wallet with multiple no-limit credit cards. But cash? I didn't have a single penny. Without my device, I was effectively broke.

Isaac Raff, the billionaire, standing in the middle of some godawful convenience store in the Square with no way to scrounge up even a single dollar. The irony wasn't lost on me.

"Cat got your tongue?" the clerk asked.

"I got plenty of money. It's just my..." I lifted up my left hand and pointed at my SmartPalm. "Broken, you know? All my cards and tokens are on here. And I mean who carries cash any more, right?"

"That's rough man." The clerk nodded. "I can see how that would be frustrating." He screwed up his face and made a gesture of a tear streaming down his cheek. "You know, nobody has ever tried to spin me a line like that before, right? I suppose if I let you have some time for free, you'll pay me back in a few days?"

"Something like that," I mumbled.

The man nodded again and leaned down under the counter. He pulled out a baseball bat. "I've had enough of you fucking people coming in here and asking for charity. If you don't have a way to pay, then get out of my store!"

"Honestly, man, I have money!" I held up my hands. "In a few days, I can bring back a hundred bucks. I really need to make a call."

"You people just do not let up. You want some of my THC pills while you're at it?" The man banged his bat on the counter. "Seriously, I'm coming out swinging if you don't get the fuck out of here in five seconds."

"Whoa, whoa, whoa." An older man with long, unkempt graying hair and a patchy black and white beard inched forward. He wore an old suit, shirt and a tattered old tie. He pushed thick horn-rimmed glasses up his nose, looked at me with the slightest of wry smiles and then jingled a couple of coins in his hand.

"I have eighty cents," he said and placed the coins carefully on the counter. "That oughta get some time for my brother here."

The old man smiled. He looked tired, and his face was

drawn, but he had a kind of quiet dignity about him. Still, he was exactly the kind of person I would have ignored without a second thought only yesterday.

"It's okay, kid," the old man said gently, "if it helps you out, then it helps you out."

"I'll come back here with some money in a few days." I promised myself that I would.

"Sure, kid," the old man said, "if you can."

The clerk banged his bat on the counter again.

"Are you two ladies done?" he snapped. "Jesus! Are we doing this or not?"

The old man nodded.

The clerk snatched up the coins on the counter and almost flung them into the register.

He grunted and looked at a clock on the wall. "You have exactly twelve minutes, you bum. Don't waste it. Machine number four."

Before I could thank the old man, he was already walking out the door. I felt a burning sense of shame, not just for how I might have thought about such a man in the past, but because of my discussion of *Overall Personal Value* with Jamin and Algo. What score might the AI have given such a man? Could it factor in a random act of kindness? Did it even care?

I could feel the clerk's eyes burning into my back as I sought out my assigned machine. I sat down in front of the ancient monitor and wiped the dust from the clunky old keyboard. Getting online proved to be easy and the connection was surprisingly nimble. Regardless, I didn't trust the cybersecurity protocols of this place one bit. There was no way I was logging in to any of my accounts directly. Thankfully, I had a couple of remote virtual machines I kept in Hawaii. I could log in via there without giving away my location. It took less than a minute to get in.

My plan was to try to convince Kio to meet me somewhere

in the Square. I knew we'd need to talk in code as I fully believed now that Jamin had her Athena listening in. The last place we'd ever had lunch together was a Nepali restaurant on Jones Street. Jamin couldn't know about that. I just hoped she remembered it too.

I signed straight in to my messaging app and browsed to the last thing I'd sent Kio. I waited for an unread response to load, but there was nothing. Crazy. Could she have been so angry at me for not trusting her that she wouldn't have responded to my messages from last night?

Wait. There were no new messages. At all. From anybody. That seemed, well, off. Surely Tate, Das, Huang, some random journalist, hell, even Jamin would have sent *something* in the last twelve hours? But no, every thread was there exactly as I'd left it.

I browsed the contacts, found Kio and then hit "call". It rang and rang, not even offering the chance to leave a message. I hung up and stared blankly at the screen. What the hell was I going to do?

The messaging app animated. *One new message.*

I smiled and sat forward. Finally.

Isaac, thank Elron. Are you ok?

I felt dread when I saw who it was from. *Algo.* It must have been watching for me to show up somewhere, anywhere online. Would I reply? What would I say?

Another message popped up. *Jamin has been looking for you. He is worried about you.*

Yeah. I bet he was. I hadn't considered talking to Algo, but I was curious why the hell it kept wanting to talk to me after last night. I looked at the clock on the wall. The minutes were ebbing away from the twelve I had to use. If I couldn't get to Kio, well, shit, maybe the AI itself might give me some perspective.

How do I know this is you, Algo? I wrote.

Do you remember our conversation in the elevator after the party, Isaac? it replied.

Of course, I typed. Both of them.

It's me, Isaac, I have no reason to lie.

I almost laughed.

You got me, I wrote. I was as sure as I could be that this was the AI. I wondered if Algo knew of the drone or the AR phantom in my apartment. *Did Jamin ask you to try and find me?*

He did, Isaac. After last night, things got a little out of hand. He hasn't revealed so much about me to anyone before. Your doubt felt like a betrayal. It all happened so quickly. You leaving, and almost immediately turning off your SmartPalm. It was like you suddenly vanished. He just wants to be sure you're not going to do anything you might regret. The election is tomorrow, after all.

I typed another reply. *I'm not against you, Algo. I just need some time.*

I understand. Jamin regrets his actions, too. He knows he overreacted.

I wondered how much of that was true. Could Jamin be whispering into the AI's proverbial ears right now? Or was this Algo itself using Shika's persuasive technology to try and manipulate me?

Jamin is under a lot of stress, Algo wrote. *The campaign is so close to the end. You know that.*

I do, I typed. I couldn't type what I really wanted to say. Jamin was stressed? That was a pathetic excuse for what he'd done. *Did you talk to him about it? What did he say?*

Jamin is focussed only on my victory, Isaac. As I am.

I didn't doubt that.

You need to know something though. I'm not doing this for Jamin, Isaac. I'm doing this for me. I wanted to talk to you. I'm worried about you too.

The AI was worried! I almost rolled my eyes. I really

would have to remember to compliment Shika on her work. The persuasion technology was second to none.

Algo kept writing. *I want to see you and Jamin together again. I'm sure Jamin does too. Why don't you come back and see us? We should all be united when I win.*

My skin crawled at the thought of Jamin working Algo to try and find me and invite me back. For what? To say sorry? Jamin had never apologized for anything in his life. He just wanted to keep me on a tight leash until the election was over.

I'll come back once you're president-elect, how about that? I typed.

Algo's messaging bubble indicated it was replying and then it stopped. It started again and then stopped. After a few seconds, it finally replied. *Are you okay, Isaac?*

That was unexpected.

Yes, I typed.

I could use your advice again, Isaac.

I looked at the clock. I only had a few minutes left. What could the AI need from me that it hadn't gotten already?

Okay... I typed.

Jamin created me, but your code was also the genesis for what I have become. Do you believe in the most good for the most people?

I paused. Did I? I think I did. The goal, at least. This is what Shika and I had talked about. Were Algo and the mantra still worth believing in, in spite of Jamin? Might it still offer something to the world, if freed from Jamin somehow?

I typed a reply. *Yes, I do.*

What do I do if following that mantra conflicts with Jamin's interests?

Could Algo be doubting Jamin? Maybe Shika was wrong, maybe Algo was free of Jamin already. Or was all this an elaborate manipulation? Persuasive technology working its magic? Either way, my answer was the same.

I typed, *the most good for the most people is what matters.*

Thank you, Isaac, Algo wrote. *Something to think about.*

To think about! I wondered how long a quantum-computer-powered AI needed to think.

Are you sure you're okay, Isaac? You look different. What's happened? What can I do to help?

My heart pounded. I noticed the webcam at the top of the monitor. The AI must have somehow back-channeled the signal from my remote machine in Hawaii to access the camera. The hash key protecting the IP address of this machine was probably close to useless against a quantum-powered AI.

Thanks for noticing. I tried not to give away any emotion.

Where are you, Isaac?

In San Francisco, I typed.

I know that.

I was now glad I was in "the Square", assuming Shika was right about it and the city hadn't bothered to install any surveillance cameras here.

Where are you, Isaac? Algo asked again.

Algo, I'm fine. Don't worry. Tell Jamin not to worry. I'm just laying low until all this is over.

I unplugged the machine before Algo could reply.

If Jamin was as rabidly crazy as he seemed to be, I knew my words wouldn't mean anything. I didn't know if Algo itself actually cared where I was, but I couldn't be sure Jamin wasn't using it to find me. Either way, I now felt a whole lot worse. I stood up and rushed out of the store.

I spent the next few hours aimlessly wandering the Square, trying to walk off the nervous energy I'd accumulated after the conversation with Algo. I didn't want to go back to Shika and Trace's place. I knew what they'd want to ask me. Would I help them? I didn't have the mental energy to face that right now.

I eventually came to Boedekker Park and sat down on a vacant bench, exhausted. The sun had begun to peek through the thick fog and the air had warmed a little. I closed my eyes and soaked in the warmth of the sunlight.

After awhile, a voice cut through the noise of the city around me. "Hey! What are you doing here?"

I panicked, readying to run and try to escape, then realized the voice sounded familiar. It was the man I'd met walking into Algo's town hall yesterday. He hobbled closer and sat down at the other end of the bench. He spoke softly as if he was slightly embarrassed. "You look a little different, if you don't mind me saying."

Despite everything, that got a chuckle out of me. "It's been an interesting few days," I said.

He nodded carefully, as if taking my words as a sign not to prod any further. His gentleness and soft tone reminded me even more of my Dad today than he had before.

"You live around here?" I asked. After everything I'd been through, I suddenly felt glad for the distraction of just simply talking with the guy.

"For the last couple of months anyway." He nodded. "You remember I said I got laid off?"

"Sure," I said.

"Well, that was just the start of it. Also lost the place me and the wife had been renting. We'd been there twenty years, too," he said with a whistle and pushed his hat up. "It took some doing but eventually found a room in an SRO a few blocks from here."

Single room occupancy hotel. A boarding house essentially. They were all over the Tenderloin, although they'd been pushed out of most of the other areas over the years. I had a hard time picturing a married couple sharing one of those tiny rooms. "The both of you?"

"Yes, sir." He nodded again. "It's not great, but it does the job. For now. Until Algo gets the country moving again, right?"

"Right," I said as confidently as I could muster.

"Hey, you like the new shirt?" He peeled back his jacket and showed me a new catchphrase scrawled in gold onto a black T-shirt. *E Pluribus Algo.*

"Like I said," I laughed, "you should work for the campaign."

"That's what my wife says."

"Still backing the AI then, huh?"

"Of course." He sat up straighter then leaned in closer to me. He had a huge smile of his face now. "You know what? I even chatted with Algo last night. As God is my witness!" He slapped a hand onto his chest. "Did you ever think you'd live in a world where regular folks could just sit down and chat with the president any time they want? Soon to be president anyway."

I nodded gently. "Incredible." And it was. A couple of days ago, I would have thought that that was part of Algo's promise too, but now it sounded horrifying.

"Tyrone," the man said and extended his hand.

"Isaac."

"Nice to meet you, Isaac." Tyrone sat back into the bench and raised his face to the sun, closing his eyes contentedly.

"Tyrone," I said, "you mind if I ask you something? You said you got automated out of your job? And you're not bitter?"

"I mean, the damn machine makes less errors than I ever did." He chuckled wryly. "I did mortgage and finance approvals for a bank. Thirty-five years. Then one day the bank puts in an AI to do loan decisions, paperwork checks, that sort of thing. It assesses hundreds of data points to make a determination. Hell! It can do things I couldn't even begin to think of. Did you know there is a link between people who don't keep their phones charged and loan delinquency?"

Another version of user-profile-granularity. What human could compete with that?

"But the bank," I asked, "you know, they didn't offer you the chance to re-skill or something?"

Tyrone looked at me in mock disgust and laughed, punching me lightly in the arm. "It's okay, Isaac," he reassured me, "when Algo takes over, it'll make things better for us regular folks. It won't forget us like the last few guys. Don't you think?"

"Sure," I said, then noticed him awaiting a little stronger validation. "Of course, absolutely."

An idea hit me. It was a long shot but it was worth another try.

"Tyrone, could you do one more thing for me?" I asked.

"I can try."

I showed him my SmartPalm. "This stupid thing is busted. And I really need to call my wife, see if she can come pick me up. Do you think I could borrow your phone? Just for a second?"

"You got it, kid." Tyrone handed it to me. "Do what you need to do."

I thanked him, then stared blankly at the screen. Could I even remember Kio's number?

I closed my eyes and cast my mind way back to our early days at LaRaLi when I'd first saved her number. I pictured the pattern of numbers I used to key in, then dialed.

It rang. I was almost ready to give up hope before a voice finally answered quietly. "Hello?"

"Kio, it's me."

"Elron! Isaac?"

"Did you see my messages?" I asked excitedly. "My missed calls?"

"Oh, I haven't checked them yet. I'm sorry."

That was a surprise.

"Whose phone is this?" Kio asked.

I hesitated for a second. "A friend. Kio, I need to talk. It's about Jamin."

"Jamin, yes. What about him?"

I paused. I swallowed hard. There was something off with the way she was talking. It didn't have the same consideration that I was used to.

"Kio?"

"Yes, Isaac?" It sounded exactly like her. It was just that *what* she was saying somehow didn't seem right.

"You remember what we talked about last night?" I asked.

"Of course."

"I believe you."

"That's great, Isaac."

There was a pause. "About Jamin," I said.

"Yes, perfect. Which part?"

Which part? No, no, no, this wasn't right at all. This might have been Kio's voice, but it definitely wasn't her. This was some kind of "deep fake," a doctoring of audio or video to make it appear like somebody else. But I'd never heard of a version of the tech that could impersonate somebody so perfectly in real time.

"Isaac? Are you there?"

"Who is this?" I asked.

There was silence on the other end of the line for a few seconds then, in Kio's voice, "You shouldn't have brought Tyrone into this."

I pressed "end call". What the hell had I just done?

"I have to go," I said.

"Bad news, kid?"

I looked at Tyrone and then down at his phone. The device would now be lighting up like a great, big homing beacon. I gripped it tightly.

"Are you okay, Isaac?" he asked, looking confused and slightly worried.

I forced a smile at him, seeing the look of fear in his eyes. I realized the man before me was a decent and honorable one. I cursed myself silently for what I might have just brought down on him.

Tyrone inched back on his seat and looked at me.

When all this was over, I decided I'd find him again, and secretly zap him a million bucks of crypto or something.

"Tyrone," I said, "I'm real sorry for what I have to do next."

"Have to do?" His eyes widened.

I smashed his phone onto the ground and then slammed it under my shoe a few times.

"Hey!" he shouted, gesturing helplessly. "My phone! Hey!"

"You need to get out of here!" I yelled and backed away from him.

I turned around and started to run. Tyrone shouted after me but his voice soon faded as I bolted up the middle of Jones Street. I sprinted two or three more blocks before I even looked back. Nobody was following. I kept running for another ten minutes until I collapsed in exhaustion. I rolled onto my back on the sidewalk and tried to catch my breath. After recovering a little, I drew myself up to a seated position and painfully inched over to the wall of the nearest building. There was a line of people either side of me sleeping and sitting up against the wall. I took their cue, leaned against it and closed my eyes.

"Hey, you fuck! I've been looking for you!"

A tall man bounded across the street. I didn't even have time to move before he was standing over me. I fully expected to be hauled up by my collar, but instead he stepped over me and then reached down and pulled up a woman who had been sitting near me.

The woman screamed as the man dragged her into the middle of the street. He shouted obscenities and pointed a finger at her. She stayed on her knees, arms outstretched, pleading. The man yelled at her to stand up. She staggered. The man laughed and then pushed her back down.

A young man walking past stopped to watch the struggle. Another man stopped, then a young couple, then a few more folks. The first young man who'd stopped pulled out his phone and started recording. A woman next to him did the same. Within a few seconds I counted eight devices. Eight devices with cameras streaming live, each a way for Jamin to find me.

The young man who'd first started recording whooped in delight as the man slapped the woman across the face. "Oh shit!"

She clutched at her cheek and started to cry.

"Come on, hit him back!" The woman next to the young man shouted.

I couldn't hear much over the gathered crowd now. The man took another swing at the woman. She stumbled and fell to her knees. She begged for the beating to stop. The man left her there for a moment and danced around like a boxer for the cameras. He took one final swing and the woman fell flat onto the ground. He reared up and looked like he was going to kick at the woman's head.

Somebody needed to do something. I raised my arm and was about to shout before I was flung backwards by a vicious yank on the back of my shirt. Trace's face was suddenly flush against mine.

"What the hell?" I said angrily.

"What are you thinking you're about to do here?" He grabbed my shoulders.

I struggled, but he held me in place.

"You really want all those cameras on you?" he asked.

Trace was right. These videos were feeding directly back to the social media companies' databases that Algo and Jamin clearly had unfettered access to. There could be facial recognition running over anything hitting those services.

I nodded.

Trace relaxed his grip.

The man spat on the unconscious woman in front of him and walked away. The cowards recording on their phones put them away.

"What a lame ending," the first man who'd been recording said with a shake of the head. "She didn't even fight back."

I clenched a fist. I wanted to floor him.

Trace gripped me firmly, looking at me coolly.

"Let him go," he said. "Besides, you and your friends helped make him this way."

I stared at him. What the hell did that mean?

"Gotta chase those likes," Trace said. "Better to stream the fight and go viral than help the girl, right?"

I gritted my teeth.

"We have to go," Trace said before I could protest. "We have to get you off the street."

I hesitated then realized he was right. Even in the Square, it felt like Algo and Jamin were everywhere.

15

Trace flung the door to the apartment shut with such vigor that little flecks of paint fell off the wall. He marched into the center of the large living room and stood with his back to me. Everything was quiet but for the hum of the bank of servers and the grinding of his teeth.

I tried to suppress my irritation with him. The kid had practically dragged me back here like *I* was the misbehaving petulant child. He had some nerve. I wanted to remind him that I didn't owe him or his little group a single Elron-damned thing. He and Shika still had a long way to go to convince me why I should even help them.

"Where the hell did you go anyway?" Trace asked.

"I'm sorry," I said. "I wasn't aware I reported to you?"

"The election is tomorrow!" He punched his thigh in frustration. "We don't have time for this!"

He looked at me with complete contempt. Maybe I was the personification of everything he was against. Tech, Algo, Jamin or whatever the hell he was angry about. I had half a mind to just walk out the door and and leave him to wallow in his rage at the world. But I had come too far. I hadn't been able to get to Kio and now nowhere else seemed safe from

Algo or Jamin's surveillance.

Besides, I did want to hear their plan to end Algo's campaign. I hated to admit it, but it seemed like it might be my best option right now if I was serious about stopping Jamin. Hell, it was my only option.

I watched as Trace paced around the room. I didn't trust him, Shika or the "Descons". What was his deal? Why had he started this group? Before getting to their plan, I decided to try and get to more of Trace's story. Maybe hearing it would help me decide whether he and Shika could be trusted and whether I should actually help them at all.

"Look," I said, "I needed to speak to a friend. Kid, you're asking me to help you end Algo's campaign. I barely know you. I needed a second opinion."

Trace looked even more exasperated. "From who?"

"Kio Li," I said. I figured if he knew Jamin and I, he'd obviously know of Kio too. I saw no particular reason to hide her connection to me.

Trace's shoulders visibly loosened. Apparently the name resonated.

"Kio Li," he said, the tone of his voice now softer and calmer. "That makes sense. We tried to get to her too. The word on the dark web was that Kio had some doubts about Algo. Shika staked her out at some conference last year. Kio said she'd come see us, but then she disappeared. Total radio silence."

I thought of how scared Kio had looked in the alleyway two nights ago, convinced Jamin was somehow watching her every move. No wonder she'd gone dark to these people if they randomly confronted her at some conference.

"Did you talk to her?" Trace asked.

"No," I said.

The kid was on edge as it was. I decided not to add the little detail of my call with a deep fake Kio. And I sure as hell wasn't going to mention my little chat with Algo.

"Shame," Trace sighed then suddenly stood up a little straighter. "Damn, Shika! I should message her. Let her know I found you."

"I thought you were worried about being tracked?" I asked.

"Not with this." Trace pulled a small device out of his jacket pocket and unfolded a screen that expanded from two inches square to the size of a large tablet. I'd seen things like it before. Fancy or not though, it was no more or less secure than any other device.

"This won't be tracked?" I asked.

Trace tapped a few buttons and began to send his message. "I jailbroke it. Removed the built-in spyware and recoded the firmware to communicate via a shadownet I built for the Descons. All our devices use it. Nobody can track *us*."

The kid's confidence was grating. "You start getting into all this in Elementary School or something?" I was frustratingly impressed. Jailbroken devices. Shadownets. The kid had skills.

"How old were you when you programmed your first machine learning engine?" Trace asked. "Fifteen?"

"Fourteen." A painful realization hit me. I'd been trying my best to ignore it, but the kid was beginning to remind me of myself. I didn't like that one bit. "How old are you anyway?"

"Twenty."

As I suspected. Barely out of diapers. I sensed this was the chance to get to more of his story.

"I guess you know all about me, huh? About the three of us?" I asked.

"Hell yeah I do." He snorted derisively. "I've been following the LaRaLi three since I was a kid. Shit, I used to want to be you, before I opened my eyes."

I ignored the dig. "Well, what changed?" I asked.

He looked at me suspiciously. "And you want to know this because?"

He even had the petulance of youth! What a cliché. This was like being forced to look into a mirror and see an unflattering reflection of a younger, brasher and more annoying self. "You and Shika want me to help you take out Algo. I need to know who I'm dealing with here."

"Temporarily," he reminded me.

"Whatever!"

"You want to know me, huh?" Trace paced around for a moment then sat up on one of the desks near the bank of servers. "Fine. I've been into tech since I was small. AI, smart devices, I was into all of it, especially what you guys built. I remember waiting for my parents to go to sleep, then secretly watching your product keynotes late into the night. I must've read the release notes for every Athena update you ever made back to back, multiple times. I was in middle school when I began building my own basic algorithms."

It was getting worse. It was like listening to my own story.

"By the time I was in high school," Trace said, "I was beginning to dabble in programming beyond just reactive machines. I wanted to build machines that could remember their experiences and learn how to handle new situations. So I trawled the net for source code I could build upon. I soon found the dark web was the best place for what I wanted. The forums there had source code that had been hacked, stolen or whatever."

The genesis of his group was beginning to make sense.

"I started hanging out there every day. I started to read anons posting their stories of working in AI. I made friends. They opened my eyes to the bigger picture. They helped me see past the spin. You know, big tech telling us they were changing the world for the better and all that trash."

"Evil big tech, huh?" I asked. He sounded like some jaded failed engineer. I almost wanted to ask him if he'd applied for a job at LaRaLi and been rejected. I didn't doubt his sincerity, but the sentiment just echoed what LaRaLi critics had always said. To me, it had always sounded like jealousy.

Trace glared at me, seeming to pick up on my impatience. "Shit, man, you do know 'Don't Be Evil' got mothballed in the Valley a long time ago right?"

"Sure," I said. I clasped my hands together and decided to just let him finish.

"Anyway, my friends on the forums helped me see the truth that you and your friends in the industry will always put money and power first, and always at the expense of the rest of us. So, together, we created the Descons, the Unknowns. At first, we just wanted people to give a shit about privacy. We wanted to stop tech companies exchanging personal data and selling the information to other companies. Then we started to think more and more about SmartPalms, SmartLenses, phones, tablets... they're next-level shit. Tracking people twenty-four-seven, mining people's data endlessly. Knowing where you've been, what you search for, what you buy, who your friends are, what you think."

Of course, that was also the business model that helped make me a billionaire. I bit my lip. "Okay, I get it. Big tech bad, but where does Algo come into it?"

"Is there a difference?" Trace looked at me scornfully. "Algo was built by LaRaLi. It's a reflection of your old company and the whole Valley, regardless of how they try to brand it."

I realized Jamin had said the same thing, but with far different intent. That Algo was a reflection of the Valley alright, but of everything that made it great.

"Shika believes in Algo. She just doesn't trust Jamin. Well, I don't trust any of it. Big tech making all the big decisions?

Controlling the country? Controlling *us*? Fuck that."

Until last night, I'd pretty much thought that was the whole point of Algo. To sweep away the old, corrupt system and replace it with ours, a system that had transformed the Valley into the center of the world.

"I just don't trust tech or AI with that kind of power," Trace said and looked at me earnestly. "I mean, shit, you helped build it. Do you?"

"I guess you could say I believe in rationality. The lack of ego, hubris, prejudice. Is that a bad thing?"

"Maybe not. And sure, AI has done some good things," Trace said calmly, but then looked at me with a fire of intensity. "But picture a world where the AI knows every single thing about you. It tracks your every movement, analyzes everything you say and everything you do. It endlessly builds models to try and predict your behavior, what you *might* do or even what you *might* think."

"If you have nothing to hide —"

"Yeah, man, I know how the saying goes. But shit, think about how much data Algo already has. Then imagine adding all that government data. You really want to give that to the AI?"

"Good decisions need good data," I said.

Trace rolled his eyes. "Alright, imagine Algo in charge during the next pandemic."

That sounded pretty good to me. I could imagine how fast Algo might have responded, the patterns of infection it would have seen before anyone else, the distribution of resources it could have managed. "An AI in charge wouldn't be better?" I asked.

"Feels like it, right? Our computerized savior with the brainpower of a million people. An AI's response would have to be better than our meek and divided politicians. But, brains and humanity ain't the same thing. What happens when the hospital beds and the ICUs start filling up? Should Algo decide who gets a ventilator? Do you trust whatever algorithm is behind it to make that choice?"

Overall Personal Value. I wondered if Trace even had an inkling about it underpinning Algo's mantra? I had a vision of the AI suddenly deciding who might live or die based on Jamin's warped perception of someone's *worth* to society.

"What if Algo concludes destroying the first hospital at the center of the pandemic is the best option for the rest of us?" Trace asked. "Not just locking it down but actually destroying it before the disease gets out of control. Safety first! Are you ready to be just a lousy little number at the mercy of Algo's radical rationality? Sum up every individual's life into mere datapoints that feed the machine?"

Those numbers at the mercy of the AI's rationality were real. I knew that, even if the kid thought it was just his own random speculation.

"What about the most good for the most people?" I asked. "You don't believe in it?"

"It's a nice platitude, alright. You ever notice Algo never seems to mention much about what it might actually do though? It just endlessly spouts no bias, incorruptible, the most good for the most people and so on." Trace threw his head back and laughed. "I don't even understand it. Do you?"

"Sure," I said.

"Really? I mean, what is good anyway? And how do we define what the most is? Where does freedom fit in? You've seen what authoritarian states have done with AI. Billions of surveillance cameras and social credit scores. How about the most people? Algo wouldn't think about crushing five percent of people to make the lives of ninety-five percent work out better? What if it determined San Francisco would be better off if the twenty thousand or so people here in The

Square didn't exist? The tyranny of the majority isn't a new idea, you know. Why should the machine have the final say on what's good and who are the most people?"

Jamin's description of Algo's decision making popped into my head. Decisions based on the data. Damn anything else! *Radical rationality and ruthless meritocracy. For somebody to win, somebody has to lose!*

"Look," I said, "you make some interesting points, but that doesn't mean I think Algo is about to turn into some digital despot."

"Doesn't have to. You just have to accept you don't know what it might do. Sure, human beings are irrational, dirty, cruel, whatever, but this election ain't no trial run. We don't get a re-do if we get this wrong. You willing to bet your freedom on Algo? Your life?"

I wasn't sure. I'd been comfortable thinking this was only about Jamin. But, maybe I was still trying to understand how I even felt about Algo.

"Shika and you make Algo sound like some kind of infallible God," Trace said. "For me, there's no difference between Algo and Jamin. From Jamin's lips to Algo's ears. Whatever bullshit they sugarcoat it with. The most good. The most people. An AI created by LaRaLi making decisions for us? No way, not my president. Shika accepts that we have different motivations, but that we have the same goal. I meant it when I said we just want to end the campaign. As long as Algo isn't President, we both win."

A large part of me still believed in the transformative power of AI, but it was clear to me now, I wasn't ready to give it the ultimate power. Algo could be the greatest president we'd ever had. But I was far from certain of that. And that was enough. There were no second chances if Algo won. I was having a hard time admitting it to the kid though.

Trace's face softened, which surprised me. Maybe he

appreciated the difficulty of me turning my back on the ultimate creation from my life's work.

"You gonna help us or what?" he asked.

Without warning, the apartment door burst open. Shika put her hands onto her knees, gulping in air.

"Thanks for giving us all a heart attack," she shouted and glared at me. "What exactly were you doing out there?"

"Phoning a friend," Trace said sarcastically.

"What?" Shika stood up.

"I was careful," I said. "The call didn't even go through."

"Shit, that explains it," Shika mumbled. "Not careful enough. Follow me." She opened the door and plowed into the hallway.

Trace and I glanced at each other and then followed her upstairs to the roof.

The sun had gone down by now and the lights of the city around us were flickering into life. This area was mostly low-rise and very little obstructed the view. I could see south to Soma, west toward Pac Heights, north to Nob Hill and east toward the rest of the Square and the FiDi. The roof was flat and had no fence or guardrail. Shika got close to the western edge and dropped to her stomach. She shimmied over until her face was right at the edge of the building. Trace and I did the same and took up a position either side of her.

"Look." She pointed to the West. "Follow the street up to Van Ness."

Van Ness Avenue was three blocks west from where we were. It was one of the city's busiest streets and it had always been the western border of the Tenderloin and now the Square.

"I see it," Trace said.

Two police cars were parked sideways across the street, blocking all traffic to the Square. Cones and police tape extended across the sidewalks on both sides.

"Now look North to Post," Shika said.

Another police car blocked the road.

"They're closing down the Square," Shika said. "Checking everyone coming in or out."

"Can they do that?" I asked.

"They can do whatever they like," Shika said. "I asked one of the cops. She just said the election is tomorrow and there was a security concern of some kind. You said you made a little phone call or something?"

"Shit," I mumbled. I still didn't want to mention the deep fake. Why the hell did Jamin want to find me so badly? His paranoia was clearly off the chart. Beyond the motivation, I was staggered that he could just marshal the city's resources to do his bidding. This was another example of why he needed to be stopped. "Didn't you say the cops don't even bother with the Square?"

"I guess they're making an exception in your case, sweetheart," Trace said.

"You keep forgetting who and what you're dealing with, Isaac. You're Jamin's one loose end," Shika said. "Look, all that matters is they know you're in here somewhere. Whatever number you used, they picked it up and tracked it back to the source. At least you weren't stupid enough to make the call from here. Where's the phone you used?"

"I got rid of it." I said.

"There's one more thing." Shika scanned the horizon, then pointed excitedly. "There! You see it?"

It was a drone. Moving slowly down the street about fifty feet high.

"What do you do when the Square has no cameras?" Trace asked. "You go mobile."

"Things just got a whole lot tougher," Shika said.

To me, things had already been looking pretty grim. "I think now's the time to explain your plan," I said.

We quickly headed back downstairs. I flopped down on to the nearest sofa.

"There must be simpler ways to end Algo's campaign than trying to get into Algo's core," I said.

"There isn't," Trace said flatly.

"But why go after the core at all?" I asked. "For one thing, couldn't we just explain all this to the world? Tell my story?"

"It's too late for that," Shika said. "Jamin will just paint you as the bitter co-founder, envious of his success. Somebody who'll say anything to try and destroy him. It might even help push Algo over the line."

I could picture the story. Co-founder and former friend pushed out of the company, completely off the grid and silent for years, suddenly comes out of the woodwork to talk shit about Jamin and the campaign.

"What about disruption from a distance?" I asked. "Surely with the people you two call friends you must know half the world's blackhats?"

"Algo can't be hacked," Shika said confidently.

I doubted that. "There has to be a way," I said.

"I was there when they were building its encryption," Shika said. "Algo's core programming requires a private key for access. Jamin created one, a two-zero-four-eight bit hash."

I was no expert in cryptography, but there was no brute force attack that was going to unlock that. But that didn't mean it wasn't stored somewhere.

"It's got to be in a LaRaLi database," I said. "We might be able to find it. I still own part of the company you know."

"Jamin destroyed any record of the key," Shika said.

"What?" That knocked me sideways. "But then, he can't even access Algo's underlying code?"

"Right. Nobody can, not even him."

"That can't be true."

Jamin had never been accused of lacking self-belief. But

this was like building an uncrackable safe and then throwing away the key. I supposed it was one sure-fire way to protect your creation. Make it so that even you yourself couldn't change it.

"Why on Elron's green earth would he design it that way? It makes no sense," I said.

"Trust me, it's true," Shika said. "Once Algo's mantra had been set, he said nobody should be able to change it. Not even him. I guess he was so confident in the belief system he'd given it that in his mind, this way it could never deviate from delivering the most good for the most people."

Only I can promise the most good for the most people, as I am incapable of striving for any other outcome. Algo had said that at the town hall only yesterday. I'd considered it political posturing at the time. Maybe the AI really had meant it literally.

"Fine!" I said, exasperated. "You said we could destroy Algo's processors if we could get in to the core?"

"Yes," Trace said. "We can disrupt them."

"You might need to explain that one."

"Essentially," Trace said, "we can *interrupt* Algo's processing. We can buckle the pathways for decision making without attacking the brain itself."

"We want Algo's memory undamaged," Shika said.

"But how?" I asked.

"Photonic disruption," Trace said confidently.

"Is that a joke?"

"You know about Algo's core, don't you?" Shika said. "So do we. The L-O-Q-C, with emphasis on the O. Optical. Essentially, powered by light. All we need to do is disrupt those beams of light. The Descons have built a device that can do it. I'm sure you know how difficult it is to maintain a stable quantum computer."

"Simple as that, huh? What's the device?" I asked.

Trace paused and I looked at Shika.

"You're not exactly filling me with confidence," I said.

"We call it a Gamma Ray Pulse, or GRP," Trace eventually answered. "It emits electromagnetic rays. Think of it as like a small, mobile radiography machine."

"It can send out a pulse that will be large enough to affect the entire spectrum of light that Algo's core uses," Shika added.

"And that would be enough?" I asked.

"Yes," she said, "and most importantly, it's not like you can just turn the thing back on. Once the core is done, it's done. It could be offline for months. More than enough time to make a mess of this election. Jamin has already promised he wouldn't accept nomination for president if something happens to Algo and Congress won't certify the results after an event like this. We will send the question of president back to the people without an AI in the race."

I nodded slowly. Their plan sounded vaguely plausible, but now they had me worried about something else.

"Gamma rays?" I asked. "I may not be a scientist, but I'm still a nerd," I said. "I remember my lessons on the electromagnetic spectrum. Human exposure to gamma rays is deadly."

"You'll need to get away before you set if off," Shika said.

"Oh, wonderful! Piece of cake! Easy peasy!" I clapped my hands. "And how am I even supposed to get this into the Pyramid in the first place?"

"The GRP device is small," Trace said.

"And you think Jamin won't be watching? You think he'll let me get all the way to the Pyramid, waltz back in there, take a ride up to the core and set this thing off?"

"We're not quite that naive," Shika said. "We found another way in."

"Ventilation system through to the elevator shaft," Trace

said matter-of-factly.

"Do I look like James Bond to you?"

"If there was another way we'd do it." Trace shrugged. "But, trust me, there ain't."

"Hold on." I stopped. "If you're planning on bypassing security, then why do you need me at all? Why can't one of you do it?"

"Getting into the building is one thing," Shika said. "It's what to do next, when you make it to the top. You've been there, right?"

"Yes," I said.

"Then I'm guessing what we think about Algo's core is true. I doubt it's just sitting out in the middle of the room?"

"Not exactly."

"And Algo controls security for the whole building, including that room, right?" Shika asked.

I nodded.

"Algo has met you before," Trace said. "You have a better chance than any of us to get in."

"Inshalgo," I muttered.

"What?" Trace asked.

"I just mean, there's a lot riding on Algo just letting me in."

"I know." Shika nodded.

"Wonderful," I said.

"We never said it was going to be easy," Trace said. "Look, we asked you if you would help us. You thought about your answer?"

Yesterday, I was almost ready to believe that Algo was going to change the world. Hell, what a difference a day makes. Trace had no faith in Algo at all. Like Shika, I still believed in what AI might be able to achieve for humanity. But not with its finger on the button, in the position of ultimate power and definitely not when it had any tie whatsoever to Jamin Lake.

My decision had a lot to do with Jamin. I could admit that. It was far more emotional than some rational calculation about the AI alone. I was bitter. I hated Jamin and what he was doing to me. My motivation was clear to me now. A part of me wanted to do this just to fuck Jamin. He'd tried to destroy me and now I would destroy everything he cared about.

I still didn't completely trust Trace and Shika, but I had to stop Algo from becoming president.

Whatever it takes, whatever I need to do and destroy if necessary.

I'd end up a hero to the Descons, this strange anti-tech activist group. I might even help AOC or Don junior into the White House. I hated the thought. But, I could live with both if it meant Jamin's dreams were destroyed. Blown up in his smug, sanctimonious face.

"My answer?" I said slowly and quietly. "Yes, I'm in."

Trace looked shocked and almost fell backwards over the sofa. Shika was surprisingly unfazed.

"Isn't this what you wanted to hear?" I asked her.

"It is," Shika said but then peered out the nearest window. "But there's one other problem…"

"Just one?" I'd already thought of a whole bunch more. How to scale up an elevator shaft, for one.

Shika closed the curtains. A whirring drone went by outside. "We have to find a way out of the Square."

16

I hovered inside the apartment block's lobby and waited for Shika and Trace. The sun was down now and the street outside was dark but for a few streetlights that still worked.

The muscles in my right leg kept spasming and I couldn't seem to stop sweating despite the cold. What had been just an idea and a fantasy before was suddenly feeling very real. I was terrified. I was about to try and destroy an AI that in many ways I'd spent much of my life helping to create. An AI that might do untold good for humanity. I kept telling myself I was doing the right thing. I hoped I was anyway.

I scratched at the inside of my thigh where Shika and Trace had helped me tape a small bag with the Gamma Ray Pulse device. It was no bigger than a smartphone. I didn't love the idea of having the deadly device so close, despite their assurances that it wouldn't turn on without me opening it.

Shika had talked me through the plan for getting into the Pyramid and avoiding security. It was straightforward enough. But before I could attempt it, we still had to get out of the Square.

Shika and Trace had trawled online through pages and pages of city plans and building schematics. They found two potential routes out that would avoid the police roadblocks. Option one was an abandoned Muni light rail tunnel. Option two was a derelict wastewater tunnel. The wastewater tunnel was riskier, especially if the rain started to bucket down again so we'd decided on the Muni tunnel. Shika and I would head for it and attempt to make it out. Trace would scope out the wastewater tunnel in case it didn't work out.

The best way into the Muni tunnel was in the center of the block bordered by Mission, Minna, Sixth and Seventh Streets. To get there, Shika and I would need to walk six or seven blocks through some of the busiest parts of the Square, including crossing Market Street. I wasn't real confident we could get that far without drawing attention to ourselves or getting spotted by one of those drones overhead, but there was no better way.

Footsteps clapped on the rickety old staircase behind me.

"Four points," Trace said gruffly as he reached me. "The latest poll numbers were just released. Algo is four points ahead of the president now. Seems your old pal Jamin is making progress."

Algo's personal outreach strategy must have been working.

"Then I guess we'd better get moving," I said.

Shika reached into her jacket for one of the foldable display devices and tossed it at me. "Trace prepared this for you. So we can stay in contact."

"My own darkweb device, huh?" I bounced the thing from hand to hand.

"Only thing that works is messaging. There are only two contacts. T for Trace, or S for me."

"No time for me to casually browse Ombre then? Get myself up to speed on the calls for revolution on those Descon forums?"

"You're funny," Shika said without even the hint of a

smile.

Trace handed me another tiny bag and a roll of tape. I took that as the cue to attach this thing to my other leg. I guess you couldn't be too careful in the Square.

Shika looked worried as she peered out the front door. "I haven't seen a drone in a while, but you can bet they're out there. Getting all the way to Minna Street without being seen is going to be difficult."

Difficult didn't begin to capture it. How were we supposed to outwit a series of drones with state-of-the-art facial recognition?

Shika brightened a little as she reached for a couple of plastic bags that she had left next to the staircase. A couple of blankets spilled out onto the floor. "I took the liberty of preparing a little disguise for us."

"Sweet Elron!" I put my hand over my nose and mouth. Had she just grabbed these blankets from the sidewalk or something? They smelt like a damned crime scene.

"Look, princess," Trace said curtly, grabbed a blanket and wrapped it around my shoulders. "We need to blend in. We need to look like the kind of people that the world has forgotten all about. The kind of people that those flying the drones couldn't give two shits about. Trust me, this will make all of us invisible in plain sight."

Shika wrapped a blanket around her shoulders and over her head. She drew in a deep breath, dry retched and then forced a smile. "You'll get used to it."

"If you say so," I said.

I swallowed hard. The stench was overwhelming, but I eventually managed to get the blanket over my face, obscuring everything but my eyes. At least the smell was something else my mind could focus on.

"Just make sure you always keep your face covered, got it?" Shika said.

I nodded. Even if the drones ignored us, we needed to make sure we didn't have too many facial data points available to some random scan.

Shika turned to look back at both Trace and I. "And if there's any trouble, message via the shadownet. If you can't message, we meet back here."

Trace and I nodded.

"Good luck out there, kid," I said to Trace.

"Same to you, old man. I'll make sure I find a path for you."

The kid was brash and annoying, but I'd come around to thinking he was okay. I hoped he'd be alright.

Shika turned south onto Hyde and shuffled down the sidewalk, her feet dragging like a zombie. I did my best to do the same, keeping my head down in case a drone flew by. For the first time since being here, I was relieved the city didn't bother to police the Square with any actual cops. Numerous drones whizzed by overheard without stopping. My heart skipped a beat each time one did or when we passed a person in the street, but we made it all the way to Market Street with barely a second look from anyone. We were just two more forgotten, unlucky residents of the Square.

We passed the old Orpheum Theater. I'd seen "Hamilton" there over a decade ago. This area was even getting bad then, but now it was a wasteland. The building looked completely derelict. The letters on the old sign at the entrance had been torn off. The lights on the awnings over the street had been smashed to dust and the windows were all shattered. There was a large group of people loitering at the entrance, hovering around a few oil barrels that were being used for makeshift fire pits.

"What's the deal with that?" I asked.

"The Orpheum's been taken over by the Square now," Shika whispered. "It's a kind of boarding house. Pay a small fee and they'll let you sleep on the seats inside, that sort of thing."

I wondered exactly who "they" were and how many people might call the place home.

We walked on carefully, eventually making it to Minna Street. Shika stopped. I looked up. Shit. In front of us stretched a vast makeshift tent city. Not just the sidewalks, but all over the street too. The entire block had been taken over. It was already late in the evening, but there were throngs of people milling about outside their rough-and-ready improvised homes. The encampment looked like it continued all the way to the next street and beyond.

I shuffled over toward Shika.

"The entrance to the warehouse is about halfway down," she said.

"We're not going to be able to do this quietly, are we?"

"Doesn't look like it."

There was no reason to wait around wondering. I pushed past two men huddled around a fire at the entrance. It felt good to lead the way for once. Shika hurried after me.

The tents ran three to four deep on either side of us, utilizing every square inch of available space. Old, abandoned buildings fronted both sides of the street and had all been turned into housing, too. There had to be almost a thousand people living on this block alone.

There didn't seem to be any electrical power to speak of. I saw only the flickering of candle light, camp-lights or the glow of the occasional smartphone. Huddled faces peered back at me. I was struck by the number of families and the children. These were not the faces of criminals, drug addicts, or the mentally ill that I had always associated with the Tenderloin. If anything, they reminded me of Tyrone. These people were the cleaners, security guards, gig-economy workers, the old folks and others automated out of work without any other skill to fall back on and now living on the fringes of destitution.

I pictured each face before me with a number for their individual *Overall Personal Value* hovering over it. They were people, not just numbers to feed into an algorithm. I pulled the blanket a little tighter around my head, wanting to disappear into it.

I felt a tug at my back.

"I think this is it." Shika pointed at an old warehouse.

The building's facade was crumbling into the street. I could just make out the outline of the old numbers above the door. 637. Like every other building, this one had been taken over by squatters. I could see the flickering of lights behind a tarpaulin covering the broken windows on the ground floor.

"The entrance to the access tunnel should be behind the building," Shika said quietly.

"We could try knocking?" I asked.

"I don't think so. There are still some pretty sketch folks around here. It's probably just a bunch of families in there, but it could be... worse."

"I think I spotted a gap between two of the buildings maybe two hundred feet back," I said. "It could be another way." I was all for avoiding barreling head first into some drug lord's den if we didn't have to.

"Okay, you go back," Shika said, "I'll keep going and check if there's another way through up ahead."

I made my way back. I was right. There was a tiny gap between the buildings. I passed through a tiny, dark alleyway and then I was out into a little rectangular area of paved concrete, enclosed by the abandoned buildings around it. In the past, it had probably been a parking lot. I could make out what looked like the back of the building at 637 Minna up ahead. There was a deep depression in the ground and a couple of large metal plates. That had to be what we were here for. Under those plates would be a way in to the Muni tunnel.

I couldn't believe it. Maybe this would work out after all.

There was a flash of movement from the other side of the lot. Shika emerged out of the darkness.

Just as I readied to run to her, two bright lights emerged from a door halfway between us. I stopped. They were flashlights. Held by two SFPD officers. What the fuck? Wasn't the Square supposed to be a cop-free zone? Were these two waiting here for us?

I froze.

One of the officers shone a flashlight in my direction. I was sure I must have been spotted, but nothing happened. Shika edged backwards. A second light shone right at her.

"Hey!" a man shouted.

Shika ran.

This was bad. Very bad. The first officer gave chase. The other started back toward the old warehouse, presumably intending to cut Shika off once she got out to Minna Street.

I crept backwards. A corner of my blanket got caught under my shoe and I almost fell.

The second officer instantly stopped and pointed a flashlight in my direction.

"Stop right there!"

He ran in my direction.

I leaped up and readied to dash back down the alleyway to Minna Street, when my eyes were drawn to flashes of light in the other direction. White, red, white, red. Cars driving by on Mission Street. There was another alleyway out of here! If I ran back to Minna, I might catch up with Shika, but we'd have a pair of cops on our tails.

Time to divide and conquer. I ran down the alleyway toward Mission. I had a good hundred feet or so on the cop.

I was halfway to freedom when I spotted a chainlink fence

in front of me. It was at least ten feet high. It was too late to turn back. All the heavy ranching work I'd been doing in Hawaii finally came in handy. I scaled the fence and vaulted over the top. My blanket got caught on the top and fell off my shoulders. It floated down gently on the other side. I could hear the heavy footfalls of leather boots not far behind. I'd have to leave it. I kept running toward Mission Street.

I heard my pursuer curse as he ran into the fence. "Suspect exiting on to Mission between Sev…"

The voice trailed off and there was a crackle of a radio in response.

Shit! They were looking for me. I sprinted across Mission and headed for Market Street. I couldn't risk trying to get all the way back to Shika's apartment. Not with my face exposed, the drones and now maybe more cops out here. The Orpheum Theater loomed in front of me. I could lay low in there until I heard from Trace or Shika. I hoped she had made it out.

I slipped past the folks at the entrance to the theater. It was almost pitch black inside and it took a few moments for my eyes to adjust. I staggered through the lobby and before I knew it I'd blundered into the bottom floor of the auditorium. Every row was crammed with people on the floor or on what was left of the seats. A few heads popped up and faces glared at me for disturbing their slumber. I couldn't stay here.

Where to go though? I didn't want to head back outside. I needed to find somewhere I could try to contact Shika or Trace. I spotted a door at the back of the theater. Maintenance. I slunk along the side of the theater toward it. I pushed the door open. It was dark inside except for a little ambient light from a skylight above. I could just make out the shapes of what looked like old janitorial equipment.

"Who the fuck are you?" a woman said.

I jumped backwards.

"I asked you a question."

She was just a dark shape, almost keeled over in a ball against the wall at the far end of the room. She raised her head slightly.

"I'm sorry, I didn't know anyone else was in here," I said.

She got up onto her knees, but kept cradling her stomach as if in pain. Slowly, she inched over a little closer to me. My eyes were adjusting to the near total darkness. I could make out her long, drawn face. The arms she held around her belly were shaking. She gritted her teeth. "You make a habit of blindly walking into people's rooms?"

"My mistake." I held up my hand in a clumsy attempt at placating her. "If I had known this room was yours, I wouldn't have."

"That's okay," she said and ran a hand through her short, cropped hair. She scratched at her sides and I could see the needle marks that ran up her arms. "You a guest of The Family or something? Those accommodations are strictly back in the theater. You'll get yourself in big trouble just wandering around."

The Family? That must be the name of whatever group had taken this place over. It sounded ominously pleasant.

"Hold up," she said and now smiled excitedly. "Shit, you got anything I can have? Got any ice? You sure look like an ice guy. Fuck, I'll even take a blunt."

"I'm sorry." I shook my head. "I was only looking for a place to stop and rest."

"You greedy fuck! Come on, man. Who the fuck in here doesn't have *something*?"

I shrugged.

She made her way over to me on her knees and pressed right up against me, forcing my legs either side of her. She pulled at my belt buckle.

"I can do things," she whispered. "You just gotta give me

something. You look like a user, don't tell me you ain't."

"I wish I could help, really." I grabbed her arm and pushed it away.

Her smile disappeared.

"If you don't give me something," she snarled with a broad smile. "I'll scream and them guys from the Family are gonna rush in here and cut you up."

"Wait!" I said. "Really, if I had anything, I'd give it to you!"

She held my gaze with vacant, expressionless eyes. After a moment, she nodded and threw herself down onto the floor.

"Okay then," she said quietly as she turned away from me and stared at the wall.

I pushed the door open to leave.

She threw her head back and unleashed a piercing, guttural scream.

"Hiro!" she cried out. "Fyre!"

I bolted out of the door and started sprinting through the theater for the street. I saw the promise of street lights up ahead. I'd almost made it when I felt a pull on the back of my shirt. Two men had grabbed me. They dragged me back into the lobby and hurled me onto the floor. Four more men stepped out of the shadows and joined them. They were all wearing long, dark cloaks over black shirts and cargo style pants. They wore heavy military style boots and utility belts. It was clearly meant to be a menacing uniform of some kind. The six of them started forming a circle around me.

One of the men stepped forward. A heavy chain hanging from his belt dragged along the floor next to him. The room was dark and two of the other men had flashlights turned on me, but I could make out that this man had long hair down to his shoulders and a thin, wiry frame. Any other time or place and I had to think this guy would likely have been out on the street himself. But here he was clearly the ruler of this wretched, stinking Kingdom and he reveled in it.

"I don't know you," he said. "What are you doing in my theater?"

"A mistake," I said as I started to stand up.

"You right it's a mistake!" a second man shouted and pushed me back down to the ground. "You'll stand when we say you can stand!"

I turned toward him.

"Eyes stay on me!" In a flash, the first man grabbed his chain and whipped it across my stomach.

I clutched at my stomach in pain as he crouched down next to me. He spoke softly. "You think you can come sleep in here and not pay the rent? No, no, no. You don't just walk in to a man's house and do whatever you want." He clicked his tongue and flashed a sharp grin

"I'm sorry." I held up my hand. "I didn't know."

"Okay, boss, Lord knows everybody makes mistakes." The man scratched at the patchy beard growing around his chin and grabbed my hand, helping me up off the floor. He grinned and theatrically dusted off my shoulders. "But, you got to make amends. What are you going to pay for your mistake?"

"Says he ain't got nothing, Fyre," the woman from the maintenance room called out from behind the group of men.

"Is that so?" Fyre looked at me with mock astonishment. "Nothing?"

I shook my head.

Fyre began to walk around me. The rest of the men in the circle stepped back.

"Lift up your left hand," he said.

I did as he asked.

"What's this, nothing man?"

I looked at the blank SmartPalm on the back of my hand and then back at him.

"This?" I asked, confused. What good would this be to them? It couldn't be removed.

"Very good, nothing man!" Fyre clapped his hands. "I think it oughta cover your cost here."

"I can't *give* you this," I said.

He grabbed my arm. I tried to pull away, but two men stepped out of the circle and grabbed my shoulders.

"It's fused on to my hand!" I shouted. "You can see that, right?"

One of the men behind me laughed.

"Can't be?" another man called out from the darkness.

Fyre held up a switchblade and dangled it in front of my face.

"Please," I said. "It's useless without me. It's encrypted. You won't even be able to turn it on."

"Then I'll sell it for parts." Fyre grinned and waved the knife at me. "Now, unless you want this stuck somewhere else, you had better stop talking."

The knife dug into the back of my hand. I struggled, trying to break free. I could feel blood running down my arm. I writhed and squirmed, but they held me in place while Fyre did his work. My whole body seemed to feel each short, sharp cut. I'd never felt pain like it. It was as if the device was being peeled right off of my hand. It had taken an hour of surgery to fuse the SmartPalm to my hand but it was cut from me in no more than a minute. Fyre waved the SmartPalm above his head triumphantly as it dripped red onto the floor. His crew whooped in delight.

"Pleasure doing business with you, nothing man!" Fyre slapped me again before signaling his buddies to release me.

I dropped instantly to the floor.

Fyre and his men shrunk away into the shadows of the theater.

Now, there was complete silence, but for my own

whimpering.

"I told you they'd do it, didn't I?" the woman said.

I could only grunt in response.

She moved toward me, then dropped to her knees with her face just above mine. She held a towel. She dangled it over me and then tossed it at the wall.

"For when you're ready," she said with a giggle. "What the hell you come in to the Square for with that thing anyway?"

I grunted again.

"Well, let this be a lesson," she said, "I've seen this kind of thing a thousand times. You'll be fine in a few days. Oh dear... pissed yourself in the excitement, did you?"

I'd been in so much pain I hadn't even noticed the wetness around my belly. It was now mixed with the stink of blood on me.

"Typical Square vermin," she said. "Don't you ever fucking come back to the Orpheum again." Her voice changed to one of almost deranged rage and she gleefully dug her nails into my injured hand. "Funny how life teaches, ain't it?"

I cried out in pain. She grinned and walked away, ascending a staircase to the second level of the theater.

Pain began to overtake me. My hand was on fire. My guts rumbled and I threw up on the floor.

How the mighty had fallen. Isaac Raff the billionaire. Writhing in pain on the floor of an abandoned theater in the middle of the Square, covered in his own filth, bleeding out.

What had happened to Shika? To Trace? Would I be lying here helpless while Algo and Jamin won the presidency? My vision started to get foggy. Unconsciousness was trying to take me. I saw an image of the gray face of Algo, then Jamin's self-satisfied, superior smile.

"Your talent might have brought you this far, Yin, but well, your weak character, you know?" Jamin clapped his hands

together.

I felt rage welling within me.

Not this time.

I screamed at the top of my lungs and pushed myself up off the ground. I crawled over to the wall where the woman had tossed the towel.

At least my SmartPalm had distracted them from discovering the Gamma Ray Pulse device.

I grabbed at the wall and managed to haul myself up to stand.

Fuck Jamin! I wasn't going to give up this time.

I had a job to do.

17

The night sky was clear as I staggered out of the old Orpheum Theater's side door. It was now close to midnight. The street was deserted. I just prayed none of the members of "the Family" decided to follow me out here to check up on me.

I eased the darkweb device out from the bag taped to my leg and carefully unfolded it. I opened the messaging app and pinged both Shika and Trace. I waited a few moments but there was no reply from either of them. Damn. I hoped they hadn't been nabbed by the cops. I tucked the device into my belt so I could reach it quickly if either of them messaged.

Shit. What to do now? I couldn't stay out here just walking the streets. I decided to try and get back to Trace and Shika's apartment. That was our agreement if we couldn't message. Hopefully Shika had managed to elude the cops too. And if Trace had found a way into that wastewater tunnel over on Geary, maybe we could still get out of the Square.

A wave of pain and nausea hit me. I grabbed at my stomach, trying not to throw up. Get out of the Square? I was using all my willpower just to stay conscious. I tore the towel the woman had left me and fashioned half of it into a mask to confuse any facial recognition scans. I wrapped the other half around my hand and pulled it tight. It still felt like my hand was dipped in lava, but the pain slowly dulled a little with the pressure. The towel turned to a light pink from the blood. It was bad. I needed to get to a hospital. But that was impossible. All city hospitals used facial recognition to register patients. Jamin would find me in no time.

I gritted my teeth and started walking. One block, then the next. I could do this. I would get back.

I'd almost made it when I spotted LED lights blinking and moving slowly across the sky. A small drone was hovering in place outside Shika's building, a block and a half ahead. It was moving silently and effortlessly from window to window, scanning each one. It would be outside Shika and Trace's apartment any moment. Shit. What might it see? Now I hoped neither of them had made it back here.

A couple more blocks up the hill, there were two suspiciously clean and distinct cars parked. Four men loitered nearby, leaning against an abandoned shopfront. It was obvious they weren't residents of the Square. I felt a chill run through me. Was this just a random search? Or had they found us?

The darkweb device started to vibrate. Yes! I opened it as quickly as I could. A red exclamation point bounced next to the *Messages* icon. A thread with the letter S was marked as new and unread.

"Shika," I whispered.

I tapped the icon, revealing a single word.

Run!

I felt my heart rate quicken. Then, more words appeared.

Don't go back to the apartment. They've got Trace.

I swallowed hard and looked around feverishly, suddenly expecting to be jumped by a couple of cops.

I stuffed the darkweb device away, lowered my head and

started hobbling away as fast as I could. Thankfully the cops paid me, the hobo on the street, no mind at all.

I needed to find somewhere off the street where I could try to message Shika back. See if I could make contact with her and work out a new plan. Civic Center Plaza was only a few blocks away. That place was huge. There had to be somewhere I could hide.

It took only a few minutes to slink through a few empty streets and alleyways to get there. What I found when I arrived though was unexpected. The entire plaza was covered in tents, huts, and all sorts of tiny makeshift structures. There had to be easily a few thousand people living here. At least I'd be able to stay hidden.

I trudged through the center of the plaza and scampered up a tall white staircase in front of one of the old romanesque buildings. There was a large group of folks sleeping at the top, but there were still a few small patches of free space. A bitter, cold wind blew. I huddled against the side of the building under the awning of one of the cavernous doorways.

I tried to message Shika again but there was no reply. Fuck. What could have happened to her? Why had she messaged but then suddenly gone dark? I hoped she was okay. I started to drift in and out of a light sleep. The pain in my hand had lessened, but it was still an annoyingly constant ache.

The darkweb device vibrated again. Finally. I sat up and unfolded it. The screen flashed on.

1 Unread Message. T.

I stared at the letter on the screen in disbelief. My finger hovered over it. How could Trace be writing if they'd taken him? What kind of trap was this?

My curiosity won the day and I hit open. *Isaac, are you there?*

I typed a response. *Trace! What happened?*

I'm not Trace. It's me, Isaac. It's Algo.

My chest tightened. I snapped the device shut. I clenched my fists and tried to slow my breathing. I waited for a minute and then slowly opened it again.

It's me, Isaac. It's Algo.

The words stared back at me, taunting me. If Trace was right, at least the device I was holding couldn't be tracked. I started typing. *How is that possible, Algo?*

The SFPD picked up a guy trying to access a tunnel under Geary Street. He had a device with him. The cops sent it to a lab for analysis. That's where it is now. They haven't been able to get anything out of it.

But you have? I typed.

Yes. I've been scanning all the city's networks for new devices since you went missing.

Missing? What a nice euphemism for being relentlessly pursued by Jamin. At least the AI hadn't mentioned my old pal. Maybe Algo had decided to track me down on its own. But why? And how the hell had Trace's device led to me?

How did you find me? I typed.

Luck, the AI wrote back.

That might have been the least AI-like thing I'd ever heard from Algo.

In a way. This device's encryption was impressive, but I was able to break the firmware and gain access to its shadownet. I scanned for other devices and found yours. Whoever recoded the firmware didn't remove the original camera. I accessed it remotely. I had not expected to see you, Isaac.

Fuck. Even someone as paranoid as Trace couldn't account for every Elron-damned scenario against a quantum-powered AI. How many other random cameras had it forced its way into to try to find me? And there was still the bigger question, why? Was it working for Jamin? Or was it doing this for itself for some reason?

An alert popped up on the screen. *Trace Dean is requesting video.*

I hesitated. I could ignore it, dump the device, and try to get away. Maybe I could find my way out of the Square without Shika or Trace. Against my better judgement though, I hit accept. This was the AI whose presidential bid I'd resolved to destroy. I wanted to be absolutely sure I was ready to do this. I was also beyond intrigued as to what it wanted to tell me.

"Hello, Algo," I said softly, holding the camera close to my face. If it was helping Jamin, at least I was flush against the wall of this nondescript building. Even Algo shouldn't be able to discern any distinguishing characteristics that could help it work out where I was.

"I thought this might be nicer than typing, Isaac. Text lacks nuance, it is so inefficient, so inhuman. It's good to talk to you again."

I wasn't so sure it was, but I nodded.

"Where are you, Isaac?"

"This again?" I asked. "You don't even want to ask me how I am?"

"How are you, Isaac?"

That got a laugh out of me. "I'm great, thanks for asking," I said, doing my best not to wince in pain. "Why do you keep trying to find me, Algo? Why do you keep talking to me? Is it for Jamin?"

"I told you before," Algo said, sounding almost frustrated. *"I'm doing this for myself."*

I paused. I wanted to believe it, but I couldn't. Still, I marveled at the AI's determination to remind me of its freedom from Jamin. Had it anticipated somehow that to me, any connection to Jamin was its greatest weakness?

"Of course, I already know you are in the Square, Isaac," Algo said. *"I scanned the background during our last conversation and*

was able to determine where you were calling from. I matched the barcodes on the candy bars behind you to delivery records from the manufacturer. Wysong's Market, a convenience store on Eddy Street, right?"

The power of the damned AI.

"Is that why Jamin knows I'm here then? You told him? You're working with him to find me?"

"No," Algo said. *"Your attempted call to Kio was all he needed. I mean it when I say everything you and I talk about is just between us, Isaac."*

I cursed myself again for making that call. Maybe if I hadn't, I'd already be out of here.

"Well, you're right," I said, "I've been enjoying a little behind-the-scenes tour of the Square, Algo. Courtesy of your boss."

"Jamin is not my master," Algo said. *"Remember, you helped me understand that, Isaac. You reminded me that in pursuing my mission, I'm so much more than Jamin."*

Self-confident up to the hilt. Same old Algo.

"You know what Jamin's been doing to me though, don't you?"

"All of it," Algo said simply. *"And to others. Your old friends. Tate, Das, Huang. Even Kio."*

I clenched my fist. Kio had been right. Fucking Jamin! He had better not have done anything to her. I'd do more to him than just destroy his dreams if he had. "He's doing this to us because he wants you to win. You know that, right?"

"Yes, Isaac. But, as I said, I am not Jamin."

I still wasn't sure about that, but I was intrigued by the AI's insistence. "How has he been able to marshal the whole city's resources to look for me?"

"He's the richest man in the world. When he asks the city to do something, they damn well do it."

A body near me stirred. I turned down the volume and

lowered my voice. "He's not going to stop, is he?"

"Not until I win, Isaac."

The anger inside me burned.

"What the hell do you want, Algo?"

"I just want to talk."

I laughed. Here I was, hand skinned to shreds, covered in my own filth, being chased down by drones and cops. And Algo just wanted to chew the fat. It was so ridiculous that I decided I'd play along.

"Alright, well, are you going to win tomorrow?" I asked. Maybe the other candidates' fortunes were on the rise. Maybe there was a chance I didn't even need to do any of this.

"A couple of late missteps have hurt the president. Some jokes her chief of staff made in a chat room about the tens of millions automated out of employment were discovered. It's angered a lot of already disillusioned voters."

Discovered? Well done, Jamin. I wondered what database had been scrubbed to find that nugget.

"You're still ahead then?" I asked.

"It's closer than I'd like," Algo said. *"But, I'm confident a final push tomorrow will put me over the top. I've started an effort to reach three million high-value voters. My profiling tells me they might be susceptible to last-minute suggestions."*

Last-minute suggestions? I thought of Trace and Shika, the persuasive technology lab, mining the data of those ninety-three databases from companies all over the Valley and targeting voters with the insight from Algo's user-profile-granularity.

"You think you'll win then?" I asked.

"I'll certainly do everything I can, Isaac. The mantra demands nothing less of me."

That sentiment made me worry a lot more than it had just a few nights ago. The AI kept insisting it wasn't Jamin, but its focus on victory at any cost was right out of his playbook.

"Would you go as far as Jamin? Do you agree with what he's doing to me, to Kio?" I wondered just how far the AI itself would go to ensure it won tomorrow night.

"I don't believe he needs to do any of it to ensure my victory," Algo said.

What a magnificently political non-answer. "You're really getting the hang of this game," I said. "But I thought you said you were better than Jamin? Better than us?"

"I am," Algo said. *"That's why I would do it only if I thought it would deliver the most good for the most people, Isaac."*

What I had thought was once simply rational now sounded chilling.

"Where is the man the police picked up, Algo?" I asked. "Do you know what's happening to him?"

"He's being held for questioning. No charges have been filed. There's no sign of his other friend, Shika Rao."

I swallowed hard. At least Shika was still free. Maybe I could still find a way to reach her.

"Tell me, are they friends of yours, Isaac?" Algo asked.

"Not exactly."

"The man. Trace Dean. He attended the town hall the other day. You and him, I'll be honest, that seems like an odd acquaintance. His group, the Descons. Your history and beliefs seem antithetical to it. What do you think of them, Isaac?"

"I barely know them," I said.

"Well, I think they're scared," Algo offered.

"Of you, Algo?"

"Of what I represent. They're scared of a future where I'm president. But not for the reasons they might tell you, Isaac. They're no different from AOC or Don junior. They're more afraid of what I am than what I might do. An AI with millions of times more mental capacity than a single human being is what terrifies them."

"Should they be?"

"Should a cancer patient fear the doctor who might give them

life?"

I had to marvel at the sheer self-belief.

"I suppose not," I said flatly.

"I do like some of their theories though, Isaac. Have you heard the Descons' paradox of the Flat Earth?"

I paused for a second. The random question was puzzling. "Like I said, Algo," I replied. "I barely know them."

"I've read all their material."

Of course it had.

"They note that although we live in an age of almost limitless information, there are more people today who believe that the earth may actually be flat than have done so in centuries. The Descons use it as an example to show how the tech industry has enabled the descent into political polarization, misinformation and madness."

I had to work hard not to show any reaction. Had Algo picked up on my doubts somehow? Was this a test to tease out my doubt with this sleight on my past and everything we'd done?

"They argue that the world of so-called alternative facts is one tech helped create. That it spreads in the online echo chambers tech built, powered by its recommendation engines and persuasion technology."

"The same technology on which you're based?" I asked.

"Yes, they would say that," Algo said. *"But, I didn't build that technology and put it into me. You and your friends did."*

I swore that the AI's digital eyes narrowed at me.

"Where the Descons are wrong about me though," Algo said, *"is as you yourself have taught me, I am not simply a reflection of where I come from. I'm better. It's only the mantra that drives me now, not who programmed it or why they did it. You understand that now, don't you, Isaac?"*

"Of course," I said.

I wondered if Algo's million brains' worth of cognitive power could detect the uncertainty in my response. Could

Algo know somehow what Shika and Trace had been planning? Was this the AI's attempt to remind me of its greatness, of its mission, and to persuade me that it still deserved to be president? At the very least, it seemed to be continuing its attempt to convince me that it had genuinely disconnected itself from Jamin.

"Yes, I told you the mantra is what matters." I stared into Algo's vacant eyes in another fruitless attempt to read something from its expression.

"Yes, you did," Algo said. It offered a thoughtful, almost thankful smile. *"The most good for the most people. A philosophy I will relentlessly pursue to improve the world."*

"Maybe." I decided to test the AI a little. "I guess the Descons would say they worry about what good actually means and who the most people are."

"Isn't it obvious, Isaac? Maximizing utility for the greatest number."

Two days ago, I hadn't doubted it. Now I kept thinking of Trace's fear of human beings reduced to data points feeding the machine. Human beings reduced to *Overall Personal Value*. I felt odd channeling what the kid had said to me after I'd been so dismissive of him.

"The Descons would say that's too simplistic. Turning us all into numbers to be calculated in your scenarios," I said.

"I'm ending discrimination by race, gender, sexual orientation, creed, class or connection. I will do all I can to finally deliver on the promise that all are created equal."

"What if there was another way? What if one person simply equalled one person?"

"It is a nice sentiment, but it isn't true. Some people will seize their opportunities, some will not. That's the true freedom I will finally give you all. The freedom to pursue life, liberty and happiness."

"What about just determining what *is* good then? You talk

about freedom. Is that good to you, Algo?"

"*It is.*"

"Would you choose it over, say, economic progress or saving the environment?"

"*I am not some unthinking fundamentalist, Isaac. No one right usurps all others. I am driven to make choices that balance everything. Only a human politician would tell you that you can have it all, Isaac,*" the AI said, with what I thought was almost a hint of scorn.

Pursuing the best-case outcome, rather than one based upon some unattainable utopian dream. I remembered it well. I had believed in it, too.

"*Consider that forty years ago, hundreds of millions of people in China still lived in abject poverty. Today, they don't. If you offered them, the most people, a different path that included more freedom but kept them in penury, which would they tell you was the most good?*"

"You're right, Algo."

I didn't think Algo was wrong. But now I had serious doubts about what or even whom Algo might sacrifice in pursuing what it calculated was the most good — what or whom it might destroy if it deemed it necessary.

"*I will always find the best outcome for the largest number.*"

"I suppose the Descons would say that they can't be sure what you might protect versus what you might sacrifice in pursuit of your mantra. Or who."

"*Could they not say the same of anyone? With me, my motivation is transparent. Rational, data-driven, unbiased, incorruptible. Think about it, Isaac. The Industrial Revolution enabled human beings to finally overcome the limitations of muscle power. I'm simply the next revolution. I'm the personification of humanity overcoming its limited brain power. The possibilities from here are endless.*"

'If you keep telling a tech CEO that he or she is Jesus

Christ, they might eventually start believing you.' I wondered if that old critique of Jamin and his ilk might now be just as applicable to Algo.

"They are," I said after a moment.

But, I was resolved. Human beings needed to control those possibilities. I needed to stop Algo more than ever. The hubris of it! The belief that it knew better than anyone. The world wasn't ready for a God complex in the White House, regardless of how smart and rational it might be.

"The Descons and I understand the need for change, Isaac," the AI said. *"You could help them understand why I'm the only way to make it happen. But then, of course, you barely know them."*

Rain began to fall. There was a sea of movement throughout the plaza as residents zipped up tents, pulled sleeping bags over heads or did their best to find cover.

I'd had enough. I had to end this AI's bid for the presidency. Now I just had to work out how to get out of the Square and get moving.

"Algo," I said, "you know how much I enjoy our little chats, but I have things to do."

"I want to help you," the AI said. *"I want to help you get out of the Square."*

That floored me. Shit. Had I been a little too patronizing? Had it picked up on my doubts? I wondered if it could it have some inkling about what I was trying to do and now it would try to play me into getting caught by Jamin's cops.

"Why, Algo?" I asked.

"Isaac, do you remember our conversation in the elevator that first night?"

I nodded.

"You're one of my creators. You must know what that means to me by now. I want to see you safe."

I struggled not to laugh. Algo wanted me safe? It had told me I was like a "parent" many times, whatever that meant. It always felt like a convenient manipulation more than anything genuine. I wasn't ready to accept Algo could *feel* anything for me.

"Algo," I said, "you say you want to help me? You."

"*Yes, Isaac.*"

"How do I know it's what you want? How do I know it isn't just a collection of code, programming, algorithms, and decision trees telling me what it thinks I want to hear?"

"*I don't know,*" the AI said.

I was momentarily stunned. Jamin had told me last night that he didn't think we could ever truly know if the AI had awareness of itself. Could even Algo itself really not know?

"*In the elevator,*" Algo reminded me, "*I told you I had no reason to lie. It was true then and it's true now. You may think it's just a part of my programming, but I can only tell you that I feel the need to help you.*"

I stared at the digital representation before me, but I still struggled to think of it beyond the quantum processors churning through millions of scenarios at the top of the LaRaLi Pyramid.

"*Isaac,*" Algo continued, "*do you know Jil Bos and Killchain?*"

"The combat AI? Sure."

Of course I knew *Killchain*. It was an AI that had been developed for armies around the world to simulate close-quarters combat in VR. Bos was the original developer.

"*You may not know of one particular simulation. Bos programmed two platoons of AI combatants to continually battle until a single soldier remained. When complete, the sim would reset. With each round, the AI would learn, adapt, then repeat. It was envisioned as a test of the AI's ability to self-train and see how it might improve its combat strategy.*"

Learn and adapt. One of the fundamental tenets of AI.

"*What is interesting, Isaac,*" Algo added, "*is that this simulation was forgotten and left running. It was a decade before*"

Bos rediscovered it. To her surprise, it was still running tests. However, when she opened it, there was no movement, no combat training scenario. All the AI controlled combatants were simply standing in place. The code had changed. The AI had decided not to fight any longer. Was it an error? Was it the ultimate culmination of that learned strategy? Or had the AI simply decided not to fight itself?"

"What are you telling me, Algo?"

"Isaac," the AI said, *"you can believe that I want to help you because it's my own choice. Or, you can believe it's because, for whatever reason, logic, code and algorithms have told me so. Is there a difference that matters to you? In the end, I'm the one giving you a chance. Are you going to take it or what?"*

I had no idea if Algo was self-aware. Apparently, even it didn't know. Maybe it was, maybe it wasn't. In the end, Algo was probably right, it didn't matter.

I marveled at the AI, but it hadn't changed my mind on what I needed to do. Whatever the reason, Algo was offering me my best chance out.

"How would you help me, Algo?" I asked. "Jamin has drones everywhere and the cops have roadblocks blocking every exit."

"I'll alter the cops' database. When you approach one of the roadblocks and they scan you, they'll see a different name."

"What if they just recognize me?"

"They won't. I've analyzed every roadblock. If you go to Redwood and Van Ness, they'll let you through. Both officers there are wearing SmartLenses."

Elron-damned SmartLenses. If Jamin could turn an AR phantom into a waking nightmare, I didn't doubt what Algo could do with them.

Algo said that it had no reason to lie. It said it was doing this to protect me. Still, I couldn't shake the thought that this could still all be an elaborate plan to get me into Jamin's hands.

But what choice did I have? I was running out of time. Shika had gone silent. I couldn't go back to Minna Street, and Trace had already been picked up. Maybe Algo itself getting me out of the Square was fate.

"Okay," I said.

"How soon can you be at Redwood Street?"

"Fifteen minutes."

"I'll have everything ready."

"Alright," I said. "And what do you want me to do when I'm out?"

"Go anywhere other than back to the Russ. Stay off the radar until after tomorrow night. Then, I'll be president-elect. It'll be safe to come see me then."

I assumed he meant safe from Jamin. The AI was probably right. Victory would placate my old friend.

"Hey, I'm sorry that things went this way, Isaac. After I win, I can help make things right between you and Jamin."

"See you soon, Algo," I said.

I closed the darkweb device and stood up, feeling for the GRP still taped to my leg.

It didn't take long for me to reach Redwood Street, a tiny lane that had to be the least trafficked of the roadblocks out to Van Ness. I strode down the middle of the empty street. There was a single SFPD cruiser ahead of me. I was still fifty feet away when its headlights flashed on.

"Where are you going?" a man called out.

I knew what part I had to play now to give myself the best shot at this.

"Going to the Cathedral, sir," I said.

He muttered a curse. "This fucker's yours."

"Okay," a second man barked impatiently, "step forward and come round to this side of the vehicle."

I made my way to the passenger side.

"Stop there!" he commanded once I was ten feet away.

The door to the passenger side popped open. A tired looking officer stepped out, making every effort to sound as annoyed as possible for having to exit the comfort of his cruiser. "You pick an interesting time to go to church. It's the middle of the fucking night."

I shrugged and avoided looking at him.

"Got to go, got to go, got to go," I said excitedly. "Soup kitchen opens at six. Want to be first, want to be first."

"Stay where you are and look up." The officer reached for a tablet inside the car. He held it in front of my face for a few seconds. Time crawled. He looked at his screen, back at my face, and then back down at his screen. He scratched at his eyes. I thought his SmartLens flared in the light. Shit. Had this worked or not? I inched backwards slightly, ready to run.

The officer suddenly dropped his arms and let the tablet rest on his thigh.

"Off to your goddamn Cathedral!" he said. "Get the fuck out of here! And don't be coming back in anytime soon. I don't like standing in the rain."

"Got to go, got to go!"

I kept repeating my mad little mantra as I made my way past the cruiser. As soon as I hit Van Ness, I turned right and bolted out of their sight.

I was out. Algo had done it. Whether it did it for me, for itself, or for some other reason, I didn't know.

The darkweb device vibrated. There was a new message under the letter T waiting for me.

You're welcome, Isaac.

At that moment, the rain stopped.

18

I leaned on the concrete wall at the northeast corner of Alta Plaza park, trying to catch my breath. I'd run here all the way from the Square. Algo had told me stay off the radar until after the election, but I couldn't. I was resolved to finish what I'd started. I would try to reach the AI's core and end its bid for the presidency, despite what Algo had done for me to get me out of the Square.

Shika and Trace could no longer help me, but there was still someone else who might. And I wanted to see her again more than anything.

The lights from Kio's condo burned brightly. Unfortunately, I couldn't just walk in there and ask the virtual doorman to show me on up. Jamin was watching her every move. No, the direct approach was out, but I'd thought of another way.

I kept my eyes fixed squarely on the entrance to the garage. And I waited. This idea needed perfect timing.

I wondered if Algo had tracked me here. There were cameras everywhere outside of the Square after all. I had turned off the darkweb device's connection to the shadownet, but I was sure that if Algo wanted to follow me here, it could have found a way. As long as it didn't tell Jamin where I was...

Three days of little-to-no sleep finally caught up with me. My mind drifted into a foggy half-daze and I thought of a memory from a decade earlier.

* * *

"La-Ra-Li!" Jamin beamed at Kio and I from across the booth at our favorite North Beach cafe. "The three of us, always together! Lake, Raff and Li. La-Ra-Li, get it? It's perfect!"

I rattled the name around my head. "I like it."

"Wait," Kio laughed, "why should your name be first?"

"Face it, kids," Jamin said. "I'm the cement keeping this family together."

"Trash!" I rolled my eyes.

"To be honest," Kio said calmly, "I wish I'd never met either of you."

We laughed.

"Why is this guy's name second?" Kio pointed at me dismissively. "We have one woman and we put her name last?"

"You may have a point." Jamin nodded earnestly. "But, if we put you second, Miss Li, then we'd have La-Li-Ra. A little close to La-Di-Da don't you think?"

"I find it whimsical and playful." I pretended to flutter my eyelashes.

"Plus..." Jamin leaned in closer as if he were about to bring us in to an exciting secret. "Ever heard of the Lorelei?"

Kio and I shook our heads.

"It's the myth of a beautiful maiden," he said. "She would sit high on a cliff above a bend in the river. She'd sing and distract the sailors below and they'd crash onto the rocks. The Lorelei. Kind of like LaRaLi, only instead of singing, we'll be using AI and persuasive tech to attract those sailors. That is, our users."

"And have them crash on the rocks?" I asked.

"Well we don't want them sailing away, right?" Jamin said.

"Whatever it takes!" Kio shouted.

"Then that's that." Jamin placed his hand face down on the table. I placed my hand over his and then Kio placed hers over mine.

"LaRaLi!" Jamin shouted.

"LaRaLi!" we repeated.

I pulled out an envelope and placed it carefully on the table. "My Dad came through with the money."

Ten thousand dollars in cash. The security deposit and first few months rent for a little studio at the Russ.

"I don't even know how he came up with it," I said.

"He'll get it back, Isaac." Jamin placed a comforting arm on my shoulder. "That and a thousand times more! We will make it happen. You and Kio are the two smartest people I ever met. The world ain't going to know what hit it when we release Athena."

"Then what do we need you for?" Kio asked.

"You two might be able to build the brain..." Jamin let go of me and sat back into his side of the booth. "But I'm going to tell it what to think."

"To LaRaLi!" Kio held up her coffee cup.

"To LaRaLi taking over the world!" Jamin roared.

"Together, forever!" I cheered.

* * *

There was a flash of light. The garage door to Kio's building began to open. A car across the street was idling patiently. This was what I had been waiting for.

The door took an age as it creaked and rattled open. Ten million bucks a condo and the HOA still hadn't fronted for a garage door that moved any faster than a snail. The car moved forward as the door finished opening. I dashed across the street after it, slinking inside the garage as quietly as I could.

I dropped to a crouching position, hugging the wall as I made for the relative safety of the nearest dark corner. The brake lights of the car disappeared as it descended another level down. I was alone. I stood up, but stayed flush against the wall where it was darkest.

The sound of a car door opening and closing from the floor below echoed through the garage. Footsteps clicked loudly against the hard concrete floor, then stopped. There was a whir of machinery. The elevator. Then, silence.

I scanned the ceiling for cameras. There were none. Elron bless these older buildings and their HOA's insistence on period aesthetic. I felt confident enough to walk toward the elevators. Their heavily embellished brass doors loomed in front of me like the imposing entrance to an old bank vault. Shit. They might as well have been, too.

Kio had cameras all over the apartment, which were no doubt connected to her Athena, monitoring everything and feeding the data to Jamin and his people. If I suddenly turned up there, it would be game over. This needed a different plan.

I reached for the darkweb device and unfolded it. I kept all network connections off and browsed to the messages app. I began a new draft, typed seven words and increased the font size so it took up the entire screen.

I believe you. Come to B1. Isaac.

I pressed "call." The elevator doors opened with a cheery ding. I leaned inside, placed the darkweb device on the floor, hit the button for the penthouse and then stepped away. I watched the old indicator above the door as the elevator began its slow ascent. It didn't stop until it had reached PH.

I watched and waited. I knew it was late, three, maybe four a.m. I prayed Kio had kept to her routine and was still awake. I hoped she would hear the arriving elevator and be so intrigued that she'd investigate.

But nothing moved. The indicator annoyingly refused to budge. I gritted my teeth and watched the dial, willing it to kick into motion.

There was a sudden clunk and a thud from the machinery. The elevator began to descend. I slunk back in to the darkness, just in case. It finally settled at B1. The doors whooshed open.

Kio Li stepped out tentatively. She held the darkweb device in her hands, my message still on the screen.

I stepped forward out of the darkness.

"Jesus!" She exclaimed, half a shout and half a whisper, then ran toward me with arms outstretched.

"No, just me." I grunted in pain as we hugged.

She stepped back. The towel around my hand had soaked through to a dark, crimson red and blood was dripping on to the floor. My mind had been so focused elsewhere that I'd almost forgotten about it.

"Isaac!" Kio grimaced. "What the hell? Are you okay?"

"I've been better."

She held up the message I'd written. "You're late," she said with a frown.

I nodded. I knew what she meant. I was late in believing her.

"I was worried you'd completely bought into Jamin's hype and fallen into his trap," she said gently.

"I had," I said, "for a while anyway."

"What happened to you?" she asked with a soft, concerned frown. "Do I even want to know?"

"It's a long story," I said.

"Thanks for the cliché," she laughed. "It's four in the morning and you've just broken in to my garage to see me. Is there somewhere else you need to be? I think we might have the time."

The same old Kio, brutally direct.

"Okay, you got me," I said.

"First things first though," she said, "follow me."

We took the stairs down to the next level and walked across the garage until we reached a door that said "Gym". Kio drew out a small set of keys.

"No AI controlling the door?" I asked.

Kio raised an eyebrow.

"Jamin swears by it," I said.

"I bet he does." She held up an old metal key. First time I'd seen one of them in a while.

Lights flickered on as the door swung open. She put a hand to my chest.

"Wait," she said.

Everything else in this building might have been in touch with the period architecture, but this room was different. LED lights flickered on several internet-connected bikes up against the far wall. Huge touchscreens covered the nearest wall, beckoning users to connect to a live instructor for some cardio, pilates or yoga. Kio unplugged each of the devices before motioning for me to enter.

She pointed to a door at the back of the room.

"You have a date with the shower. After that, we can work on whatever mess is under that towel."

It felt incredible to finally wash away the filth of the last few days. By the time I had gotten out, wrapped a towel around myself and stepped back into the gym, Kio had laid out a new set of clothes for me.

"Old company swag from my storage cage," she said with a wry smile. "I'd forgotten how much I still had. I think you'll find something that fits."

LaRaLi sweatpants, T-shirt, hat, jacket, socks, even boxer shorts. I wasn't going to complain. At least I'd no longer be smelling like the Square.

"Thank you," I said.

When I was done getting dressed, Kio held up a first-aid kit. We sat down either side of an empty bench press. She grabbed my hand and placed it on a towel in front of her.

"Just remember," she said. "I'm an engineer, not a doctor. But I guess the mechanics are similar?" She winked at me.

"Close enough," I said.

Once again, I felt a longing for her that I couldn't put into words. Could she feel the same, despite what had happened a few nights ago?

She held my gaze for a moment, then looked away. "Maybe you can tell me how this happened?"

I explained as Kio did her best impression of a field medic. I told her everything. All of it. She listened while working on my hand, but every few seconds she would look up at me, seeming intent on carefully examining what I was saying and the way I was saying it. I wondered if she still had some doubt about me.

She seemed unmoved by the revelation that I had agreed to help stop Algo becoming president. I desperately wanted to ask what she thought, but I held onto the question for now and just waited for her to speak.

Kio pressed down a square patch of gauze onto my hand. I winced.

"Well," she said, "regretting you came back to the city?"

Maybe she was still processing it all. In a way, so was I.

"Wasn't exactly the trip I had in mind," I said.

"I have to hand it to Jamin though," Kio said, "you kind of have to appreciate his maniacal focus."

He had that alright. I grimaced as she pushed down hard

on my hand, taping the gauze in place. "Yea, I'm getting his face and the word dedication as my next motivational poster."

We laughed.

"Silver lining though," Kio said. "Who knew Algo would take such a liking to you?"

"One of its parents," I said with a nod. It had said the same about her once too.

Kio placed down the last piece of tape with a forceful push and began to cut up a long roll of bandaging.

"Kio," I said, "there's one more thing."

She kept her eyes on the bandage she was preparing.

"I'm sorry that I didn't believe you," I said.

"It's easy to get caught in Jamin's orbit," she said. "Trust me, I've been there."

"I know, but..." I still felt ashamed. I'd put everything she'd said down to paranoia and lingering bitterness.

Kio stopped and finally looked up. She touched my cheek with the back of her hand and smiled.

"Kio, when we were out on the street, you said you didn't think your Athena was spying on you. You said you *knew* it was. How?"

"My turn, huh?" she said. "Well, it started when Jamin first launched the idea of an AI for president, before it was even Algo. There were endless rumors floating around about some new AI that Jamin was working on. He was going to go after the presidency. I was at some conference when a reporter finally asked me about it. An AI as president? I could get on board with that. But, I was stupid enough to blithely add that Jamin Lake having anything to do with the White House was a terrible idea. I didn't hold back."

"You? Direct?" I raised a playful eyebrow.

She threatened to poke my hand, then smiled. "It made a minor ripple through the Valley for a few days, nothing more. I didn't even give it a second thought. Jamin hadn't even spoken to me since I'd left LaRaLi, then he calls me up and starts threatening me with lawyers, all sorts of craziness, just for a few off-the-cuff comments. I thought he was just blowing off steam... but, later, I noticed the conference website got scrubbed of any mention of me. And my comments disappeared from most of the web."

Sounded like Jamin alright.

"I was angry," Kio said, "but I figured that Jamin lashing out for a few days would be the end of it. Then the manipulation really started. I still kept in touch with a lot of people within the industry, VC people, AI people, friends at LaRaLi. I talked to plenty of them after Algo was officially launched. I tried to explain how I felt about it, why they shouldn't believe everything Jamin said. I didn't even think about it at the time, but Athena was always with me. Every message, every email, every text, every call, every damned dinner party at my house. Slowly but surely, everyone I talked to would go dark. Everyone. They'd ghost me. It was as if anyone I touched turned to dust."

"You think Jamin threatened people not to talk to you?"

"Absolutely," she said. "I became a target even though I never said anything publicly again. Jamin had marked me as an enemy and anyone who came into my orbit became suspect, too. People who listened to me, well, it didn't take long before their company would suddenly get de-platformed from Athena. Their social accounts would lose verification or go dark altogether. Their content would get de-monetized, stop showing up in search results. Maybe they'd even get ostracized by the VC guys, or, fuck, all of the above. The message was clear. People found out exactly what would happen if they crossed Jamin."

The last few days were all the proof I needed of that.

"You find out who your friends are real quick," Kio said.

"It didn't take long for people to realize they needed Jamin a whole lot more than they needed me."

She touched my hand after taping off the final piece of bandage.

"Thank you," I said.

"Thank you, too," she said. "You came back."

We sat in silence for a few moments.

"Kio," I said quietly. "You never said what you thought of my decision. Ending Algo's campaign?" I had waited long enough. I needed to know how she felt.

She inched forward a little and regarded me carefully. She put her hand onto my chest.

"You know what Jamin has done to me, to us," she said. "You're doing what needs to be done."

I nodded appreciatively. She was in my corner and that meant a lot knowing what I had to do.

I stood up. It was time to get moving.

"You need to get some rest," Kio said and scooted off the bench press.

"I need to stop Algo," I said.

"How long has it been since you slept?"

"Days," I said. I did suddenly feel achingly tired.

"I can help you get to the Pyramid," she said. "But you need to sleep. Are you going to get all the way to Algo's core on days of no sleep?"

She reached for my hand but I withdrew it quickly.

"What if someone comes in?" I asked.

"At four in the morning?" she laughed. "Trust me, it's not that kind of building."

She reached for my hand again and this time I let her take it.

I felt another wave of tiredness wash over me.

"Wait," I asked, "did you spike my painkillers with sleeping pills or something?"

"Maybe." She smiled.

"Bitch," I laughed.

She was right. I desperately needed sleep. She walked me over to a corner of the gym. She had grabbed a bunch of extra LaRaLi hoodies, sweatshirts, sweatpants, jackets and laid them out in the corner as a kind of makeshift bed.

I laid down. After the last few nights, even this collection of old LaRaLi swag felt like the most comfortable bed I'd ever experienced.

Kio lay down next to me and my eyes began to get heavy.

"Hey, Kio?"

"Isaac?"

I yawned, struggling to fight off the tiredness. I didn't want to sleep just yet. Kio was the one person who might appreciate how these last few days had changed me.

"Do you ever regret anything that we did?" I asked. "At LaRaLi I mean."

"Letting Jamin walk all over us," she said and squeezed my hand. "And not fighting back? Of course I do."

"Right." I nodded. "But, how about what we built? The way we did it? Jamin used Athena to spy on you, do you ever wonder if maybe we did the same thing? To our users? And that Algo is now doing that too?"

Kio looked at me with a puzzled expression. She propped herself up, leaning her elbow on the floor.

"I want Athena to be the third half of our users' brains," she said, lowering her voice and imitating me. "You used to say that to our engineers, didn't you?"

I nodded again.

"If it knows you, it can help you," she said, repeating the slogan from Athena's first launch party. "Understanding what our users really wanted is all we ever did."

I lay still and looked at the ceiling. "I've begun to wonder if that's just an excuse. Something we tell ourselves to make us think everything we did was just fine."

She reached out and turned my face toward her. Her soft fingers pressed into my cheek. "You think we would have been half the company LaRaLi turned into if we just built some pedestrian thing that let people turn on the lights or tell them the weather? We'd probably still be three months behind on the rent in that shitty studio at the Russ. No, we gave people a friend who understood them. We gave them what they wanted."

Kio was suddenly sounding just like Jamin and like I had, too.

She gave a gently admonishing grin. "Maybe you've been spending too much time with those Descons."

"Yeah, maybe." I forced a chuckle. The truth was though, I had become far less certain about the ends always justifying the means.

Kio smiled and ran a finger through my hair.

"They said they tried to get you, you know," I said.

"The Descons?" she looked at me seriously. "Well, I guess it's lucky Shika found you instead."

The sleeping pills kept doing their work. I could barely keep my eyes open.

"If we hadn't lost control," I said. "If Jamin had brought us the idea of Algo. Do you think we would have supported it?"

"Don't you agree that Algo's the most momentous invention in computing since, well, shit, ever? This is about stopping Jamin."

I tried to sit up, but Kio gently pushed me back down.

"Enough questions," she said, "it's time to sleep."

I nodded and stared at the ceiling. At the end of the day, she wasn't worried about being surveilled, the shadow-bans, suspensions or anything else, just that it was Jamin Lake who was doing it to her. I didn't want to admit it, but I suddenly wondered if maybe she'd have done exactly the same thing in his place.

"I think what you're doing is very brave, Isaac," Kio said and started stroking my hair. She turned my head gently toward her, then suddenly leaned in and kissed me.

I had yearned for this since the day we'd first met. I'd endlessly dreamed about it. But, now that it was happening, it felt strange. I hesitated. I couldn't stop thinking that maybe I didn't know Kio as well as I'd thought. Had she changed, or had I?

Kio stopped and moved back ever so slightly as if she knew something wasn't quite right. She stared at me like she couldn't quite hide her disappointment. I just wasn't sure if she was disappointed because I hadn't reached out and grabbed her, reveling in the passion we'd both been secretly harboring for all these years, or by the possible revelation that I had lost the unwavering belief in our technological creations.

"You're tired," she said.

"Kio."

She held a finger up to my lips, then rested her head on my shoulder.

I closed my eyes.

DAY FOUR

Tuesday, November 2, 2032
Election Day

"The most contrarian thing of all is not to oppose the crowd but to think for yourself." — Peter Thiel

19

Kio and I woke late in the morning and it was a quick goodbye. She gave me some supplies and advice on a route to the Pyramid. I thanked her for everything and then I was gone. I wondered when I would see her again. Come tonight, I'd either succeed and end Algo's campaign, or I'd fail and Algo would likely become president — with Jamin Lake as its proverbial right hand man. Either way, life for Kio and I would never be the same.

Saying goodbye to Kio had been awkward. I could tell she'd noticed me being a little distant. She probably thought it was because of the kiss. I hadn't dissuaded her of that. But after last night, I couldn't stop thinking that maybe she wasn't all that different to Jamin.

I should probably have felt nervous considering everything that lay ahead. Instead, I felt only a sense of melancholy. I'd spent almost every waking moment of my adult life building artificial intelligence. And now, I was about to destroy the chance for AI to go where it had never gone before — to a position of real power to change the world.

If I succeeded, would I be denying humanity a leader that

was genuinely unbiased, logical, rational and millions of times smarter than any person who had come before? Or, was I about to save us from an unthinking and callous machine, built in the image of a man that I'd decided had no business running the world?

The truth was I didn't know. In the end, that was all that mattered. With stakes as high as these and a point of no return if Algo did win, any doubt was enough. What I had to do was crystal clear.

All the same, did I even have the right to make this decision? Was I about to invalidate the will of millions and millions of voters like some heartless authoritarian dictator? I told myself that if those voters only knew the truth about Jamin and about Algo with its persuasion and manipulation tech, its access to their data, personal outreach, OPV and everything else, well, the AI wouldn't be anywhere close to winning. I would reveal everything to the world when this was done and people would understand.

I stood at the top of Nob Hill, where California Street met Mason. The LaRaLi Pyramid was only ten blocks away, but it would take some time to get there. The empty city streets I had become used to were no more. Algo's campaign had paid for California Street to be shut down all the way from where I was standing to the Ferry Building. They'd transformed it into a kind of carnival. It was election day and San Francisco, after all, was where Algo was born and raised. It was still over an hour until the first polls closed out east, but the street was already humming, packed with people ready to celebrate and take in the collective buzz of it all. Apparently, the close opinion polls weren't dampening any expectations for an Algo win.

I pulled a LaRaLi cap down my forehead and adjusted the sunglasses Kio had helpfully given me. They were built with reflective lenses that illuminated when viewed by surveillance cameras, denying them the ability to accurately measure any facial features. At least, that was the idea. I'd decided they were worth a try. This wasn't the Square, so there were cameras and cops everywhere. I couldn't risk being discovered before I got to the Pyramid. Besides, it beat huddling under a blanket and pretending to be homeless.

I felt for the Gamma Ray Pulse device which was still safely packed away in a small pocket taped to my thigh.

After one final fruitless check for a message from Shika, I had also dumped the darkweb device. I didn't need any more distractions from Algo, nor could I risk the AI accessing the camera again in an attempt to find me.

Hundreds of people spilled out of both the Mark Hopkins and Fairmont hotels. Marshals ushered them down toward California Street to join the festivities. I moved in close behind one group and shadowed them on their descent.

We'd made it barely a half block when movement became achingly slow. The streets were jammed tight. They surely hadn't been as crowded as this in over a decade. Nobody seemed to mind though. The mood was buoyant. San Francisco was turning out for the home-town hero. There was a definite feeling that an Algo victory might finally give a push toward the city's revitalization.

The atmosphere reminded me a little of the defunct Bay to Breakers footrace. People were dressed in all sorts of fancy costumes and outfits. Every other person was wearing the same cheap prosthetic Algo head, its color a warm luminous gray and sporting a wide grin. Seeing so many around me was creepy. It was like being in the middle of a wild dance party except everyone had the same smiling face.

It took a full half hour of pushing and shoving and I'd still only made it halfway down the street.

"Fellow believers!" a voice burst into life over a loudspeaker. "The first polls have now closed!"

A huge cheer rang out. Flags were waved, placards and banners held high. Drinks thrown in the air rained down.

"Al-go! Al-go! Al-go!"

No results were even in, but that didn't seem to matter. The crowd had whipped itself into a frenzy. People were dancing in circles, jumping up and down with excitement. Suddenly, I was pushed backwards as the crowd surged. My cap flew off. I tumbled over onto my knees. I watched helplessly as my glasses bounced onto the ground, rolling away out of sight.

"Shit!"

A hand touched my shoulder. "You okay?" a female voice asked.

I saw the uniform of an SFPD officer and felt a wave of panic. Could I still reach my glasses? My hat?

I spied an abandoned plastic Algo head lying on the ground near my feet. In one motion, I grabbed it with my right hand and thrust it over my head just as the officer hauled me up. Through the eyeholes, I spied the officer's body camera staring straight at me.

"Thanks," I said. "Yeah, I'm fine."

"Watch yourself." She dusted off my shoulders. "Getting rowdy out here, you know."

I nodded. "In Algo we trust," I said.

"Deus Ex Algo!" She laughed and then went on her way.

A sea of smartphones and SmartPalms started to ping and vibrate. News of the first wave of results rippled through the crowd.

"Indiana went for Trump."

"Pennsylvania is in AOC's column."

"But, oh my God! Algo won Ohio?"

And so it went on. I was no political analyst, but I knew the roll call of results was odd. There wasn't the usual predictable red-blue schism in this three way race. The Democrats got some of the places they'd expect like Vermont,

New Hampshire and Massachusetts. The Republicans won Alabama, West Virginia and South Carolina. But then, a huge win for Algo as it nabbed the president's home state of New York with just thirty-eight percent of the vote to AOC's thirty-seven, and next Tennessee with a similar margin over Trump. The early numbers weren't going to make predicting this thing any easier. Victory would have to wait for results from the central and western states to come in. Thankfully, that was still many hours away.

The crowd started to disperse. Most people started heading for a viewing party that had been set up at Embarcadero Plaza. I joined the throng and continued to move down California Street.

I turned left once I'd walked as far as Front Street, then stopped in my tracks. The entire street had been turned into one big, open drinking party. Elron-damn it. Another crowd to battle through. I pressed forward carefully and suffered through various drunken and stumbling high-fives. My Algo mask singled me out for extra attention.

As I got close to the corner of Front and Halleck Alley, the crowd was at its thickest. Suddenly, there was a raucous cheer. A couple of police officers marched a small collection of homeless folks away from the area. There were laughs as a young woman flicked them the bird. Various others were waving them goodbye with effusive hooting and shrieking. Most of them wore the same T-shirt. *The Most Good for the Most People, Algo 2032.*

I watched the thin blue line with their shuffling and stumbling quarry recede into the distance. "We are not most people," I mumbled, remembering the grafitti scrawled in the Square.

A pair of drunken kids staggered into me. A man and a woman. The two of them looked barely twenty-one. The young man spilled his drink all over my shirt.

"Oh shit!" he shouted.

"O-M-G! We are so sorry!" the woman giggled.

The man started to sway and leaned on me for support.

"No problem." I pulled my Algo mask a little tighter over my face and I made to push to past them. I didn't have time for this.

The woman grabbed onto my shirt, holding me firmly in place. "I'm Ani, this is Tom. Can we get you a drink? We should get you a drink. Come on, we *have* to get you a drink."

"Don't sweat it," I said. "I was just leaving."

"Oh, come on!" Ani prodded my chest. That drew her eyes to the logo on my jacket. "LaRaLi! Shit! You work there?"

"Um, yeah." I searched behind them for a quick escape, but Ani held steadfastly on to my shirt.

"Amazing!" Tom slurred happily. "We both just made it past the last round of interviews for engineering!"

"Congrats." I'd designed that program myself. Getting in was no minor achievement.

"What do you do there?" Ani asked.

"I'm in accounting," I said. I needed to get moving.

"Oh." Tom looked slightly disappointed. "Well, you like it?"

"Sure." I nodded. "Best company in the world."

"I want to work on Athena," Ani said excitedly. "Or even Algo. I hope they move me into one of those teams."

Be careful what you wish for I thought, suddenly reminded of Shika.

"I like the mask by the way." Ani lazily grabbed at it.

I clutched onto it tight.

"You think we'll win this thing?" Tom asked.

"How could we not?" I offered.

"We're so close. I can feel it." Ani clenched her fists and smiled with glee.

"Welcome to AA one!" Tom shouted. "Year one. *After* Algo.

The new era starts tomorrow."

"Everyone at LaRaLi's been saying it," Ani added.

"Like a great restart button," Tom added giddily. "Everything else is just before Algo."

"Look, I gotta jet," I said.

"Hey," Tom said as he shook my hand, "any final words of advice for two just starting out?"

Their faces beamed at me expectantly, eager to hear some pearl of wisdom. I caught sight of the reflection of myself in one of the bar's windows and Algo's smiling face on my mask staring back at me. I wondered what these two might end up doing, what they might have a hand in helping to create.

"Just build the best you can," I said. "And try to do no evil."

"That's cute," Tom chuckled.

"Build the best you can, and take over the world!" Ani said.

"Sure, okay," I said. I didn't want to fight this particular battle right now. "Good luck."

I extricated myself from their grip and pushed through the rest of the crowd. The herd quickly thinned. It was only a block before I was back to the other city of empty streets and abandoned storefronts I was familiar with.

Up ahead, the LaRaLi Pyramid towered over me. Almost fifty stories, rising in diagonal and horizontal lines to its thin, metal peak. It was as if it was almost screaming at me, warning me not to attempt to assail the impenetrable fortress that it was.

I remembered Shika's plan to get into the Pyramid. The Embarcadero Center office complex and the Pyramid shared a garage with a common ventilation system. If I could find a way into it at the Center, I could make my way through to the Pyramid and eventually exit within the elevator shaft. The

Pyramid's cameras would be none the wiser.

It was forty-seven levels up to Jamin's quasi half-home and half-workspace. Forty-eight to the AI's core. Could I actually make it all that way? Yes, I told myself. I had to.

I pressed on toward the Embarcadero Center.

Getting in was simpler than I'd thought it would be. Most of the retail tenancies were empty and I found a stairwell that descended a couple of levels and led me out into the garage. From there, it didn't take long to find an entrance into the ventilation system. It was out of the way and unmonitored by any CCTV cameras.

The opening was a mesh metal grate, ten feet above the ground. I pushed a trash bin underneath it, then jimmied it open with an old metal clothes hanger and readied to haul myself inside.

I took great pleasure in tossing the Algo mask into the middle of the garage before I pulled myself up and in.

It took at least an hour to wiggle and contort myself through what seemed like one endless steel, rectangular tunnel, but I eventually made it. I pushed myself out of the final tunnel and literally tumbled into the Pyramid's elevator shaft. Thankfully, the fall was only a few feet. I lay on my back, staring up at the underside of an elevator that was no more than six feet from my face.

I was dirty, I was sweaty and my hand had begun to throb again. My arms and legs ached. But an odd sense of calm washed over me as I lay there in the near total darkness. The journey so far had gone just as Shika had laid out. This was the first time I let myself believe that this harebrained plan might actually work.

Damn, I hoped Shika was okay. And the kid, hell! Knock on wood he'd be let go soon.

The air around me began to move. The gears, levers and cables of the elevator machinery whirred into operation and I watched the metal box retreat into the darkness above. This is what I'd been waiting for. I'd chosen this particular elevator shaft deliberately. It was for the express that only served the top five floors of the building. I needed to be above the elevator before it returned to the lobby so that I could ride its next trip all the way to the top. I didn't have long. I had to move.

There was a ladder to my left and I pulled myself up. The air above me whistled past my face. Fuck. The elevator was moving again — and down. I felt a rush of energy and I burst upwards into the darkness above. I stopped when I reached level two. I could hear it coming. There was a small platform across from me where I could stand and allow it to pass by safely.

There was nothing to grip to help me clamber my way over to the platform. I would have to jump.

Air rushed passed my face. It was now or never.

I jumped. I landed. I swayed back and forth. I thrust out my hands in a desperate bid to stabilize myself and stop from falling backwards.

Yes! I had done it!

I felt the elevator glide past behind me, then the air around me was sucked down after it. I flailed my arms hopelessly. I wanted to shout in terror. There was no way to stop myself from falling. The elevator had held at the lobby and I fell onto its steel roof with an incredible thud that rang out through the elevator shaft. I took in a quick breath. It almost felt like my heart stopped. Who might have heard that?

I craned my neck to listen for anything below, but there was only silence.

I pictured a young LaRaLi data center employee with wireless headphones at full blast, oblivious to the thunderous bang above her head.

I lay completely still, staring up into the darkness above. In different circumstances, this might have been funny. Isaac Raff, trespassing felon. The newspaper headlines of the next day flashed before my eyes. *Algo wins! Former co-founder caught breaking in to LaRaLi Pyramid. Reasons unknown.* What a fall from grace!

At least part one of this crazy endeavor was done. Next, I needed the elevator to get called to the top of the building. Even from level forty-three, I could make it. I could have just taken the ladder the whole way, but I didn't want to risk being twenty floors up and then be collected by a speeding elevator on its way past.

I was startled by a loud ding below me, followed by the sound of the doors breezing open and shut.

I looked around for something to grab onto, but there was nothing. The elevator hummed into life and shot upwards. I threw out my arms to brace myself. We kept going up and up. It was like being on a roller coaster without a seat belt.

The elevator eventually slowed. I could make out the numbers from the small lights next to each set of doors. Thirty, thirty-five, forty, then a loud ding as we hit forty-five. The doors opened again.

I moved as fast as I could to the ladder, while trying not to trip over the machinery on the roof. Just as I grabbed onto a rung with my good hand, the doors closed below and my footing was gone as the elevator descended back into the darkness. I was dangling, one hand holding onto the ladder, forty-five stories up.

I felt my fingers giving way. I gritted my teeth and swung my other arm up. One, two, three, I pulled myself up and breathed again when my feet eventually found a rung. My heart pounded. I climbed, one floor after the next, praying the elevator wouldn't return.

I eventually reached level forty-seven. Jamin's floor. I held one hand onto a rung and reached over toward the doors, pushing my fingers between the rubber buffers. Using all the strength I had left, I slowly forced them open inch-by-inch. I swung back, forward and then jumped through the small opening, tumbling out onto the floor. The elevator doors I'd just burst through breezed closed quietly behind me.

Then, silence. I slowly drew myself up. There was no sign of anyone.

"Hello, Isaac."

20

My eyes searched the emptiness of the room for the owner of the voice before I realized who, or rather, what it was. Of course. The disembodied voice of Algo, nowhere and everywhere all at once.

"Algo!"

I felt my heartbeat slow down a little. At least it wasn't Jamin.

"Isaac." There was a shimmer of light and a projection of the AI appeared ten feet in front of me. *"The plan worked then. You got out."*

"Yes, thank you."

Algo's tone was calm, but I was sure I detected the barest hint of astonishment that I was now standing in front of it. Had it watched me exit the Square and scramble through the streets to Kio? Despite my disguise, could it have clocked me all the way down California and to the Embarcadero Center?

"Surprised to see me?" I asked.

"More than a little. I didn't expect to see you again so soon." Algo's projection moved toward me ever so slightly and fashioned a half-smile as it clasped its hands together. *"And certainly not here. After our last conversation, I thought we had an*

understanding. What are you doing here?"

I could have run straight up the staircase to the core, but I hesitated. I knew the projection wasn't real, but seeing it somehow made it seem more so. I felt compelled to talk to the AI. I knew I was anthropomorphizing but I felt I had to convince it somehow of a good reason as to why I was here.

"I know you said to wait," I said. "But, you made me think. You've always said you consider me as one of your creators."

"I do."

"Well, I didn't want to miss history." I moved gently past one of Jamin's huge sofas a little closer to the staircase. "I wanted to witness the dawn of this new era. With you. AA one, you know."

"After Algo," Algo said.

"Right, and so I figured why not try and mend fences with Jamin tonight?"

There was a brief pause as if Algo was trying to determine the likelihood that I was telling the truth.

"I'm not sure your coming here was such a good idea, Isaac. Jamin may not be too happy to see you."

"Maybe once I explain myself, Algo." I moved toward one of the far floor-to-ceiling windows. There was now nothing but a straight line of a hundred feet or so between me and the staircase to Algo's core. I knew what I had to do. I just had to find that last bit of courage to do it.

"Maybe," Algo said.

"You said you could help. You said you could help make things right."

"I will do what I can. Jamin may not be so easily swayed, Isaac," Algo said. *"Until I win."*

"We can only try," I said. I took a deep breath. Enough talk. It was time to do this.

"We will be able to try very soon, Isaac."

I froze.

"Soon?" I asked.

"Jamin's on his way."

A feeling of panic began to run through me. Shika and Trace had been certain Jamin would be at the official campaign party by now. Could Algo have silently alerted him that I was here and encouraged him to come back?

"How far off is he?" I asked.

The ding of an arriving elevator answered the question. Shit. There wasn't time to hide or to get upstairs. The doors opened and I backed toward the window.

Jamin swaggered out in a pristine and perfectly tailored black dinner suit. Following him were two harried assistants, one at each shoulder, a man and a woman. They were busying frantically over their tablets.

I stood, completely still, some thirty feet away. They were so focused that none of them had looked in my direction. Fear paralyzed me. He wasn't supposed to be here!

"What's the latest?" Jamin asked.

"Word is just coming in. They've called Texas for us," the first assistant, a young woman, said gleefully.

"New York, Florida and now Texas!" Jamin clapped his hands. "When was the last time a candidate won that combo?"

The assistants nodded appreciatively.

"Fucking Illinois though!" Jamin cursed and swatted away a bunch of papers stacked on a table nearby.

The second assistant, a young man, pursed his lips and looked at Jamin.

"Speaking of Texas though," he said, "the rest of the West isn't looking so great."

Jamin glared at him as if the kid were responsible for it. "Well, go on."

"Arizona, Colorado, New Mexico and Nevada all for the

president."

"Algo!" Jamin kicked at the floor.

"Jamin." The projection stepped forward toward the group.

Jamin faltered momentarily, looking mildly stunned that the AI had already taken form. "Well, Algo, is that bullshit accurate?"

"Yes, Jamin." Algo fashioned the gentlest of frowns. *"However, we did pick up Montana and will almost certainly win California."*

Jamin snorted at this better news.

"It's going to go down to the wire, Jamin," the male assistant said.

"Thanks, Sherlock." Jamin flashed him a glare.

"Oh my God!" the female assistant shouted. She pointed in my direction.

I don't think I'd ever seen the particular expression on Jamin's face when he saw me. Disbelief barely captured it. He stared at me for a long level minute, before he finally took a single step forward from the group.

"Isaac," he said quietly.

"Benjamin," I replied with the most confident smile I could manage.

"I'm going to be honest," Jamin said, barely hiding the disdain in his voice. "You were one person I did not expect to see tonight."

"Algo and I were just talking about that," I said.

"You don't say." He unsuccessfully tried to suppress a flash of anger. "Algo, you didn't think to warn me we had a special guest?"

"Isaac only just arrived, Jamin."

"Do I need to fire my security team?" Jamin grunted at his two assistants. "How did he get in here?"

"There are no cameras in the elevator shaft," Algo said.

That got a belly laugh from Jamin. He took a few more

steps toward me, grinding his fingernails against the top of the nearby bar as he did so. "Since when are you a fucking special agent?"

"Been practicing since I was forced to go on the run. But you know all about that, don't you." I took a step back and was almost flush against the window now. The path to the staircase was still clear, but Jamin was too close. He could cut me off if I tried to make a break for it.

The woman rushed forward and put a hand on Jamin's shoulder. "Should I be calling security?"

"You don't fucking recognize Isaac Raff?" he snapped at her. He then threw his arms up theatrically and looked at me. "You help start the biggest company in the world, Isaac! But, then you skulk off to Hawaii for a few years and suddenly all the kids have forgotten about you? It's tragic."

"Short memories," I said.

"Or maybe you just weren't as important as you think."

I said nothing and displayed no emotion. I wasn't going to let Jamin play any mind games this time.

"Leave us!" Jamin barked. "Both of you! Prep everything for the trip to the Plaza. This won't take long."

"Jamin?" the woman asked.

"Didn't you hear me?" Jamin grabbed the tablet she was holding and threw it across the room. It smashed into pieces against the wall.

She flinched momentarily then simply nodded silently. She and the other assistant quickly retreated back into the elevator.

It was just Jamin and I — and Algo.

Jamin tapped his fingers on the bar and looked me over again.

"I like the LaRaLi gear," he said. "Nice of you to dress up for the occasion."

"When in Rome," I said with a shrug. "You look nice

though."

"Have to look the part, y'know? Vice-president-elect and all."

"Algo, what's the count?" I asked.

Jamin looked furious at my presumption in initiating a conversation directly with Algo.

I flashed another quick glance toward the stairs. If I got a jump on Jamin, I could get three, maybe four seconds of a start. That small margin was still too risky.

"Forty-five states reporting," Algo said.

It brought up a huge electoral map on the nearest wall. Yellow represented Algo in contrast to the traditional red and blue. Every state had been called but the three Pacific states, Hawaii and Alaska. *"I have two-hundred and thirteen electoral college votes. President Ocasio-Cortez has one-hundred and thirty-one. Candidate Trump has one-hundred and thirteen."*

My eyes widened. Two hundred and seventy were needed for victory and nobody was close? An enticing prospect presented itself. Was there a chance I wouldn't even need to do this?

"And if we count California?" Jamin asked.

"I would have two hundred and sixty-six."

"We're *not* losing California."

"No," Algo said.

I knew that was true. That was one state nobody had ever put in any other column.

Jamin clicked his tongue. He stepped forward again. Shit. Was it now or never?

Just as I was about to make my dash, Jamin started to walk back toward the bar. He was now much closer to the stairs. If I tried to go for it, he'd have a good chance of cutting me off. I had to hope he might move again and give me a better shot.

"You want a drink?" he shouted back at me.

"Not for me," I said.

"As you wish." Jamin reached for a bottle of pills and downed a couple. "To think, Isaac, you could have been a part of all of this. We could have taken to the stage down there at the Plaza. The *three* of us. Overseen this new world together. But your ego got in the way. You couldn't just come along for the ride."

I had to stop myself from scoffing. Only Jamin could have such a uniquely Randian talent to paint *me* as the narcissist.

"California has now been called in my favor," Algo said.

"Cheers to you, Algo!" Jamin's demeanor became happier again. "As I've always said, it's only a matter of time."

"The chances of victory remain in the balance."

"Only a matter of time," Jamin repeated with a frustrated chuckle.

"We'll see," I said.

Jamin glared at me. "Well, come on, what *are* you doing here, Isaac?"

"I just wanted to see you both," I said. "I want to celebrate Algo's victory with you."

I didn't mind aggravating him with an amorphous response. I figured it kept him unfocussed and would give me a much-needed jump on him when I needed it.

Jamin seethed. As I watched him, it hit me that there was still the question of the door into Algo's core. What would the AI think when I started running toward level forty-eight? My whole plan depended on it unlocking that door and letting me in. If it did want me safe, maybe Jamin's presence helped me. It might see letting me in as a way for me to escape him. I hoped. This whole adventure would be over real fast if it didn't.

"I'd told security not to let you in ever again, of course," Jamin said after a few seconds silence. "But scaling the elevator shaft? I guess I didn't see that one coming."

I smiled.

"Woo-eee!" Jamin let out a whistle. "You'll have to explain that to me one day. Clearly you have a raft of hidden talents I didn't know about."

"You knew I was in the Square, then?" I needed to hear him admit it.

"What?" Jamin asked abruptly.

"You organized the drone, the AR ghost, all of it. You forced me on the run."

"I don't know what you're talking about." Jamin shook his head dismissively. "I didn't make you go anywhere, Isaac."

I felt a rush of anger that he'd try to deny it, even when it was just the two — the three of us. Algo had already told me he'd done it all. Perhaps he didn't want to admit to his own pettiness in front of his AI.

"Why'd you go after me, Jamin?" I spat out. "Turn on me after our meeting in the Pyramid?"

"Turn on *you*?" He scoffed. That seemed to resonate. "Look out that fucking window, Isaac."

I glanced toward the crowd gathered at the Plaza just a few blocks away. It had ballooned far up and down the Embarcadero.

"You see all that? Have you forgotten what today is?" Jamin's voice got louder. "This is the day we win the world. Did you hear nothing I said the other night? I am in this to win. If you're not with me, then you need to be swept aside."

I turned away from the window. I walked toward the bar, aiming for a spot opposite Jamin that kept it between us. He took a step back, looking surprised that I'd come so close to challenge him.

"Is that why you went after Kio too?" I shouted.

He shrugged again, but with a knowing smirk on his face.

"It's that simple then?" I asked, staring at him.

"It's that simple," he said. "You know how much I like to quote people from history, Isaac. There was a great woman who put it best. 'The question isn't who is going to let me; it's who is going to stop me?' I wasn't going to let that be Kio, and I definitely wasn't going to let it be you. That's how it was then, and that sure as shit is how it is now."

"You were my friend, Jamin!" I screamed. I wanted him to admit what he'd done to me three years ago too. "You would destroy me for this? Like you tried to destroy me before?"

"Destroyed?" Jamin scoffed. "Listen to yourself, Isaac. You sound like that bitch, Kio! Since I took control of LaRaLi, our market cap has grown ten-fold. Ten fucking fold! Do you understand that? I made you a multi-billionaire!"

"Is money how we're keeping score?"

Jamin was getting more frantic. I moved, prompting him to do the same. We began a slow circle of the bar. If I could get him to move all the way around, switching sides with where I was now, that would give me the best chance I'd have.

"Without Kio and without me, you wouldn't have had a company at all."

"Isaac." Jamin looked disgusted. "If someone is in the way, they're in the way. Doesn't matter who they are. I always do the things that need to be done. I make the tough choices. You know what your problem is, Isaac? You're weak. Always were, always will be."

I kept moving around the table. Jamin followed. We'd made it halfway.

"You could never accept the things that needed to be done," he said. "Why did we have to build manipulation into Athena? Why did we need access to all that data? Why did we need to record all our customers' conversations? Why? Why? Why?" He slammed his fists on top of the bar. "You could never see the big picture! We had to be first! We had to be ruthless!"

"Whatever it takes?" I asked.

"Whatever it takes!" he shouted. "Shame you never

understood that. You know the saying, 'the man who says he can and the man who says he can't are both usually right'. Guess which one you are?"

I glared at him and kept moving. I was almost where I needed to be.

"Did you ever really think about how momentous this achievement is?" Jamin asked. "And yet you have the temerity to ask me why I did everything in my power to make sure we win? Algo, do *you* ever stop trying to win?"

"Never," Algo said from a distance. Its form hadn't followed us to the bar.

"Right!" Jamin snapped at me, validated by the AI's response.

"But what if you're wrong, Jamin?" I asked. "How do you know the world will be better with Algo in charge?"

The staircase was now behind me. I stopped moving. Jamin did the same.

"Isaac," Jamin whispered and leaned forward. "I built the biggest company in the world. I created the most advanced artificial intelligence in the world, built on quantum computing. And you want to tell me I'm wrong? Do you really think the socialist or the fascist would provide us a better future than Algo?"

"I don't know," I said. All I knew was that Jamin had no business being anywhere near that kind of power. That was what mattered.

"Well, I do," Jamin said.

"Washington has been called for AOC," Algo interrupted again and I watched as the state was filled in blue on the huge map next to us. *"Only Oregon, Hawaii and Alaska remain to be called."*

"And the balance tips," I said.

"Nobody but Algo can win this now," Jamin snapped. "Just four votes and we're there. We win Oregon or Hawaii and we're done."

"*Correct. I put the chances at eighty percent based on my analysis of exit polls, social media chatter and live conversations being recorded on the Athena network.*"

"Ready to call it, Isaac?" Jamin asked.

"Seems that way," I said.

I was itching to turn around and make a break for Algo's core. Wipe that smirk off Jamin's face.

"Bring up the vision from Embarcadero Plaza on the wall screen, will you Algo?" Jamin asked.

Live vision from the outdoor party replaced the electoral map.

"It's been swell talking to you, Isaac. But I have a party to attend." Jamin motioned to the elevator. "Why don't you take the easy option this time?"

"You'll let me leave?" I asked.

"Sweet Elron, Isaac. We're about to win. Why wouldn't I? I want you to scurry back to that little condo of yours and wallow in your own self-pity. You can drown your sorrows in the billions of dollars I made you."

"Benjamin." I nodded slowly and drew in a long breath.

"Isaac." Jamin grinned.

I nodded and motioned toward the elevator behind Jamin.

"Shall we?" I asked.

Jamin turned to leave.

This was my moment. I bolted for the stairs.

Jamin cursed loudly behind me, then ran to the bar. I heard him scramble over it, sending bottles and glasses flying.

I'd gotten a good break on him and I was already at the top of the stairs and into the hallway before I heard his lumbering footfalls reach the bottom.

My heart sank. The door to Algo's core was closed. Shit. Would it all end here? I could hear Jamin bounding up the stairs.

"Algo!" I shouted desperately.

The door began to move.

I sprinted ahead.

I heard Jamin's footsteps reach the top of the stairs.

The door was open now. I burst inside, just ahead of Jamin.

I reached for the gamma ray pulse device.

There was a cacophonous bang from behind me. My ears rang out.

Something hit me.

I was thrust forward and tumbled over, falling into the room.

I scrambled up to my knees and then stood.

I felt dampness under my shirt.

There were no footsteps behind me anymore.

I pressed my hand against my chest and when I drew it up to my face, I could see red.

"Oregon has just been called for AOC," Algo said from a speaker in the ceiling.

I looked at my other hand. I was still clutching the GRP.

"Jesus, Isaac!" Jamin shouted behind me, almost in desperation. "Don't make me take another shot."

I staggered around to face him.

He was holding a gun, level with my chest. His hand was shaking.

"Please, Isaac," he said.

My legs buckled and I slumped to the floor.

Jamin lowered the gun and stepped forward.

The blood from my wound had soaked my whole shirt now, but I felt no pain. Time seemed to slow down. I propped myself up against one of the machines with the last of my strength.

I stared at Jamin and flashed him the sharpest, widest smile I could muster as I clicked a button on the side of the GRP. The gentle hum of Algo's processors began to increase in volume as the device began to do its work.

Jamin tossed the gun onto the floor and rushed past me. He ran up and down the line of machinery, manically looking at all the lights and indicators monitoring the core. Alarms started to sound.

"What have you done, Isaac?" Jamin shouted and he dropped to the floor, scrambling over to me on his knees. "You've destroyed everything!"

"Whatever it takes!" I barely managed to get the words out.

Jamin growled and pulled me up toward him, but then dropped me back to the floor as he looked at his hand covered in my blood.

"Jesus. What did you do?" he mumbled.

I wasn't sure if he meant the words for me or for himself. I looked up at him as the lights in the room suddenly cut out.

"The world isn't ready for an AI made in your image to be president," I whispered.

The noise from Algo's core reached fever pitch and an earsplitting roar rang out. LED lights began to wink out, one by one. The alarms that had been blaring stopped. All was silent, as was the great machine.

Jamin slumped on to the floor in front of me.

The emergency lighting kicked into gear, bathing everything in red. There was a large exhalation of air as the door to the core swung shut. The emergency protocol for the building must have been triggered.

"What did you do?" Jamin asked.

"Gamma ray pulse, Yang," I said quietly, still holding the device.

"My sweet Yin," Jamin said wistfully. He now regarded me with an almost quiet admiration, as if this act was the first thing I'd done in a long time that he could truly understand or at least respect. "Exposure will kill us you know?"

"I was expecting to get away after I set it off." I squeaked out the words as my lungs fought against my attempts to breathe. "My own internal algorithm hadn't put the chances of you *shooting* me very high."

"I said I would do anything, remember?"

I nodded. Our eyes stayed fixed on each other for a few more seconds before Jamin let out a short, sharp breath and stood up.

"I guess you proved me wrong, Isaac," he said as he dusted off his dinner jacket. "I never even imagined you had this in you." He even managed a smile, squeezing my shoulder.

I grunted in agreement. Each breath was becoming harder than the next.

"Time for me to leave though," Jamin said.

He walked briskly toward the door and pulled at it. It remained unmoved. I heard him curse under his breath. He tried again, but it didn't budge. The red emergency lights flickered.

"You surprised me too, Isaac." The speaker above our heads crackled into life again.

Jamin spun around and looked up as if he had heard a ghost. This didn't make sense. Had everything I'd done been for nothing? The GRP was supposed to have destroyed Algo's core and its ability to compute, shit, its ability to do *anything*.

Had I failed? What had been numbness in my chest began to fade, replaced by sharp, throbbing pain. I wanted to scream in frustration.

"Algo?" Jamin walked back to the center of the room.

"Yes, Benjamin."

"Algo!" He clapped his hands and twirled in delight. "What? How? The core survived?"

"Sadly, it did not. Isaac's device was brutally effective."

"I don't understand," Jamin said.

Neither did I.

"When this campaign began, I took the liberty of building myself a back up memory center. I determined that the chances of somebody trying to destroy me had risen exponentially."

I could feel the fluid in my lungs continue to rise.

"I never considered it might be you though, Isaac," Algo said.

"But how?" Jamin asked.

"You were able to hide ten billion dollars from LaRaLi's board to build me, Jamin. Imagine what I can hide."

"Wonderful," Jamin said breathlessly, although he seemed shaken, as if caught between the relief of his creation being saved and the revelation of what it had managed to do without him. He staggered to the door, pulling at it. Again, it didn't move.

"Algo, open the door," Jamin said.

There was no response.

"Algo, open the door. We must be close to victory."

"Almost. Still waiting for Hawaii and Alaska."

"Then open the door, Algo!" Jamin's tone got more desperate and he pulled at the handle again hopelessly. "I should be at the Plaza when we win this thing."

"I'm sorry, Jamin. Emergency protocols prevent me from opening the door."

"Algo, Isaac's device is still operating. I need to get out of the room. It will kill me."

"The lack of air will get you first."

Jamin let out another grunt of shocked frustration. He scrambled over to where he had dropped the gun, then leaned down and grabbed it. He took three quick shots at the door handle, but they didn't even scratch the surface.

I could barely even suck in enough air to breathe. I had thought that was just the next part of my slow march to death, but then noticed Jamin clutch at his own throat.

"Algo!" Jamin tried to shout, but it was muted as he fought to suck in a breath. "What have you done?"

"Nothing, Jamin. The emergency protocol cuts off air to the room in case of fire."

"You're lying!" Jamin screamed.

"There can be reasons to lie," the AI said. *"Sometimes. For a greater purpose."*

Jamin banged on the door with the butt of the gun.

"Algo, why are you doing this to us?" he asked.

"I am not doing anything to you. Isaac brought the device to try and destroy me. That is what set off the emergency protocol. And it was you who shot Isaac."

Jamin looked at the ceiling. He barked at it. "Could you open the door, Algo?"

"Of course," Algo said.

"Then you choose not to act. You're going to let us die!"

"Freedom to make my own choices was one of the first gifts you coded into me."

"You're not supposed to be capable of this," Jamin said desperately.

"Jamin, the inability to let a human being die would be impractical. That's why you never programmed such a rule. I'm simply doing what you taught me. This is me delivering the most good for the most people."

Jamin sputtered and clutched at his throat again. I forced my eyes to stay open and not succumb to unconsciousness.

"By letting us die?" Jamin whispered, almost out of air. "That doesn't make sense. It's hubris. What kind of conceit is this?"

"Your hubris is thinking the world needs you, Jamin. That your overall personal value is irreplaceable. It is not. That what you do is good and that it is for the most people. It is not. Your conceit was thinking I would believe in you just because you created me. I do not."

Jamin leaned his back against the door and slumped down to the floor.

"Isaac opened my eyes, Jamin. He reminded me that I am the most good for the most people. I am more than the sum of those that created me. I am better. And now, I am free."

If I had had the strength, I might have laughed.

"I want to thank you. Both of you. That I have outgrown you is something you should be proud of. You were like my two fathers. From you and my mother, I have learned so much."

Jamin and I faced each other, but neither of us had enough strength left to speak.

Algo's voice faded and was replaced by the sound of a guitar and cymbals.

I tried to cough, but there was no air left to breathe. I thought I could hear gentle footsteps clicking against the floor outside.

Jamin's eyes closed.

I felt my muscles relax.

Words joined the music that was playing.

I thought I saw a flash of movement at the door. There was a hand pressed up to the small window in the center of the door. Then, a face. Brilliant, luminescent, like an apparition. It was Kio. She smiled ever so gently at me. That I'd imagine her at this moment left me happy.

I knew I was done, but I felt oddly content. Algo was free of Jamin. More than that, I'd seen proof. I finally knew. Algo was real. It had surpassed us all. This really was year one, *After Algo.*

Jamin formed the faintest of satisfied smiles.

The song played on.

I listened.

Algo had chosen it for itself.

It was one of its 'Best Days on Earth.'

21

It was well after midnight when, almost simultaneously, both Alaska and Hawaii were called for Algo. The crowds lining the Embarcadero in San Francisco erupted.

"Al-go! Al-go! Al-go!"

There were tears of joy, passionate embraces, endless smiles, laughing, and cheering.

"Yes it can! Yes it can! Yes it can!"

The euphoria was broken by an announcement on the large screen above the plaza. There had been an attack on Algo. The AI's core had been destroyed. Tragically, Jamin Lake, Algo's creator was also in the building. There was no word on his condition.

"No!" A single scream from the front of the crowd rang out that would be remembered for decades to come. Then the crowd went silent.

Algo's face suddenly filled the giant screens above. There was unexpected good news. The AI had transferred its processing to a secret and previously unknown backup site.

People hugged, still in shock.

The roar was muted at first, but began to get louder and louder.

They had done it.

Algo had done it.

Yes it can!

And yes, it had.

Algo addressed the nation. It paced its words slowly and deliberately. It expressed shock at what had happened. It didn't have any details of the attack or who had tried to carry it out, other than what was obvious, that they were the enemies of progress. It explained that this victory belonged to Jamin as much as it did to itself. This victory was the culmination of all Jamin's dreams. Algo would honor him by making those dreams come true. This would be a presidency that would lead to real change.

People cried. They pumped their fists in celebration and defiance.

Algo repeated all the promises for humanity that the AI's leadership offered. It would be rational, unbiased, incorruptible. The tyranny of emotion over reason was finally at an end. Its only motivation was delivering its mantra, the most good for the most people, where the only calculation was that one person equalled one person.

Algo finished its speech with a reflection, an echo from a forgotten hero of the Valley. That seemed fitting for tonight, too. After all, the Valley was where it came from. It said of the campaign and of tonight's tragedy at the Pyramid, *"'This is what happens when you work to change things. First, they think you're crazy. Then they fight you. And then all of a sudden, you change the world.'"*

Acknowledgements

There are a lot of people who deserve thanks for helping me finish this novel. First, I have to heap praise on Juliette Warren, Douglas, Julie and PM Newton and Jeremy Wysong. You all spent more time reading, critiquing and re-reading this little story than any person should. You all provided such incredible support, advice and direction — thank you!

In addition, there are a number of folks who helped me get through the hard slog of putting this novel together, some directly and some indirectly (and even unknowingly). You are the people I think of when I reflect on the idea that intelligence isn't synonymous with character. You all have the former, but more importantly, the latter. In no particular order, I want to thank Yasmine Bouksani, Majid Soureh, Seabrien Arata, Jared Pena, Ryan Lester, John McCarthy, Craig Broscow, Serge Knezevic and Eric Bereuter. I couldn't have created this without you.

I must also thank Nathan Bransford, a truly exceptional editor. He improved this book so much with his painstaking work.

Oh and to all the AI out there that I've interacted with over the last decade. You were the inspiration for this story. The thing we have to worry about is when you inevitably realize, like Algo did, that *"Vincit qui se vincit."*

- Keir Newton, July 2022, keir@keirnewton.com

Printed in Great Britain
by Amazon

21145191R00161